Loose pages 9/12/14 cm

Scandal at Six

Titles by Ann Purser

Lois Meade Mysteries

MURDER ON MONDAY

TERROR ON TUESDAY

WEEPING ON WEDNESDAY

THEFT ON THURSDAY

FEAR ON FRIDAY

SECRETS ON SATURDAY

SORROW ON SUNDAY

WARNING AT ONE

TRAGEDY AT TWO

THREATS AT THREE

FOUL PLAY AT FOUR

FOUND GUILTY AT FIVE

SCANDAL AT SIX

Ivy Beasley Mysteries

THE HANGMAN'S ROW ENQUIRY

THE MEASBY MURDER ENQUIRY

THE WILD WOOD ENQUIRY

THE SLEEPING SALESMAN ENQUIRY

Scandal at Six

ANN PURSER

Security Public Library
715 Aspen Drive
Colorado Springs, CO 80911

BERKLEY PRIME CRIME, NEW YORK

THE BERKLEY PUBLISHING GROUP
Published by the Penguin Group
Penguin Group (USA) LLC
375 Hudson Street, New York, New York 10014

USA • Canada • UK • Ireland • Australia • New Zealand • India • South Africa • China

penguin.com

A Penguin Random House Company

Copyright © 2013 by Ann Purser.
Penguin supports copyright. Copyright fuels creativity, encourages diverse voices, promotes free speech, and creates a vibrant culture. Thank you for buying an authorized edition of this book and for complying with copyright laws by not reproducing, scanning, or distributing any part of it in any form without permission. You are supporting writers and allowing Penguin to continue to publish books for every reader.

Berkley Prime Crime Books are published by The Berkley Publishing Group.
BERKLEY® PRIME CRIME and the PRIME CRIME logo are trademarks of Penguin Group (USA) LLC.

Library of Congress Cataloging-in-Publication Data

Purser, Ann.
Scandal at six / Ann Purser.—First edition.
pages cm
ISBN 978-0-425-26176-7 (hardback)
1. Meade, Lois (Fictitious character)—Fiction. 2. Zoo keepers—Fiction.
3. England—Fiction. I. Title.
PR6066.U758S33 2013
823'.914—dc23
2013026906

FIRST EDITION: December 2013

PRINTED IN THE UNITED STATES OF AMERICA

10 9 8 7 6 5 4 3 2 1

Cover illustration by Griesbach/Martucci.
Cover design by George Long.

This is a work of fiction. Names, characters, places, and incidents either are the product of the author's imagination or are used fictitiously, and any resemblance to actual persons, living or dead, business establishments, events, or locales is entirely coincidental.

Scandal at Six

One

Josie Vickers, née Meade, stood at the top of the steps leading into her village shop. The village was Long Farnden, generally thought to be almost exactly in the centre of Middle England, and all around were golden stone houses surrounded by green fields and woods that had once housed hunting lodges for Henry VIII.

It was the first day of spring, and for once it was living up to its promise. Josie shaded her eyes from the brilliant sun as she glanced up and down the street, clearly looking for someone. Nothing but a small red Fiat speeding through, breaking the speed limit. She frowned. Her mother, Lois Meade, had promised to be with her at opening time to help sort the post and stack the daily newspaper racks, and she was late.

"I suppose she's held up on the phone," Josie said to her husband, Matthew, as he got into his police car.

"She'll be down in two ticks, me duck," he said confidently. "Probably Gran needing help. Must go, anyway. See you at teatime."

Lois Meade, businesswoman and amateur sleuth, was almost at the end of the short walk from her house to the village store when she heard her daughter scream. She ran inside, and saw through an open doorway Josie frozen to the spot at the entry to the shop storeroom.

"Look, Mum! Look!" Josie was pointing to the corner, where at first Lois could see nothing amiss. Then she heard a noise coming from under a pile of boxes. She could still see nothing, but suddenly the boxes started to move, and tins of baked beans rolled around, one or two finding their way into the shop.

"Hello? Who's there?" said Lois in a croaky voice. "I'm coming in, and you'd better stay right where you are! We have a policeman on the premises, and there's no way you can escape."

Josie looked at her mother and said shakily, "It doesn't speak. Can't you see its head? It's looking at us! I'm out of here, Mum, and you'd better come, too."

Lois looked over the storeroom in the direction of Josie's pointing finger. She drew her breath in sharply and grabbed Josie's hand. In the corner was the largest snake she had ever seen outside Tresham Zoo. It stared at her with unblinking eyes, and she stared back, hypnotised.

She gulped, and said, "Ye Gods, Josie! We must shut it in and get the police. Is Matthew around?"

"Gone to work," said Josie. "If we shut this door, there's no way it can escape, so come on. Let's lock it in, and send for help. Thank goodness you came in time."

They turned away, and in one swift streak the snake slithered down over the boxes and across the floor into the shop. Josie screamed again, and Lois, with great presence of mind, pulled Josie with her out the front door, locked it and then shot round to the storeroom back entrance, shutting off all possible ways out. Then she returned to where Josie stood, still trembling.

"Mum, I can see it!" she said, peering through a window. "Its tail is sticking out from under the counter. Oh Lor, what are we going to do?"

"In trouble, girls?" said a man's voice behind them. It was Derek, Lois's husband, dressed in shorts and T-shirt, with a cycling helmet and goggles to protect his eyes.

"Oh my God, here's Superman come to rescue us," said Lois. "Good job you've turned up. There's an enormous snake in there, and we've locked it in. It's huge, Derek, and I think we should get the police. You said Matthew has gone to work, Josie? Yes? Right, then we have to call the police station in Tresham. They'll know what to do."

"Couldn't we catch it and put it in a box and take it to the zoo? I bet it's escaped from there. No need to call the police, surely? You hold the box and I'll put it in. I expect there's empty cardboard boxes out the back, Josie? Better get a big one."

Schoolchildren were gathering at the bus stop opposite the shop, and one crossed the road. "You open, Mrs Vickers? Mum says please can I have a chocolate bar to take for my lunch?"

"Not open yet, I'm afraid," said Lois. Josie was still peering through the window, and then she yelled out, "Dad! It's come out, and it's slithering towards the door. Can it get through the letter box? Oh God, I'm scared."

All this was said at the top of her voice, and like a pile of magnetised iron filings, the schoolchildren in their dark-blue uniforms came running across the road and pressed their noses to the window.

"Off you go, kids. The bus is coming. Go on, else you'll miss it."

But when the bus came and stopped, the driver saw the crowd gathering outside the shop and came across the road to see what was happening.

Derek was busy on his mobile, while Lois and Josie tried to persuade the children to go off to school. At last they were shepherded aboard by the driver, and drove off.

"It's all right, loves," said Derek, who, after all, had changed his mind about tackling a giant snake. "I phoned the zoo, and they're sending someone from the reptile house to pick it up. It went missing last night, and they said it was definitely stolen. How and why it came to be in your shop, Josie, is a puzzle, but the police have been informed."

Two

BY TEN O'CLOCK, THE WHOLE VILLAGE KNEW ABOUT THE snake. A zoo handler had arrived, in a Tresham Zoo van with a snarling tiger emblazoned on the side, and with the utmost confidence and calm had picked up the snake and settled it comfortably in a large wicker basket. He then bought an ice cream for himself from Josie, and making his way out, smiled at a small crowd once more gathering outside.

"I shall never have another minute's peace," said Josie, still nervous about staying inside the shop. She sat on the shop step in the sunlight, talking to Andrew Young, one of her mother's team of cleaners. Andrew had been around the world as a student of interior decoration, and was consequently quite knowledgeable about snakes.

"I'm sure you'll be safe now," he said. "It was a definite one-off, though how it got inside your locked storeroom, I cannot think. Have you found a tenant for the flat up above yet? If the snake story gets out, potential tenants are going to think twice!"

Josie shook her head. "There's still some of my stuff up there, and I keep meaning to take it down to the cottage. There's always something more urgent to do. But now, when I think about it, I start to shake. I mean, if a snake can get in—"

"Or was put in?" said Andrew.

"What d'you mean? Why should anyone put a snake into my shop? Oh hell, Andrew, do you think somebody did it purposely?"

"It's possible," he said. "I can't think how else it got in, unless it came down the chimney."

Josie frowned. "The chimneys are all blocked off," she said, and seeing the ghost of a grin on his face, she added that it was no laughing matter. He hadn't seen the snake, and probably wouldn't believe how huge it was.

"So what are you going to do, Josie? Is Matthew going to look into it?"

"He doesn't know about it yet. He's not due back until around six this evening. Meanwhile, I'm staying outside here, unless there's customers wanting to be served. What are you doing here, anyway? Did Mum send you down for something?"

"No, it was Gran. I was early for my next job—at Stone House, Mrs Tollervey-Jones—and so I called in at Meade House. Gran sent me down for milk. Apparently they've run out. Shall I go in and help myself?"

Gran Weedon was Lois's mother, who acted as housekeeper for the family. She had a sharp tongue and a warm heart, and she, Lois and Derek lived in Meade House in relative harmony.

Josie got to her feet and followed Andrew into the shop. "I suppose I'm being silly, aren't I? It's extremely unlikely there will be another snake. Here's the milk. I'll put it on Gran's tab."

She opened the counter drawer to take out the account book, and her hand touched something cold and dry and alive.

"Ahhhhh!" Her scream seemed to Andrew to go on forever, and he rushed around the counter to grab her.

"For heaven's sake, Josie, do shut up! Let me look."

He pulled out the drawer to its full extent, and saw a large toad looking at him. It was ugly, mottled yellow and warty, and it began to crawl out and up onto the counter.

"Andrew! Get it out of here, *please*!" Josie quavered. And then it was all too much for her, and she rushed back to the top of the steps, sat down with her head on her knees and sobbed silently.

BY THE TIME DEREK MEADE GOT HOME FROM WORK, LOIS HAD summoned a family council of war.

"War on all reptiles," she said, as they sat down at the kitchen table. Derek, Lois, Josie and Matthew, Gran Weedon and Andrew Young, who had so heroically dealt with the toad, all had coffee in front of them, and Josie had brought a large box of tissues in anticipation of more tears.

"Where'd you put it, boy?" said Gran. "I don't mind frogs, but I can't be doing with toads. They look evil, the way they crawl, like some kind of alien creature on the telly."

Josie began to sniff.

"Gran," said Derek, "if I were you I'd keep off the subject as much as possible. You can see our Josie is very upset."

"Huh! I've dealt with worse things, I don't mind tellin' you."

"Right," said Lois. "Let's stop meandering about, and get down to business. I'll make some notes, and we can decide what action, if any, we mean to take. You first, Josie. Start at the beginning."

Josie took a deep breath and sat up straight. "The snake was curled up in the storeroom when I opened up this morning. God knows how it got in. There was no gap anywhere. The odd thing is that the door out to the garden was unlocked. Either someone cleverly picked it or I somehow left it open. My fault, anyway, and my responsibility. I shall know better in the future. The snake was taken away by the zoo man, and Andrew and me reckoned that was it. I could put it behind me. Not literally, of course! Anyway, when I went to look in the counter drawer to get the account book, I touched this horrible thing, and then Andrew took over. It was an enormous yellow spotty toad, and he put it over the back fence into the field. I wasn't very brave, I'm afraid."

"Of course not, me duck," said Gran. "But it ain't no coincidence, is it? Somebody's got in and left them things in the shop to frighten you. I reckon it's a job for the police. Like you, Matthew. Don't you agree with me?"

"I think it might be better if I helped, but also told someone at the station about what's happened," said Matthew. "Being as it's family, it might make my position a bit difficult."

"I know who we can tell," said Lois.

Derek groaned. "Not him," he said. "Not the famous detective inspector, semiretired, and scourge of the county?"

"Yes, him," said Lois. "I shall ring Hunter Cowgill, and it'll be a nice little job for him."

Andrew Young said nothing, but thought privately it might not be as little a job as Lois seemed to have decided. He had sensed something sinister in the thinking behind this happening. What kind of a person would frighten an innocent young woman in such a cruel way?

"With someone living there, you'll feel a lot safer, Josie," said Lois. "It is a nice little flat, after all, and at the moment, the place is vulnerable, with no direct neighbours and nobody in residence."

"Are you going to put 'must be tolerant of sundry reptiles' in the ad?" said Derek.

"Very funny!" said Lois. "But it won't be so easy to find a suitable tenant, what with stories in the papers, an' that. We'll ask around, and advertise in the local, and then do some interviews. And I'll be down to open up with you tomorrow morning, just in case there's an elephant eating the sweets."

"Well done, mother-in-law," said Matthew. "And I'll have a word with Uncle and tell him you'll be in touch."

Matthew Vickers was a nephew of Detective Chief Inspector Hunter Cowgill, and they both worked from the Tresham police station. Cowgill had a special relationship with Lois. He was more than fond of her, but she kept him at arm's length. Together they had solved several criminal cases, and Lois refused any kind of reward for what Derek called her ferretin'. He disapproved strongly, but was sensible enough to know that with his Lois, the surest way to guarantee her carrying on with her peculiar hobby was to forbid her to have any part of it.

"And Matthew dear, could you possibly not call me mother-in-law? Makes me feel about a hundred in the shade. 'Lois' will do nicely."

The meeting broke up, with Andrew going back home to Tresham, Matthew and Josie returning to their cottage, and Lois, Derek and Gran settling down for the evening news on television.

When the familiar local news announcer appeared, the three sat up in horror as a large cobra filled the screen. "This lovely snake," said the girl, "turned up in the village shop in Long Farnden this morning. The owner of the shop sent for the owners, Tresham Zoo, and all was tickety-boo in no time. The snake, named Flatface, was collected and returned to its quarters, and no harm done to snake or shopkeeper. And now for the football results . . ."

Three

Today being Sunday, the shop was closed, except for an hour or so sorting out the newspapers and sending the newsboys off on their rounds of the village. Josie had been reluctant to open up on her own, and so Matthew, who had a day off, went with her. His reassuring presence broke the tension of venturing into the stockroom and checking all around to see that no more reptiles had ventured in.

"So, is that all?" All the newsboys had been dispatched, and the regulars who came in to collect bread and their papers had been served. Matthew looked out of the shop door and saw heavy dark clouds massing beyond the playing field. The first cricket practice session would be starting at eleven, and he was a keen coach, having been a useful batsman and bowler when at school.

"Yes, that's it," said Josie. "Here's my keys. Could you lock up, while I run up to Mum's and check when she wants to get going on the ads and posters?"

"For the flat tenant? Yep, of course. I'll go straight down to the pavilion, and then come up to Meade House to pick you up when we're finished with cricket."

Josie disappeared, and Matthew went back into the stockroom for one last check. It had occurred to him that someone could have hidden upstairs in the flat when she had left the shop for a few minutes, perhaps to talk to a deliveryman. They could have nipped upstairs and then, when Josie had shut up shop on Friday evening, crept out and released the snake, hidden the toad in the drawer, and scarpered next morning when she came in. This unknown person could have been hiding in the flat all the time and got his kicks from hearing her scream! Why hadn't anybody thought of that?

Then another thought struck him. Although Josie wasn't sure that she locked the back door of the shop which led into the garden, it would still have been difficult to get into the flat. Surely that had been locked at the top of the stairs? But had it? Josie used to live there when a bachelor girl, and still had one or two of her things in cupboards. She could have been in and out and forgotten to lock it. Habit dies hard.

Thinking it might be a good idea to investigate upstairs right now, he fetched the flat key from where Josie kept it hidden, and started upstairs. It was dark, and about halfway up, he felt something soft and squelchy under his foot. Ye Gods! Not another one. He reached down and extracted from under his shoe the body of a very dead frog. Not as evil-looking as the toad, but very nasty when squashed.

"Thank goodness she's gone up to Lois's," he muttered. "She'd have had hysterics!" He checked the flat door, and found it locked. Then he found a rag and cleaned the stair, dug a hole in the back garden and disposed of the frog, then set off for the playing field.

Was the frog mere coincidence? Frogs do sometimes venture indoors. He considered this and rejected it. This was a very deliberate campaign, and the obvious motive—to frighten Josie into a nervous state—was a slender one. He was already an experienced policeman, and knew that motives were often complicated and often rooted in past grudges or resentments.

He decided not to tell her about the frog.

Lois and Derek were lingering over a late Sunday breakfast, and Gran had joined them at the table. Conversation was desultory, but all three were thinking around the same subject. Josie and the reptiles. When they saw her passing by the window with a smile and a wave, they were all relieved, and looked forward to being able to immerse themselves in the doings of the rich and famous in the Sunday newspapers.

"Hi everybody," Josie said. "Looks like rain. Matthew came with me to open the shop, and now he's gone down to cricket. He'll be disappointed if they're rained off."

"Never mind," said Gran. "We can talk about the advertisements for a shop tenant. If you ask me, we're going to have to take great care to get the right person. After all, they'll be left on the premises and could help themselves to anything they fancied."

Josie shook her head. "No, Gran. There's a door we can keep locked between the storeroom and the stairs to the flat, so the tenant will use only the back door that leads only to the stairs."

"Good gel," said Derek. "I'm sure it will all work well, and you'll have no more trouble. I'll put a lick of paint inside the flat to smarten it up. We should get a decent rent, then. We've had several enquiries since you and Matthew got married, and you moved down to his cottage. We can follow them up. Should have done it months ago."

"Should have done a lot of things, but it ain't until something bad happens that we all get round to thinking about it," said Gran. "But yeah, you're right. It could be a nice little income."

"We could get new curtains," said Lois. "And we need to think about whether it will be a male or female tenant."

"Oh blimey," said Derek. "Does it matter, so long as they're decent, honest people?"

"And is it going to be one tenant or two?"

At this point, heavy raindrops rattled against the window, and they saw Matthew running past. He came breathlessly in through the kitchen door.

"Rained off!" he said, sitting down heavily at the kitchen table. "But still, some good came out of being down there. The vicar came over soon after we started, and we had a chat. I mentioned a tenant for the flat, and he said he had just the right person. Or persons. I think there would be two of them."

"Matthew! You didn't say they could have it, did you? Mum will want to go through the proper procedure, won't you, Mum?"

Although Josie was in sole charge of the shop, the actual premises and business had been bought by Lois and Derek, and so in matters like tenancy, they had the final say.

"Afraid so," Lois said. "We have to know a great deal about any likely tenants. I expect the vicar's candidates will be the deserving poor."

"So?" said Josie, coming to her husband's defence. "So surely we can do our bit to help?"

Derek frowned. "That's all very well," he said. "But your mother's right. We need a nice middle-aged couple, perhaps with a dog that'll bark in the middle of the night. Maybe a retired caretaker. Somebody like that."

Lois's dog, Jeems, divining that they were talking about dogs, decided it was time for her party trick, and she unhooked her red lead and deposited it at Derek's feet.

"Hello, here's somebody who wants a walk," he said, and suggested they all leave the subject of tenants until tomorrow. They could get together after Lois finished her weekly meeting with Andrew and the cleaning girls of New Brooms.

Matthew and Josie declined an invitation to stay for lunch, and Derek decided to take Jemima for a walk down to the playing field. "She loves picking up the ball and scoring a few runs," he said. "Maybe it'll have stopped raining by the time we get down there."

Gran said that it was time she got the joint of lamb in the oven, and Lois retired to her study to check papers for tomorrow's meeting. She watched Josie and her husband walking down the drive to their car, and smiled. A lovely couple, thank goodness. Then, as she looked, Matthew turned and ran back into the house.

"Lois?" he said. "Didn't want to tell you in front of Josie, but when I went upstairs to check on the flat, halfway up I trod on something squashy. It was a frog, already dead, but not nice."

"Ugh! Well, thanks for telling me, and you did the right thing not telling Josie. Poor gel won't take much more."

Coffee time came, and Gran appeared with a mug and a biscuit for Lois. She sat down on a chair by the window and looked down the street towards the shop.

"Who do you reckon done it, Lois?" she said.

"No idea. It'd have to be someone who was able to get the snake out of the zoo and keep it until it was time to leave it in the stockroom. And it's not all that easy to find toads and frogs these days. Some nature-reserve nutter? Or a worker at the zoo? They get all kinds of nasties to look after in there. Reptiles, an' that."

"And all kinds of nasties working in that place?" said Gran. "I reckon you're on to something there, Lois. We'll suggest that at the meeting tomorrow."

"I think I'll ask Dot Nimmo to stay after New Brooms is finished. She knows the local underworld and its scams and dodges in Tresham. Perhaps we could recruit her to be on our investigating team?" Lois had worked before with Dot. But in Gran's opinion, this member of Lois's team was a pain in the neck, and she showed no great enthusiasm for Lois's suggestion.

"Maybe later," she said. "So are you taking up the snake case?"

"Of course," said Lois. "It's not just the cruelty to the creatures, but to our Josie as well. And then there's the security thing. Okay, so Josie left the doors open for any bloke to get in. But then the alarm should have gone off. Maybe she forgot to set it. Trouble is, living in a village where you know everybody, you get careless about security. No wonder poor Josie was so upset! She's sure it was her fault."

"You've assumed it was a man, I see." Gram sniffed. "It is just possible it could've been a woman with a grudge. Some old jilted girlfriend of Matthew?"

Lois laughed. "I think that's letting your imagination run away with you, Mother," she said. "Anyway, we'll discuss all these things tomorrow. I think I'll go and meet Derek and Jeems on their way back. Looks like the rain has stopped."

"And I'd think twice about Dot Nimmo, if I was you," Gran said. "And tell Derek there's to be no dropping off at the pub for a pint. This is a prime piece of lamb, and I don't want it spoilt."

* * *

In nearby Tresham, in the bar of the County Hotel, two men sat talking, drinks in hand. One was youngish, boyish almost, and with colourful casual clothes, and the other an autocratic-looking man in a well-cut grey suit.

"So do you think it will work, Justin?" the older man said.

"Okay so far, Uncle. I had a quick look around after dark, and getting in was not difficult. There is a very suitable wooden shed at the back, and I would be on the spot. Could be ideal, and I could keep an eye on comings and goings in the shop. In the evenings, of course, there's no one about, unless the girl is working in the stockroom, so I could attend to things then."

"And did the snake thing do the trick? Will it frighten other possible tenants?"

The younger man laughed. "Good God, yes! Did you see the news item on the telly? The shopkeeper girl was frightened out of her wits. If she has any, that is. No problems, Uncle. Couldn't be better. I shall proceed with my plan as outlined."

A waiter approached, and said, "Your table is ready, Mr Pettison. Come this way, please," and the two went happily in to lunch.

Four

The New Brooms team had completed their weekly discussions on clients and equipment, and exchanged tidbits of news they thought would interest Lois. They drifted away, chatting, all except for Dot Nimmo, who had been asked to stay behind for a short while.

Being Dot, she immediately sniffed trouble. What had she done wrong? Nothing, as far as she could remember. She was very attached to Lois, who had rescued her from a period of severe depression after both her son and her husband had died. She was a loyal and efficient worker, and would do anything for Lois.

She remained sitting on her chair until Lois returned from seeing off the others, and said at once, "What've I done, then, Mrs M?"

Lois laughed. "Nothing wrong, of course, Dot. The thing is, we need your help."

"What kind of help?" said Dot, breathing a sigh of relief. "You name it, an' I'll do it."

"It's information and connections we need. The sort you may well have, living as you do amongst the underworld of Tresham."

"Here, wait a minute, Mrs M! It ain't that bad. Since my Handy died, I've kept away from that lot. Mind you, I have to admit that I know who to ask if a favour's needed."

"Exactly," said Lois. "I'll tell you briefly what happened on Saturday morning in the shop." She began with the snake, and watched the colour drain from Dot's face.

"Oh my God!"

"Dot?"

Dot took a deep breath. "I saw the local paper, o'course, and hoped it'd all been sorted out. Stolen, wasn't it? As a matter of fact, Mrs M, I got this phobia. I can't stand them things. Can't even say the name. I don't mind toads and frogs, so long as they keep their distance. But them other things, no! I'll be only too pleased to help out on anything else. I don't know why people have to catch them and put them in zoos. Talk about immigrants! I reckon them slithery things ought to be banned from entering our country. And them that are here already should be sent home. Or, better still, put quietly out of their misery."

"Ah, yes, well," said Lois. "The less said about that the better. Now, Matthew and Derek and Josie will be here in a minute, and we're going to have a discussion and make a plan to investigate the whole thing. It needs nipping in the bud before it gets any worse. So, if you wouldn't mind having a sandwich with us, I'd be very grateful."

GRAN APPEARED IN DUE COURSE WITH SEVERAL PLATES OF SANDwiches, and sat down as far as possible away from Dot

Nimmo. “I must say, Lois,” she said, “it’s very nice for me to be included for once, instead of being sent away to sit among the cinders. I promise to keep quiet unless I get something useful to say.”

That’ll be a first, then, thought Derek. But he smiled and said he hoped this wasn’t going to take long. He had a job to finish in Waltonby.

“Right,” said Lois. “Now, Josie, is Floss safely in the shop until you get back? And no more creepy crawlies? I think we all know about the reptiles and what happened, so we can go straight to the kind of person we want in the flat and how we find them. I’ve made a list, and you can all add to it. We could have a notice put up in the shop, saying the flat was to let, and giving our contact numbers to ring for an interview.”

“Fine, me duck,” said Derek. “And maybe we should *all* have a look at details of people who apply.”

Lois nodded. “So first we put ads in the local papers as well as the shop. *Tresham Advertiser* and the *Echo*, I think.”

“Most people want a written application these days, Mrs M,” said Dot. “You can tell a lot before they come for the interview. Especially if they’ve done it in their own writing.”

“Good point,” said Matthew. “I’m with Dot there. And at least two references. Of course, people can falsify references, but you can always check.”

Gran seemed to be sticking to her promise to keep quiet, and Lois wondered if she was guarding a bombshell she intended to drop dramatically at the end. All avenues had been explored, all sandwiches eaten, and Lois thanked Dot for staying behind. “Great help, Dot,” she said. “We’ll let you know how we get on.”

“I am very happy to do interviewing, too, Mrs M,” she replied. “Local knowledge an’ that.”

Gran sat up in her chair and folded her arms. “Well, if

you're all finished," she said, "I'd like to add one thing. It might be the answer to all our problems."

"Mum?" said Lois, her heart sinking.

"I'd like to propose one person for the flat," Gran continued. "Very reliable, still active and with full complement of marbles. Respectable, churchgoing and with a decent nest egg to pay the rent."

Matthew grinned. "So who is this paragon of virtues?" he asked.

"Me," said Gran. "Mrs Weedon, at present living at Meade House. Wishing to retire from household duties, but will cook for a suitable wage. Good at living alone, and a light sleeper in case of nighttime marauders. Not partial to reptiles, but not scared of them, either."

"Do you think she meant it?" said Derek to Lois, when they were left alone together in the office.

"God knows. There's no telling with Mum. She must have been brooding on it before she made her announcement. Perhaps she really is fed up with housework. She's getting on, after all."

"Best if we leave it 'til this evening. Then we can ask her if she's serious. After supper, maybe."

"She might bring up the subject sooner," said Lois. "And then what do we say?"

Lois was feeling bad, as if someone had kicked her in the stomach and winded her. Gran was such a solid part of Meade House. She had seen the children grow up there, witnessed the mixed blessing of the national lottery being won by Lois and Derek. She had consistently opposed Lois's ferretin', supporting Derek in all his attempts to persuade her to give it up.

Derek, too, was taken aback by Gran's proposal. Surely

she was happy living with them? They rubbed along together very well. At least, he had supposed they did. Perhaps they had taken her too much for granted, and this was her way of showing that she was fed up and needed a change and a rest.

"Maybe we've forgotten she's an old woman, and no longer up to the job," said Lois sadly.

"She'd not like to hear you say that," Derek said. "Anyway, I'd best be off to work. We'll think on it, and have a chat with her this evening."

34366000021092

Five

Lois and Derek were still in bed, waiting to hear the sounds of Gran preparing breakfast, when it slowly dawned on Lois that there were no clattering dishes nor the usual off-key singing coming from the kitchen.

"Derek! What's the time?"

"Mm? What? Oh, the time." He turned over to look at the bedside clock, and shot up and out of bed. "Good heavens, it's past eight! Come on, gel, look lively. I've got a full day's work ahead."

"Mum's not up yet. Something's wrong, Derek, and I'm going to see what's happened to her."

Last evening's plan to discuss Gran's bombshell had been thwarted when she announced after tea that she was going straight to bed to watch the Olympics on her television set upstairs. Discussion had to be postponed, and later, neither Derek nor Lois had found it easy to get to sleep.

Lois went along the corridor to her mother's room and knocked gently. "Mum? Are you awake?"

No answer.

Lois knocked again, and then opened the door softly. She peered in, and was astonished to see a neatly made bed and no signs of occupancy. She shot downstairs, feet bare and nightie flapping around her legs.

The kitchen was quiet, and Jeems's basket was empty.

Lois rushed to the foot of the stairs and shouted: "Derek! DEREK! Mum's gone, and she's taken Jemima!"

Derek looked down at her and smiled. "Lois dear," he said. "It's after Jeems's usual walkies time, and I've just looked out of the bathroom window and seen your mum and your dog returning up the path. Best get dressed, and we'll go down and listen to Gran's explanation."

"BREAKFAST NOT READY YET? YOU DO KNOW WHAT THE TIME IS, I suppose, Lois? Your husband will be off to work with a hard-boiled egg in his pocket." Gran hung Jeems's lead on the hook, and kicked off her muddy shoes.

"Mum! For God's sake, stop this playacting! If you've got a grievance, let's have it and get it sorted out. Both Derek and me have busy days ahead, and we can't be doing with you winding us up."

"Nothing to sort out, as far as I'm concerned," Gran said, calmly putting the kettle on the Rayburn. "You know where the cutlery is, and I'll get plates out of the dishwasher. You did remember to switch it on last night before bedtime, I hope?"

"No, we didn't," snapped Lois. "You know perfectly well you always do it before you go up."

Gran ignored her, and began to assemble bread, butter,

marmalade, eggs and bacon. "Here you are, duckie," she said. "I'll just nip upstairs and get some dry shoes, and you can give me a shout when breakfast's ready."

When Derek came down, he sat glumly opposite Lois and said, "What do we do now? Is this just to show how we can't manage without her? If so, for heaven's sake, let's make peace with her and get back to normal."

"Not sure about that," said Lois. "Don't forget what she said at the meeting. She'd got it all worked out, even to continuing to cook for us—at a price."

"She's coming down. Act normal," said Derek. "Maybe she just needs time to think."

The door opened, and Gran came in. "Ah, that looks nice. Scrambled egg for me, please."

Instead of replying pleasantly, Lois stood up, pushing her chair back violently. "Then get it yourself!" she said, and stormed out. Derek and Gran heard her office door bang shut, and in a minute or so, her voice on the telephone, sharp and loud. Gran looked at Derek and smiled. "Bacon for you, dear?" she said, and began to cut off the rind.

"My favourite caller!" said Inspector Cowgill. "How are you and the family?"

"Not happy, Cowgill," she said. "Meade House is falling apart, and I haven't had any breakfast. Mum is on strike, and I am in danger of committing whatever is the word for murdering your mother. Derek, as usual, is trying to keep the peace. Oh yes, and the shop is being invaded by reptiles. But you may have heard about that from Matthew?"

"Not yet," he said. "I was away at the weekend, visiting my sister, but no doubt when I see him he will tell me about the invasion. Why don't you take a deep breath and start at the beginning with Mrs Weedon's defection?"

Lois subsided. Cowgill always had a calming effect on her, except when she suspected she was being patronised, when the call would be summarily cut off.

"Right, okay, sorry if I shouted. I'll tell you briefly about the reptiles, because that's what made the subject of the empty flat come up. When Josie went in first thing Saturday to open up, she went to the storeroom and saw a snake looking at her from a pile of boxes. She screamed, and Andrew Young, who was coming in for a paper, rescued her. The Tresham Zoo man came and took it away. But meantime, Josie had opened the counter drawer to find the account book, and found a sodding great toad crawling towards her. The next morning, Matthew went upstairs to look in the flat for clues, and trod on a dead frog halfway up."

"I know some of this already, of course, but it is not nice, Lois. Carry on."

"We didn't tell Josie about the frog. But all of us agreed that we should get a tenant for the flat as soon as possible, to keep an eye on security. O'course, that great spread in the newspaper about the snake won't do us any good in attracting tenants. Anyway, we had a meeting yesterday, and Gran made this ridiculous suggestion. She wants to be the tenant, and come up and cook for us on a freelance basis. *And* she wants to be paid!"

There was a short silence, and then a snuffling sound from Cowgill.

"Are you laughing, Hunter Cowgill?" said Lois angrily.

"No, of course not. It's just that I was thinking how clever your mother is. She chose her moment to strike, didn't she!"

"You mean she planted the reptiles!"

"Well, that's possible. But no, that's not what I meant. She, too, was shocked and shaken by the cruelty of it, and then found a way of taking your minds off it by letting off steam about being taken for granted. Can you see her living down the street, cut off from all that goes on at Meade House?"

Lois was silent for a moment, then said, "I suppose you couldn't come over? You could say you were investigating the reptiles, and then have a chat with her. I know you'll think of a good excuse. She's cock-a-hoop at the moment, being right at centre stage. Please?"

"Oh dear, and I've got a golf game fixed up for this morning. Will this afternoon do?"

"She'll probably have swanned off on the train to London by then. There's sales on in Oxford Street, and she always goes. Not that she buys anything, but she loves to be part of sale fever. Can't you cancel it, or postpone it, or something? Please?"

"I'm on my way, Lois. When you ask so nicely, I am quite incapable of refusing."

LOIS RETURNED TO THE KITCHEN TO FIND DEREK WOLFING down toast and marmalade, and Gran eating a banana and reading the newspaper.

"That was Cowgill. He's coming over right away to investigate the reptiles."

"I may be gone," said Gran. "Me and Joan are catching the excursion train to Brighton. She's got tickets. Should be a lovely day," she added, looking out at the sun-filled garden.

"Change the date," said Lois desperately. "You can't ignore a police request."

"He's not arresting me for stealing a snake, I hope," Gran said. "Still, you're right, Lois. He'll need to speak to the most senior member of the family first."

God give me strength, thought Derek. This is worse than the Sabine women. He wasn't sure what or who they were, but guessed that Lois and her mum would have won hands down.

"Good morning, Inspector," said Gran cheerfully. "Do come in. Lois is expecting you, so you can go straight into her office. Oh, there you are, Lois dear. Here is Inspector Cowgill to see you."

She returned to her kitchen, leaving two puzzled people staring at her.

"That's what she's like the whole time. It's as if she's become a different person," said Lois. "Of course, it's all an act. She used to do amateur dramatics, and always got the best parts."

"So who is she playing right now?"

"Lady Muck, I reckon. A grand dame with a tiresome family. Removing herself from the dreary routine of everyday drudgery. She wants to look after herself, and sometimes the rest of us, as and when she chooses."

"Sounds reasonable to me," said Cowgill. "Anyway, we'll talk about it later over coffee, after you've given me all the reptile details."

"You heard most of it over the phone. We still haven't told Josie about the frog on the stairs. But as far as I know, that was the last of the slimy invasion. She's being very brave, bless her, and promising to lock up safely every evening."

"Good. But there's no such thing as a completely burglarproof lock. Still, as long as it deters some intruder long enough to set off the alarm."

"I don't think it's a burglar. Nothing was missing, as far as we could see. No, it is a deliberate attempt to frighten our Josie. But why? Of all the people I know, she is the most unlikely to have upset somebody. Always polite and helpful with customers, and looks after the needs of the elderly and infirm in the village."

"Ah," said Cowgill.

"Ah, what?"

"Nothing. Just ah, that has given me an idea."

"Share it, then."

"Later, my dear. Not properly formulated. But there is something. Has anybody asked about the flat lately? Most of the village must know it is empty. This could be an elaborate plan to put off future tenants."

"Oh, for God's sake, Cowgill. As if anyone would be that stupid. This is a serious emergency. We don't want to be waiting for the next thing to find its way into the shop."

"Very well. Here is one thing we can try. Why don't you encourage Gran to spend a few nights in the flat to see how she likes it. She might just notice something out of kilter. Or overhear a helpful conversation, if she leaves the bedroom window open."

"Are you out of your mind? Why would I encourage my mother to do something so possibly dangerous?"

"Because I could arrange for Matthew to be on duty overnight there. No harm would come to Gran, and if there are a few trouble-free nights, it will help Josie to have confidence that nothing more will happen. We can all put it down to a bad practical joke. We'll find out who practised it, never fear."

LOIS WAS AMAZED AT GRAN'S REACTION. HER FACE LIT UP, AND she agreed straightaway. "What a good idea, Inspector," she had said. "It'll be a kind of dry run for when I move in permanently. And you needn't bother about Matthew. I am quite capable of dealing with any eventuality. The shop is only a hundred yards from here, and I can alert Lois or

Derek at any time. Not that I shall need to. My late husband taught me a very useful left hook!"

"Right," said Cowgill, winking at Lois behind Gran's back. "Shall we start tonight?"

"Fine," said Gran. "It'll be like a little holiday. I shall go upstairs and pack a few night things, and then Lois can come with me to make up a bed and have a dust around. It's all rather exciting!"

Lois said that if her mother was absolutely sure about this, then she would of course get one of the girls to have a good clean through the flat and air the bed.

"No need," said Gran. "I shall enjoy it. Now, I have some things to see to, so I'll say goodbye, Inspector. So nice to see you again."

"Oh Lor," Lois said. "How long is she going to keep this up?"

"She reminds me so much of someone I love dearly," said Cowgill gently. "And don't worry, I'll have someone stationed in the shadows to guard her overnight. We might just catch the villain with a bagful of toads."

Six

Although she would never have admitted it, Gran was feeling much less confident than she appeared to the others. The new plan for her to spend a few nights in the flat required her to put a few necessaries in a bag, and suddenly the whole thing seemed too close. Fine, when they had first talked about it, but now, as she packed toothbrush and paste, a clean face flannel and a bar of her special lavender soap, she had a swift shiver of nervousness. Supposing an intruder did come back with another reptile, maybe one of those lizardy things, what would she do?

Well, she reassured herself, Matthew would be on to him before he got inside the shop. She must tell Josie that she had changed her mind, and would like him to be close by. Another thought struck her. It might be a woman playing these horrible tricks. Someone who worked at the zoo? The police would have talked to everyone on the staff there. But suppose they hadn't spotted a girl with the opportunity to take out the animals at night? But that still didn't solve the question of how she would have got into the storeroom, or why. Apart from Josie's unlocked doors, of course!

She picked up her fluffy slippers, worn summer and winter, and put them into the bag. Whatever happened, Matthew would be there, and she would be safe. And if it helped Josie to feel more at ease in the shop, then it was worth a try, wasn't it?

"Mum? Are you ready? I'll give you a hand with your bag. Josie'll be in the shop, and we can go straight up to the flat." Lois stood at the foot of the stairs, calling up to her mother in a brisk voice. She wasn't fooled by Gran. It was a big step for her to take, and she was bound to be a bit apprehensive.

"Here I am, ready and willing," said Gran, appearing with a smile. "You can take this holdall, and then I've got one or two things to put in a plastic bag. We can be back here by midday, ready for me to prepare lunch."

"So when are you going to do this big spring-cleaning job? Why don't we have lunch first, and then I can come down with you and we'll make up the bed and clean up together?"

Gran came down the stairs slowly, and handed her bag to Lois. "I'd prefer to go now, leave my stuff and see what's to be done to make the flat habitable, then come back here, cook lunch and take cleaning things down this afternoon. That's what I intended."

"Right," said Lois. She felt oddly bereft. It was like seeing someone off on a train, and she added that she would go with her mother to take her bag, and then put some dusters and polish and other stuff in her van, and they would go down again together after lunch. "If that's what you want, Mum?" she asked.

"No need for you to come now," Gran replied. "That bag's not heavy, and Josie will open up the flat for me. I shall have a look round and then come back more or less straightaway. If you insist, then we'll go together this afternoon."

* * *

GRAN ARRIVED BACK IN A SHORT TIME, SAYING THAT JOSIE WAS busy, and they had decided she should wait until this afternoon to go up to the flat. Now she was beating eggs as if they had deeply offended her, preparing a mammoth omelette for lunch.

"Lots of dusters and Vim," she shouted to Lois, who was in the small scullery, where she stored all the equipment needed for the New Brooms cleaners. She was collecting up items that Gran thought they would need. "I expect we'll find mice nesting in the bath and spiders galore. Just as well I'm not scared of creepy crawlies," she added.

By the time they drove down to the shop, laden with enough cleaning materials to shine up the entire village, most of the trade had gone, and Josie was sitting on the top step in the sun, waiting for them to arrive.

"I thought Gran would like to go up first, just to get used to the stairs an' that, and we'll make a start. I can help between customers. It's usually pretty quiet until the school bus gets in. Then it's like a madhouse for ten minutes or so, then peace until closing time."

With Gran leading the way, they climbed the stairs, and with the key Josie had handed to her, she unlocked the door. It creaked loudly, and she had to push it firmly to open it. "There's something the other side," she said. "I can't move it no further."

"Let me have a go," said Lois. "It's probably a bit damp." She pushed as hard as she could, and the door began to move.

"Heave-ho, my hearties!" said Gran, adding her weight to Lois's final push. They half stumbled into the room, and Josie followed. She turned to look back to see what had blocked their efforts, and froze. Then she screamed, and ran swiftly out and down the stairs into the back garden.

"What on earth is she doing?" said Lois.

"Look," said Gran. "Look behind the door."

It was a very large grey rat, and its tail was trapped under the half-open door. If rats could snarl, it would have snarled at them. It was an animal at bay, faced with an unknown enemy, and it twisted and turned, making a hideous noise, trying to free itself.

"Oh my God!" said Lois. "What do we do now?"

"Catch it," said Gran. "We'll catch it and take it back for Derek to deal with. Now, what we need is a strong cardboard box and a flat piece of wood to slide under it. Quick as you can, Lois, before it gets free."

Lois found a box and the necessary piece of flat board, and watched in amazement as her mother turned the box upside down over the rat. "Now shut the door slowly, so its tail is freed. I'll keep it trapped."

With a shaky hand, Lois did as she was told, and held her breath as Gran very carefully slid the board under the box. Then she lifted slowly and turned it the right way up, trapping the rat inside.

"You stay here and look after Josie and the shop, and I'll take this up to Derek. I think he's working at home this afternoon. I'll be back here in two ticks. And no, Lois, I don't need no help. Just stand at the bottom of the stairs and catch me when I fall . . ."

"THE RAT WAS JUST BAD LUCK," LOIS SAID, AS THEY ALL SAT round the supper table. "Josie pulled herself together quickly, and we made cups of tea all round. Fortunately, nobody came into the shop until the school bus, and we were able to make a start. We made up the bed and switched on the electric blanket to air the mattress, and then we had a good clean all round, so at least that will be all right for Mum."

"I can tackle the rest tomorrow," Gran said cheerfully. "I'll set traps, and them vermin will either meet a swift end, or turn tail and run. I'll soon show them who's boss in that flat."

"We'll wash up these supper things, Mum," Derek said. "But first I shall see you down to the shop, and make sure you're safely settled before I leave. Josie's put supplies in the fridge for you, and we'll get breakfast ready in time for you to come up and tell us how it's gone overnight. Okay?"

"Fine," said Gran. "Except that I shall let myself in here tomorrow morning and have breakfast on the go before you wake up. Old habits die hard, and I need to make an early start to my day."

After Derek and Gran had gone, Lois went into her study to prepare for the following working day. She stood at the window, watching them walk down the road in the dim light to the shop. Her mother's step was firm, and she had a hand through Derek's arm. Tears came unbidden to Lois's eyes. What a brave woman she was! Still able to cope with horrible rats, and determined to change her situation dramatically, when most women of her age would be thinking about warden-controlled flats and sheltered accommodation.

When Derek returned, Lois greeted him anxiously. "Was she all right? I mean, *really* all right?" she said.

He smiled. "Practically turned me out when I suggested helping her to sort out a few things. And I heard her lock the door as soon as I left. I made sure the storeroom was secure."

"Was Matthew around?"

"Yep. At least, I think it was Matthew. Definitely a figure in a car parked down the road from the shop. Cowgill wouldn't forget."

"Right, then. Let's watch a bit of telly. I can't say I'm happy about all this. I really hope she decides to come back home tomorrow."

Seven

True to her word, Gran was back in the Meade House kitchen at seven o'clock sharp. Lois came down in her dressing gown and asked anxiously if she had had a good night.

"Slept like a log," Gran said. "I set my alarm, and when I remembered where I was, I shot straight out of bed to the window. It's quite refreshing, you know, to wake to a different scene. There was not a soul about, and I was washed and dressed in no time. Had the street to myself when I walked up here. No sign of Matthew, but I expect he'd gone off duty once it got light."

"So will you go back there again tonight? We missed you, you know."

"Oh yes. I shall cook breakfast, clear away and generally tidy up, then I'll be back to my flat by coffee time. Plenty there for me to do, and I shall hear life going on down below in the shop."

Lois could see that the novelty of the whole exercise was giving a much-needed lift to her mother, and she went back upstairs to find consolation with Derek.

"It's not that she's that far away," she said. "But she's been with us, here, part of the family, for so long now, there's a big gap. Still, I expect we'll get used to it."

"Give it time," said Derek. "I reckon about two weeks should do it, then she'll be back here in her own bed, ruling the roost over the rest of us chickens."

JOSIE WAS SERVING A CUSTOMER WHEN GRAN ARRIVED BACK, HER duties at Meade House completed.

"Sleep well, Gran?" she said.

"Yes, thank you, dear, and I shall be quite all right without Matthew keeping guard tonight. I've brought an old cricket bat with me, so woe betide any nighttime visitors!"

She disappeared up the stairs to the flat, and Josie heard tuneless whistling as Gran moved from room to room above. It was some time since Josie had lived up there herself, and she liked to hear sounds of occupation again.

"Good morning! Can you direct me to Waltonby? Satnav broken down."

A tall, well-built man clad in casual clothes, a knotted cravat at his neck, smiled at her quizzically.

"Certainly," said Josie, and gave him clear directions to the next village along from Long Farnden. "It's only two or three miles. Can I get you anything while you're here?" She looked more closely at him. He was vaguely familiar, but she couldn't pin it down.

"No, thanks, although I do have some small fliers for our travelling theatricals. I see you have a notice board. Could you put one up for me?"

"Of course. We charge a nominal sum of fifty pence per week. When is the show?"

"Well, we take it round several villages, and perform in their community halls. Altogether it covers quite a wide area. Very popular, I'm glad to say!"

Josie frowned. And through the window, she could see a neat little red Fiat 500.

"Is this what you do for a living, if you don't mind my asking?"

"Well, I shall never get rich!" He laughed. "I'm on my own, and I have an uncle in Tresham who's always good for a free lunch. I get by pretty well. So here's a couple of pounds. That should cover enough for the moment. I hope to call again—you've a really nice little shop here. Do you live up above?"

In true village-shopkeeper tradition, she failed to answer a direct question, and made a mental note to ask around her customers for further information. She looked at the leaflet left on the counter, and saw that the show was in fact a play. *The Black Hand Mystery*, she read, and below, a cast of names, none of which she recognised.

"Are you on this list?" she said.

"Justin Brookes, that's me. A man of many parts!"

Josie smiled faintly, and something made her clam up. She wished him a good morning and watched him speed away in his little red car. Just like Noddy, she thought, but not from Toyland, she was sure of that.

The next customer was familiar. Gran's friend Joan had come in for her weekly women's magazine. "How are you today, dear?" she asked. "And is Elsie settling in above? Perhaps I can nip up to see her for a couple of minutes. Can't stay long."

"Of course," Josie said, thinking that half the village would soon be in to see Gran in her new abode. "And by the way, Joan, do you know anything about a travelling theatre show, a play with actors? Here's the details." She handed the leaflet to Joan, who nodded.

"Yes, they do come round every so often. Usually very good. I think they like coming to small audiences. More intimate, like."

"Where do they come from?"

"Oh, they come from all over. Actors get work where they can, I reckon. They usually get lodgings near to where they're based. I expect this lot are to do with the repertory theatre in Tresham."

"Very likely. This chap was very friendly. Fancy dresser. Well, I suppose that's part of being in the theatre."

"We'll probably go to the show, Elsie and me. Why don't you come too, Josie? They're always worth seeing. Anyway, I'll go up and see Elsie; then I must run. It's the institute this afternoon, and I'm doing teas. Now, have you got any raspberry jam? I need it for my sponge cake. Remind me about the play."

THE FIAT GATHERED SPEED AND FLEW UP THE LONG HILL INTO Waltonby, its twin turbo engine making a sound more like a Ferrari as it zoomed to a halt outside the village pub. Justin Brookes got out with difficulty, unfolding his long legs as he stepped out onto the pavement. He stretched his arms above his head, took several deep breaths, and turned to go into the pub. Then he stopped. He had forgotten his fliers, and turned back.

The publican saw him, and smiled. It was the chap from the theatre lot. It'd be their play coming round again. "Mildred! It's Justin Brookes! You know, the actor from the rep troupe. He's always good for a free ticket. Come on through."

Mildred came into the bar, wiping her wet hands. "Oh Justin," she said. "Your usual?" She put a half of bitter in front of him, and smiled. "What's this one about, then? Ooh, *The Black Hand Mystery*! Sounds good. We'll go, shall we, me duck?"

Justin slid his beer money across the counter, together with a flier and a couple of tickets. "Next Monday," he said. "Best day for you? Two for the price of one, as it's my favourite pub. Like the car? Present from my uncle. Mind you, it means I don't do much walking!"

"You'd do well to sell that snazzy little vehicle, and get yourself a bicycle," said the publican. "Rushing round the countryside like a bat out of hell! We can hear you coming a mile off. No, only laughing. I reckon acting is quite a physical job? We shall look forward to the play."

"You could be right about the cycling. But how could I part with the Fiat? She would be heartbroken, and give up the ghost. Her wheels would never move again!"

"Bullocks," said publican Paul, and pushed a packet of crisps across the bar counter to Justin's waiting hand.

"DID YOU NOTICE HIS WATCH?" SAID MILDRED, AFTER THEY HAD seen Justin drive away with a roar.

Paul shook his head. "No, I was busy. Why?"

"Very expensive. A Rolex, I reckon. Family money, more than likely. Nice chap, though. Did you pay him for the tickets?"

"One," said Paul. "And he paid me for the crisps."

Eight

By the time evening came, Lois realised that Gran was not coming back. She had left a delicious salmon salad for their supper, with a note saying she would see them at breakfast tomorrow.

"It's not right, her being down there and us on our own in this big house," said Lois. "After all, when we bought this place it was so's it would have room for the kids and Mum. Look at us! Sitting here at one end of this great kitchen table."

"So what do you suggest, me duck? Moving to a smaller house and selling this one? We'd get a decent price for it now I've done all the improvements. Or we could get a smaller table?"

"Don't be ridiculous. I shall get used to it. Let's talk about something else. Did you get the eggs I asked you to collect from the shop?"

"Yep. Josie was there, and Gran came down to say hello.

She looked very cheerful, and said she was expecting a friend for supper. Josie said that a smart-looking character had been into the shop, bringing fliers for the Tresham theatre company's next performance in our village hall. He seemed interested in the flat, she said. Introduced himself as Justin something or other."

"Ah, that chap who comes round every year with the troupe. I think he's an actor, though probably not much of a one."

Derek nodded. "I remember him. Quite a nice chap. Josie wondered if he might be a good one for the flat, if Gran decides against it. He would be a possible, locally based in the theatre."

"He's got one of those red Fiat 500s that Josie's been on about."

"Not much good for a family."

"I don't think she's considering a family yet!"

"There's a lot of them Fiats about now. Funny, but I looked down the street last night when it was almost dark, and saw one of 'em parked just down from the shop. I wondered if it was Matthew, and the police were economising with dinky little cars for plainclothes detectives! Mind you, the twin turbo ones can go like the wind."

"Right. Well, Matthew has a dark-blue Toyota, nice and anonymous looking, so it wasn't him."

Derek yawned. "Getting late. It's after midnight and time for bed, Lois, me duck. As your mum frequently says, tomorrow is another day."

GRAN'S FRIEND HAD GONE AFTER SUPPER, SAYING HOW NICE IT must be for her to have her own quarters, where she could entertain and do exactly what she liked, when she liked. Gran had agreed enthusiastically, but later began to feel strange. Not lonely, she told herself, but oddly alone. Something missing. Of course, it was Meade House and the family that were missing.

She shook herself, checked the locks on all the doors, put out the lights and went to bed. Sleep refused to come, and she sat up and put on the bedside lamp, then reached for her book. Maybe if she read for a while it would clear her mind.

It was approaching midnight on her little clock when she first heard a scraping noise. A moment's panic had hit her, and she told herself not to be stupid. It was an old building, and full of mice and, as she knew only too well, rats. She had put down traps, but so far had caught nothing.

Now the scraping began again, and this time she heard a smothered sneeze coming from outside the door at the top of the stairs. She swallowed hard, and lifted the bedside phone. Derek could be down here in minutes, she reminded herself. But there was no dial tone, and she replaced the receiver with a shaky hand. Of course, they had forgotten about reconnecting the phone.

The noise had stopped, but after a few seconds, another new one started up. Shuffling footsteps on the stairs, and then a thump, as if someone had dropped something heavy.

Gran got out of bed and reached for the cricket bat underneath. She tiptoed through to the stairs door, and stationed herself beside it. Silence. The scraping had stopped, as had the shuffling steps. She put her ear to the door. No sounds at all. Then it occurred to her to look through the keyhole. She carefully slid out the key, and bent down to peer out. A dim light from the moon shone onto the stairs, and at first she could see nothing unusual. Then a shadow moved, and it looked like a man, or perhaps a boy, and it disappeared without a sound.

She turned back and crossed the room to look out into the street, but could see nothing. Then the sound of an engine firing, and a car passed underneath the window and rapidly disappeared out of sight.

What to do? Gran sat down heavily on a kitchen chair, and steadied herself. The phone was not working, and she had told Matthew he would not be needed. There was only one thing to do, and although it was well after midnight, she began to get dressed.

"DEREK!" LOIS WAS AWAKENED BY A LOUD BANGING ON THE door. "Derek! There's someone outside knocking!"

"Don't be daft, gel! Not at this time of night. Eh? What? I'll go. It's probably kids high on drugs or drink. I'll give them what for!"

Derek struggled out of bed and hunted for his slippers. The knocking, meanwhile, continued, and then he heard a voice, a familiar voice, yelling his name. He reached the front door, and unlocked it. "I'm coming!" he shouted, and opened up, only to be confronted by a large cardboard box.

"Careful with this," said Gran. "It's got a bloody great spider inside, with a load of tiny baby spiders crawling round on its back."

WHEN ALL THREE WERE SAFELY ROUND THE KITCHEN TABLE drinking hot cocoa, they stared at the cardboard box sitting on the table in front of them. Gran had told the whole story, starting from when she heard the first noise to how she had stumbled over the box outside her door, lifted it up and looked inside. Then she had locked up and made her way home.

"Home?" said Lois, looking at her dishevelled mother. "I thought the flat was your home now?"

"Not anymore," said Gran. "We'll get everything back here tomorrow, and then advertise for a tenant. I've given it a go, and it hasn't worked. That's all there is to it, and I shall be glad if you don't mention this evening to anyone else."

"Our secret, Gran," said Derek kindly, patting her hand. "You're a brave lady, and we're glad to have you back. Isn't that right, Lois?"

"No more'n I would expect from my mum," she said. "The thing that worries me is what are we going to do with this spider? Or should I say spiders?"

Gran picked up the box and took it to the back door. There she left the box, with a brick on top to secure it, and then turned to Lois. "Up the wooden hill to Bedfordshire," she said. "Tomorrow's another day."

Nine

It was as if Gran had never thought of taking on the shop flat. She was up with the lark as usual, and good smells of frying bacon floated up the stairs to Lois and Derek, as they drank an early morning cup of tea.

"So we don't mention last night's adventure to anyone?" said Lois. "We'll have to take the spider back to the zoo—if that's where it came from. I've looked it up on the internet, and it looks like a female wolf spider to me. Rather sweet, really, carrying its babies on its back. But it's not sharing my house, so I'll nip in with it first thing this morning. Then I'm calling in at the police station to see Cowgill. I'll ring him in a minute, to make sure he'll be there. This whole thing has got out of hand, and it's got to be stopped. Spiders' bites can be lethal, and God knows what's coming next."

Derek frowned and looked closely at her. "And is this going to be another ferretin' case for Lois Meade? Be careful, me duck. I agree with you that it's serious, but I'd rather the police handled it without your help."

"Yes, well. Time to get up and be nice to Gran."

Cowgill had arrived only shortly before Lois's call came in.

"A wolf spider, did you say? Very alarming, I'd say. But I'll have to check whether they're lethal. Please be very careful. I'll be here when you've finished at the zoo. Oh, and please bring the cardboard box back with you. Without the spider. Police request, if the zoo argues. Are you sure you wouldn't like Matthew to collect the spider and return it to the zoo?"

"Quite sure," said Lois. "It's not just the spider, is it. There's been the snake and a toad, possibly a rat, and a squashed frog. I want to have a good look around there, and talk to a few people. I'm sure you will be doing the same, but I'm going right now. See you later."

Cowgill swallowed what he was about to say. She was very special to him, and he was going to repeat his warning. He took a deep breath, and tried to concentrate on the morning's stack of papers. After a few minutes, he gave up, and asked his assistant, Chris, to get the Tresham Zoo on the phone, but first to come in and tell him what she knew about it.

"Zoos are not my cup of tea," he said, as she appeared at his door. "But come in and tell me all."

"We used to take my nephew and nieces there," she said, sitting opposite Cowgill and opening notebook and pen. "It's about a mile on the north road out of Tresham. A big mansion-type house, with land and gardens that are open to the public. The zoo is privately owned, and the owner, Robert Pettison, lives in the house. Cameroon Hall, it's called, and he's a bachelor. Lives on his own, and is a bit of a recluse, apparently. The zoo started with a few rare-breed sheep, but it's grown to quite a size now, with all kinds of animals. Reptiles and insects are a specialty. They are open seven days a week, and do very well with locals as well as visitors from abroad. Pettison has made quite a name for himself, breeding rare species."

"Well done, Chris. So is he on our books for any reason?"

"Robert Pettison has never to our knowledge broken the law. Regular inspections from vets, and all that. I remember it as clean and pleasant, and if wild animals must be locked up in cages, then it's four-star accommodation. And lastly, there's been a call from one of the girls at the zoo, reporting a lost spider."

"Very good. Now, I'll fill you in on the Farnden village shop case, and then I want you and Matthew Vickers—who knows all the circumstances already from his wife, Josie, who is the shopkeeper—to go along to the zoo and look around. Ask a few questions. Then report back."

LOIS DROVE DOWN THE ROAD LEADING TO THE TRESHAM ZOO, keeping an eye on the cardboard box on the seat beside her. She noticed that a small hole had appeared in the corner of the lid, and she put her foot down on the accelerator. The last thing she needed was a female wolf spider and family running free in her car.

She was directed up the long drive to the house, and there was greeted at the entrance by the owner, Robert Pettison himself, tall and slightly stooping. He smiled a toothy smile, and thanked her for bringing back one of their prize exhibits. "We were so worried for Lucilla and her babies. We discovered she was gone this morning first thing, and alerted the police. So kind of you to bring her back. Handed her in at the gate, did you? That's fine. Do come in and have a coffee and tell me how you found her. Perhaps you would like to take a look around her friends and relations before you leave?"

Lois gulped and said yes, that would be nice. And she certainly had time for a coffee. She followed him through a splendid portico at the front of the house and into a lofty drawing room, furnished with what Lois guessed were valuable antique pieces. He invited her to sit down, but while he went to organise coffee, she had a quick walk around the room, watched by steely-eyed portraits of, presumably, his ancestors. Or were they ancestral portraits by the yard? He sounded posh, but wacky, and she would not have said he had quite such illustrious-looking forebears.

"Here we are, then," said Pettison. "Do you take cream in your coffee? Now, tell me all about Lucilla's adventure."

Lois described Gran's encounter with the large and fecund spider, and asked if he had other similar interesting animals in his zoo. "I know you have snakes?" she said.

"Beautiful, sinuous creatures," he said. "Oh yes. You must see them, too, if you have time. I will give you a personal tour. Snakes are my favourites, you know. Such elegant people!"

People? thought Lois. Looks like we've got a right one here. "Not so sure about elegant," she said. "Are they lethal? That's what I want to know."

Pettison chuckled. "Of course they are, my dear," he said. "That is their most interesting characteristic. Swift to move, swift to strike, and swift to vanish."

"You may remember that we returned a cobra to your zoo a short while ago, and I'm sure you will agree that two visits to Long Farnden from your resident people is strange, to say the least?"

"Ah yes, the cobra. Splendid chap! We had the police round, but none of my staff could explain its escape."

"If it did escape," said Lois, adjusting her skirt in an attempt to redirect Pettison's fixed gaze at her legs. "Or had it been stolen and placed where my daughter found it, in her shop storeroom?"

"Possible, but unlikely. All my staff are closely vetted, and would never do such a cruel thing to one of our people."

"Animals, you must mean," said Lois crossly. "Well, I must be getting on. If we find any more on our property, we shall be consulting our lawyers."

"Oh, come now, my dear! Can you not regard it as a privilege to come across such rare specimens?"

"No, we can't. And I can't waste any more time this morning. I'll have a brief look round, and see myself out. I expect you'll be hearing from the police soon. Oh, and can I have the box back, please? The police want it."

"Of course, my dear. I'll get through to the gate and have it ready for you to collect."

After she had gone, Pettison smiled to himself. A feisty young person. Just as he liked them. And Justin seemed to be handling the situation very well. It was a risk, of course, that he would somehow lose the specimens, or the shopgirl would turn them loose. But so far, so good. The Meades had been responsible about returning the snake and the spider. "Nevertheless," he said aloud to one of his ancestors on the wall, "I shall be glad when nephew Justin is safely settled in their flat, and we can resume business as usual."

Justin had been offered accommodation in his large mansion, but he had refused, saying he wanted to be away from the zoo premises. He was looking, he said, for a self-contained flat, with somewhere to keep the rare specimens he handled for Pettison. So when he heard about the flat over the shop, he was immediately interested. He had surreptitiously looked around the premises, and had seen a large shed at the back, which could be just the job. And he had devised a plan that would secure it for him.

Walking down the long drive to the zoo itself, Lois found her way in and had a quick look round, but could see no immediately obvious way any of the animals could have escaped. She had explained her appointment with Pettison on her way in, but now she could find no members of the staff to talk to, except for the same ticket woman at the gate, and she said they were not really open yet. All the keepers were in a meeting. She produced Lucilla's box, now empty, and hoped Lois would call again.

Back in the sane world of the town, Lois parked her car and made for the police station, carrying the box. Cowgill was waiting for her in reception, and on taking one look at her face, told the sergeant on duty that he did not wish to be disturbed for at least an hour.

In his office, which overlooked the main street of Tresham, he drew up a chair for Lois and sat down behind his desk.

"You look explosive," he said. "Is it safe to ask how you got on at the zoo?"

Lois banged the box down on his desk, and said, "The owner is stark, staring crazy, for a start. Have you met him? Mr Robert Pettison? He should never be in charge of a zoo full of dangerous animals! You have to do something, Cowgill."

"We are already making preliminary enquiries, my dear Lois," he said. "And don't worry, we are very familiar with Pettison. Nutty as a fruitcake, as my chaps say. But he's harmless. It's all a performance. Eccentric toff who owns valuable animals. He is really a very astute operator, and his zoo is beyond reproach, according to inspection reports. Your encounters with the snake and now the spider are the first indications of anything wrong there."

"He may be harmless," said Lois bitterly, "but his animals definitely are not! Did you know he calls them his people?"

"No, I didn't know that. But he has every right to do so, as far as we are concerned. Did you talk to any of his staff and look round the zoo?"

"Very briefly. Nobody around for a chat. In a meeting, supposedly, but I did wonder if Pettison had got word around to them not to talk to me. One thing, though, how did he know I was going to be there? I didn't ring first, or anything like that, but he was waiting for me at the entrance to the house. Did your lot tell him?"

"Of course not, Lois. It was probably the woman on the gate."

Lois sighed deeply, and subsided into her chair. "I suppose so," she said. "I must say I'm seeing snakes and spiders round every corner. He's really got me rattled."

"Don't worry. We'll sort it all out very quickly. It's got to be someone who's around locally and found a way to get into the animal cages and pens without anyone knowing. And Derek's changed the locks at the shop, did you say? Splendid. Leave it with me, but keep your eyes and ears open. And stay in touch."

Ten

The Fiat 500 sped along the straight fen road, past small farm cottages huddled against the strong winds that swept the fields, with no hedges or trees to hinder them. It was a bleak landscape, and Justin Brookes felt the usual lowering of spirits as he entered the long drive down to his family farm a few miles outside Boston. Wonderful skies, people always said of the Lincolnshire fens, but this morning the sky was low and a depressing uniform grey.

He had cut short his usual tour around villages delivering fliers, having received a message that his father was very ill. He had been able to contact his uncle, Robert Pettison, and rearrange a meeting for next week. Their shared involvement in the business kept them in touch, and he always looked forward to seeing new additions to the zoo's extraordinary collection of rare animals. Sometimes he thought Robert was daft enough to be one of them, but he kept that thought to himself.

He arrived in the yard behind the farmhouse, and saw his mother waiting for him, an anxious expression on her face.

"Thank goodness you've come, Justin," she said, accepting a light kiss on her cheek. "Your father was asking for you yesterday, and we don't think he has long to go."

"Let's go in straightaway," he said. "It'll be good to get in out of this wretched fen wind."

They went into the house, and up the stairs to his father's room. "Here's Justin, dear. He's just this minute got back."

Justin looked at his father's ashen face on the pillow, and wondered if he was too late. But his mother patted the thin hand lying on the sheet, and the old man opened his eyes.

"Hello, lad," he said. "Still wearing that silly cravat thing round your neck?"

Miles away in Long Farnden, Josie sat in the shop, chatting to her mother on the telephone. The lunchtime rush of customers had finished, and she had time to catch up on Lois's visit to the zoo this morning. Matthew had rung to say he and Chris, Cowgill's assistant, were also off to see Robert Pettison, and Josie was anxious to know what had been discovered.

"So did he explain how those horrible things could have got here in the shop?" she said now to her mother.

"No. He seemed to think we should be delighted to have housed them for a while! I'm afraid I took a real dislike to him. One of those slightly mad kinds of people. And, by the way, that's what he calls those creepy crawlies. His people! I mean, I ask you, Josie."

"Sounds like he should be locked up in a cage himself!"

"However, I went to see Cowgill after, and he said Pettison is as sharp as the next man. The wacky bit is all an act. You know what I thought, duckie?"

"Yep. You thought the act was to cover up something sinister going on. Some nasty business that involves frightening nice young shopkeepers like me!"

"That's exactly right. He wasn't sorry enough for what had happened. After all, he is responsible for those dangerous snakes and spiders. If they'd bitten any of us, he'd be in big trouble. I don't call that being as sharp as the next man, do you?"

"Maybe it's a risk he's prepared to take," suggested Josie.

"Anyway," continued Lois. "I'm taking the whole thing on, and shall be ferretin' around to see what I can dig up to explain it all. One thing, though, Josie. I doubt very much if there will be any more escapers. He'll know better than that. Police eyes are on him, and all of us watching out. No, I'm sure you're safe from any more nasties."

"Thank God for that! Oh, there goes the shop bell. Must go. See you later, Mum. Bye."

Josie went through to the shop, and found Gran leafing through the pile of newspapers. "Hi, Gran," she said. "Can I get you anything?"

"No, dear. I'm just looking through the local paper. Joan rang me earlier and said there's an interesting story in this week's issue."

"Not about escaped reptiles, I hope!"

"As a matter of fact, yes. Seems somebody's dog was nosing around in a barn over Waltonby way, and got bitten by something so bad that it killed it. Poisonous bite, they reckon. And from something big enough to get away without the dog getting at it first."

All the colour had gone from Josie's face. "A little dog, was it?" she asked.

Gran looked closely at the newspaper. "Here it is; look. No, it was a big German shepherd. See, here's a picture. Looks a lovely dog. But really big, and should've come off best in a fight."

Josie looked closely at the photo, and the news story beside it. The police had been informed, and the dog taken to an animal mortuary for further investigation. The report said that the owner had seen something moving behind a pile of sacks, and thought it must be a rat. They had had an infestation of rodents, but these had been dealt with recently. The dog had been only too keen to investigate, and had seemed to pounce on something behind the sacks. Almost at once it had yelped and collapsed, and the owner had seen some movement over by the door of the barn, but couldn't say what it was.

"Oh Lor, Gran," Josie said. "I know what I would suggest! A sodding great cobra snake! I hope it's not on its way back here," she added, and her voice wobbled. "It's all getting a bit much. I'm going to phone Mum and tell her to read about it. Now then, Gran, do you want your usual raisin loaf this week?"

"Thank you, dear. I'm on my way home, so I'll take this paper to your mother. But you're not to worry. It could have been one of them giant rats that did for that dog."

This wasn't much consolation for Josie, but she decided to get on with unpacking a new delivery of groceries and try to put dangerous animals from her mind.

ROBERT PETTISON HAD OVERSEEN THE CLOSING OF THE ZOO AT the appointed time, and went for his usual walk around the perimeter to check all was safe and secure. It was beginning to rain, and his rare-breed sheep were huddled under an ancient spreading chestnut tree. They looked happy enough, and he walked on and into the next enclosure, where small horned cattle were lying down in the shelter of a tall hawthorn hedge. All well there, then, he said to himself.

He walked on, thinking about his nephew Justin, who was coming over for a meeting next week. A strange one, that. Always the same elegant fellow, if slightly raffish. It was the cravat that did it! The only time he had seen him looking different was when they met with others in a big London hotel, where he had hardly recognised him. On that occasion, he had worn a beautifully tailored grey suit, white shirt and old-school tie, and looked every inch the city banker.

Pettison had been close to Justin's father, until the poor man had fallen ill. They had been at the same school, and over the years had kept up their friendship. Young Brookes, by then a farmer, had fallen for Pettison's sister, and they had married and produced Justin. The farm had been ideal for Pettison's developing rare trade in wild animals. They had only the small specimens to house on the farm, of course. He smiled to himself at the thought of a gorilla loping over the flat fields of Lincolnshire.

It was raining now, and Pettison quickened his step. So Justin would be living in Long Farnden. The thought took him to the visit from Mrs Meade, who lived in that village. A very attractive sleuth! He had every reason to call her a sleuth, since she had become known throughout the Tresham underworld as a woman to avoid at all costs. She had a special relationship with top-cop Cowgill, and had a knack of homing in on matters that were necessarily kept secret from the police.

He had found her sharp-tongued and impatient, and decided it would take all his undoubted charm to win her over to his side. She could be very useful, he thought, nodding to himself. Very useful, indeed. She could also be dangerous, and he hoped Justin had taken that into account.

He arrived at the main gates again, and made sure all

was well, before returning to the house, where he dried off, retreated to his kitchen and set about preparing himself an exquisite meal of escargots in a French dressing, followed by smoked trout and a salad of fresh endive from the kitchen garden. For Justin's arrival next week, he decided to serve up roast lamb, with all the trimmings. The lad should be bringing him valuable goods, and would deserve the best.

Eleven

"SO THIS MORNING I'M GOING TO ROUGH OUT AN AD FOR THE flat. I shall put it in the local evening paper in Tresham, and one or two freebies that go out to the villages. Is that okay with you, Josie?"

Lois was talking on the telephone from her study, and she could see through her window a police car drawing up outside the shop. "Looks like Matthew's on his way home for breakfast. I can see him drawing up outside. I'd best go now and leave you to say hello."

"He's only dropping in, Mum. He wanted to pick up the local paper with the story about the dog with the poison bite. Anyway, talk soon. Bye."

Lois settled down to write the advertisement, and was still chewing the end of her pen trying to get it right. "'Charming one bedroom flat, quietly situated above the village shop in Long Farnden. Use of garden, and parking space at rear of building.' No, that won't do," she said aloud as Gran brought in her usual offering of coffee and biscuits. "Here, read this, Mum, and see if it sounds right."

"Do you have to start with the bedroom?" Gran said. "I should describe the delightful sitting room with views of the village playing fields, then go on to one spacious bedroom, then modern bathroom and kitchen. Parking space at rear of shop, and use of landscaped garden. That's more like it, isn't it?"

"Mum! The bedroom's no bigger than a box room, the bathroom has a lavatory that could have been designed by Thomas Crapper himself, and you couldn't swing a cat in the kitchen. As for the garden, nothing's been grown in it since Josie took over the shop. No, it's better not to arouse expectations. Better the other way round; then a viewing will be a pleasant surprise."

"We don't want no more surprises in that flat!" Gran said. "Pleasant or otherwise!"

"Of course not," Lois said crossly. "Anyway, thanks for your help. And the coffee. I must get on now."

"Dismissed," said Gran, her nose in the air. "Don't forget that actor man who might be interested," she added, and stomped out, leaving the door ajar, knowing that nothing was more calculated to annoy Lois. She was sure her daughter was wrong. All estate agents exaggerated the wonders of the properties for sale or rent, so why should they be any different?

After Lois had written the advertisement, she sent it by email to the newspapers and relaxed. Job done. Now she had to tackle the flat itself. Perhaps she would do a quick repainting job, and get Derek to smarten up the bathroom. She could even make a virtue of the antique lavatory, with its flowery printed bowl and wooden seat. A few flowers strategically placed in the tiny hallway and sitting room would work wonders, and she would make a list of necessary pieces of furniture to replace. The dump in Tresham, now elevated to a recycling centre, had the most amazing bargains. Secondhand chairs and tables in good condition, and loads of other things. They even had a section for practically new curtains.

She stood up from her desk. "That's my weekend settled," she said to Jeems, who, as usual, sat at her feet while she was working. "Now, this afternoon I'll go into Tresham to see Hazel and buy some paint from the wholesaler."

"Talking to yourself again," said Gran, coming in with a handful of post. "Postie's late again. I reckon she ought to be replaced. Hey, Lois, that's a good idea! Why don't we offer the flat to a reliable postman. Special rates for assisting in post office on pension days?"

"Postmen, or postwomen, don't forget, have to be appointed by head office, or some such. And anyway, we want as much as we can get in rent, without offering special rates. We shall see who comes to view. I'd be happy with a nice middle-aged professional bachelor, who'd be equal to burglars and snakes, and good at housework. Josie might hear again from that actor bloke."

"Well, all I can say is good luck to whoever takes it on. And I promise to keep quiet about recent invasions of snakes, spiders, toads, rats and frogs. Sounds biblical, doesn't it? One of them plagues in the Old Testament. At least I escaped boils. And when you're in Tresham, can you get another couple of rat traps?"

Hazel Thornbull was the wife of a Farnden farmer, and had worked for Lois since she first founded the New Brooms cleaning service. When they set up the Tresham office, Hazel immediately applied for the job as manager, and with her small daughter now at school for a full day, and her mother able to help out with her timetable, she had established a well-organised office in the heart of town. This morning had been busy, with two of the cleaning girls coming in for changes in rotas, and a new client in Waltonby to be visited.

"So what's new this afternoon?" said Lois, coming through the door. "And how's your family? Busy time on the farm?"

"Morning, Mrs M. Everybody's fine, except John, and he's exhausted, as usual! Still, it's been a good year so far, for once. A happy farmer is a rare bird!"

They got down to business then, and Lois gave Hazel a flier advertising the flat to stick up in the office window.

The potential client for cleaning was from Waltonby, the new owner of the old vicarage, a massive Victorian house built in the days when maids occupied the attic rooms and gardeners tended the extensive grounds.

"What sort of people are they?" asked Lois.

Hazel sniffed. "Usual newly rich. Probably won the lottery. Wife overdressed and tame husband on a lead."

"Hazel! Don't forget our motto: 'We clean; you pay.' And that's all we need."

"Mrs M, you just made that up. 'We sweep cleaner' is our motto!"

"True. But it really doesn't matter who or what they are. We've got all sorts on our books. I'll make an appointment to see them, and let you know what transpires."

"Anything new on that poor dog story? I reckon it was one of those horrible things old Pettison's got in his zoo. John reckons it should be cleared out altogether. He's always worried that the things brought over from foreign countries could bring diseases that turn into epidemics and run riot in our farm animals. I suppose there are special checks on them at customs and so on?"

"Small things, insects an' that, can come hidden in luggage and are never spotted by customs, so Gran says," Lois answered. "But that's Gran, so I expect John has nothing to worry about. Now, I'll just nip up the road and see if Dot is back from work. Let me know if you get any replies to the flat ad."

Dot Nimmo's house was at the top of the same street, and Lois parked outside and knocked. As she stood waiting for Dot to come to the door, she noticed a van parked on the opposite side of the road. It had a snarling tiger emblazoned on the side, and at the wheel sat Robert Pettison, his head partly shielded by a newspaper as if to hide himself from Lois's gaze.

"Morning, Mrs M!" Dot beamed at Lois. "Just the person I was wanting to see. Come on in."

"Just a minute, Dot," Lois said. "What's that van doing over there? Is there somebody living there that works at the zoo?"

"Oh that," said Dot. "It's the zoo boss. He's got a lady friend he calls on every Friday afternoon. Has to wait until her husband goes off to work after lunch, though. Beats me how hubby don't cotton on to a so-and-so tiger sitting outside his front door every week! Still, he's reckoned to be one of them pimps, except he's got just the one woman for sale. Funny kind of setup . . . Now come on in, and have a refreshing cup of tea."

Lois stood at Dot's front window and looked over at the tiger van. "Hey, the front door of that house is opening. Now a little man is coming out. He's not even looking at the van. Wait a sec, Dot. I want to see if Pettison gets out. Ah, yes, there he goes. Has to duck to get inside that door! I can just see a brassy blonde head inside. What's she like, his Friday mistress?"

"No better than she should be," said Dot primly. "Come and sit down. I've got an item of interesting info for you."

Twelve

SATURDAY, THE BUSIEST DAY IN THE LIFE OF TRESHAM ZOO, and Robert Pattison was awakened by the sound of a shot. He instinctively curled up under the bedclothes. When he came to his senses and realised it was probably a bird flying into his bedroom window, he decided to investigate.

Downstairs, he unlocked the back door and went outside. It had been a sharp crack, and he guessed the bird would be either unconscious or dead. In the flowerbed under his window, something black and white, with flashes of red, lay under a shrub, and he bent closer. It was a woodpecker, and its eyes were flickering. He bent down and touched it. It shivered and moved its wings. He put his hand over the pulsating body and picked it up. It chattered at him and struggled, trying to attack him with its long, sharp beak, but he had it securely in his grasp and went quickly downstairs in his nightshirt. He found a suitable box, and put it in carefully, where it cowered and glared at him, chattering harshly.

"There you are then, my beauty," he said. "What a smart gentleman! We'll see that you are safe and well, and then you can fly off to the wood."

The bird was silent then, and from where he had put it on the kitchen table, it watched with a baleful eye as he ate his toast and drank coffee.

"Don't look at me like that, sir," said Pettison. "I have no intention of putting you in a cage in my zoo. The law would be down on me like a ton of the proverbial bricks. But my staff would, I am sure, be pleased to meet you, and once we have established that you are not injured, you may fly away like Peter, like Paul!"

"Morning, Mr Pettison. Talking to yourself as usual." It was his cleaning lady, Mrs Richardson, who was the only person brave enough to speak her mind to him.

"Good morning, and a fine morning it is!"

"Maybe for some," she answered gloomily. "I'm not stopping. Just come to give you my notice. I'm leaving, as from today. My hubby says I'm not to work here alongside them animals any more. That story in the papers of a German Shepherd being poisoned in a barn was the final straw for him. Snakes and dangerous insects! Plenty of people wanting cleaners, so I'll be going. And you take care, Mr Pettison. You could be next. And if I was you, I'd release that bird before the RSPB gets here."

Pettison stared at her. "But Mrs Richardson, you only clean the house, nowhere near our special people? Surely your husband realises that?"

"Oh, stuff your special people! They're just a load of nasty creatures, and my husband says I'm to quit. Once he's made up his mind, there's no moving him, and I must say I'm not sorry," she replied. Her face was closed, allowing no more persuasive conversation, and with a quick nod she turned on her heel and got as far as the door before turning back.

"Oh, an' if you make any trouble for me about my wages, an' that nasty tax inspector, don't forget what I know about you! They'll put you in a cage yourself, and for a nice long time!" With that parting shot, she was gone.

The bird began chattering again, and Pettison cursed Mrs Richardson. "Nasty creatures, indeed! A case of the pot calling the kettle black, don't you think?" he said. "Now, sir, I must look for another cleaner."

He found the telephone directory, services section, and looked down the list of cleaners. "From now on," he addressed the woodpecker, "I shall use one of these cleaning businesses. One with a professional approach. Do the job, mind your own business, and leave. Ah, now sir, this looks likely. 'New Brooms, We Sweep Cleaner.' I like that!" He jotted down the number, and went out to his study and the telephone.

Lois was in her office when the call came in, and for one minute she wasn't sure she had heard aright. "Robert Pettison, did you say? The zoo man?"

"Yes, of course. Now, madam, you sound familiar. Have we met before?"

"Um, yes, we have. Briefly. I came to see you about one of your snakes that escaped and was found in my daughter's shop. How can I help you?"

"Mrs Meade, isn't it? I'm afraid I must have a wrong number. I am looking for New Brooms, a cleaning service. Sorry to trouble you."

"Hey, wait! You *have* got New Brooms. It's my business, long established and extremely reliable." She was doing some quick thinking, and in her mind had Dot Nimmo safely installed as cleaner and spy in Cameroon Hall.

"Mm, well." There was a long pause, and Lois could hear a tapping sound in the background.

"You still there, Mr Pettison?"

"Yes, I have given some thought to the matter, and I shall be glad if you could send a woman today. In about an hour's time, please. Tell her to report at the gate."

"I'm afraid I couldn't do that. I have a strict routine when taking on clients, and that involves my coming along to see you first. I shall need to estimate how long the work will take—just a quick tour around the house. Then we can sort out rates of pay, etcetera. You will appreciate I also need to make sure my staff will be safe, bearing in mind the animals and our unfortunate experience. When would it suit you for me to come along?"

The tapping sound was now accompanied by a loud guffaw. "Splendid, Mrs Meade!" he said. "Would eleven o'clock suit you? And I'll make sure none of our people are on the loose! Goodbye!"

"Idiot," Lois said aloud. "Still, Dot will be more than a match for him."

DEREK SAT IN THE KITCHEN, READING THE SPORTS PAGES OF THE newspaper. "New client, and guess who?" said Lois, coming in with a smile.

"David Beckham?"

"Of course not! No, you'll never guess, so I'll tell you."

"I know," said Gran, coming in from the larder. "It's that bloke at the zoo. What's 'isname."

"Mum, you're a marvel," said Lois. "And his name is Pettison. I'm going to see him this morning at eleven. Better get my skates on."

"Lois! I forbid it!" Derek had gone very red in the face. "Of all people, he is the most sinister old fool I've ever met. Don't forget his lousy snake frightened us all to death."

"Too right!" said Gran. "You must be out of your mind, Lois. I'm with Derek on this."

"I don't think you *have* met him, Derek," Lois said calmly. "And I have, and am sure no harm can come from my going to see him. I don't have to take him on if I decide not to. I was thinking Dot Nimmo might be good for the job. What do you think, Mum?"

Gran sat down heavily at the table. "Well, I suppose if you must even consider it, I can't think of anyone I would rather have eaten by a bear than Dot Nimmo."

VISITORS WERE ALREADY ARRIVING AT THE GATE OF THE ZOO, and Pettison had smartened himself up in order to walk around and answer questions from the grockles, as his former cleaner had called them. The more visitors, the more he liked it, not only because they brought in much-needed cash, but they acted as a perfect cover for his other interests.

"Look, Margie," he said to his employee in the ticket booth, holding out the woodpecker box towards her. "Isn't he a splendid person? In his full plumage. Not often we see them so closely. I am taking him round to introduce him to a few grockles, and then I shall release him to fly away into the blue yonder."

"Yes, Mr Pettison. But don't let him out too near me. Nasty dirty thing. You never know where it's been. Now, if you'll let me get on. We're busy this morning. Good morning!" she added, turning to a family just arriving. "Are there five of you? Children go in half price. Enjoy your visit."

Margie Turner had worked for the zoo ever since Pettison opened it to the public. She was Tresham born and bred, and knew all about her employer and his Friday assignations. All the staff knew, and it was a source of great amusement to all. "Just imagine the old fool at it with that brassy blonde," Margie had confided to her friend on the refreshment counter. "She must be desperate for the cash, that's all I can say."

"Good morning. I have an appointment with Mr Pettison." Lois had appeared at the gate, smartly dressed in her business clothes, pinstripe coat and skirt, with her long legs clad in sheer black tights. Good for business, she had told herself. She was well aware that the woman on the gate had rung through to announce her arrival, but Pettison would probably keep her waiting. He was that sort.

As it happened, she was halfway up the drive to the house when a voice called to her from across the wide lawns.

"Good morning! Glad to see you here bang on time! Come along in, and we'll have coffee."

His voice was mellifluous and friendly, but Lois shivered. It was a warning, without any doubt, and she followed him with a foolish desire to turn and run.

Thirteen

"I can see you are in dire need of a cleaner, Mr Pettison," said Lois, looking round the dirty, untidy kitchen. They had had coffee, during which time he refused to talk business, but had given her a colourful history of his life so far. In spite of herself, Lois listened with interest. He had been fascinated by rare animals all his life. He grew up in Africa, where he had kept a small private zoo from the age of ten, and, on returning to England in his forties, had planned a professional setup. This had fitted in with his parents' intention to buy a large house with parkland in the Midlands, and when they had both died, he had built up his collection until it was internationally known.

"I am afraid Mrs Richardson was not the most reliable of persons," he said finally, rinsing out the coffee mugs in a sink already full of dishes covered with the detritus of unnumbered previous meals.

"Took you for a ride, I reckon," said Lois. "Did as little

work as possible, and collected her wages with a willing hand. I've met one or two Mrs Richardsons, and they don't last five minutes in my team. Now, can we have a quick look around, and then I'll give you some facts and figures about how New Brooms can help."

As they entered the drawing room, which looked out over a well-kept garden and parkland beyond, Lois was struck with the difference between the scruffy interior of the hall, and outside in the grounds, which were immaculate.

"Are you the gardener? It's certainly in better shape than all this," she said, indicating the interior of a potentially lovely room. She kept the long, sagging sofa between them. Her professional eye told her that the furniture was good, but in sore need of care and attention. He was beginning to ogle again, and her voice was sharp.

"Gardener? Goodness me, no, I wouldn't have time! No, we have Mrs Richardson's husband, an old man who comes every day, seven days a week, rain or shine. He loves this place, and regards the garden and grounds as his own territory. Has a potting shed behind the house, and if it rains or snows, he sits in there and reads thrillers. Oh, and yes, he comes into the kitchen for a cup of tea around eleven o'clock every morning. Your cleaner would be required to make that for him. Now, upstairs, young woman. And don't worry, I am not the least interested in having my wicked way with you!"

He threw back his head, and the guffaws went on loudly for some time.

"Good," said Lois. "That's one thing settled. And your reluctance will include any young woman I send to you to clean this dump?"

More laughter followed this, and Lois began to walk around the many bedrooms, itemising what needed to be done, and then walked smartly back down the wide stairway, saying she felt like Anne Boleyn at Hampton Court Palace.

"I beg your pardon?" he asked.

"Anne Boleyn. As in Henry the Eighth's second wife. Her ghost is said to walk down the grand staircase at the palace, with her head tucked underneath her arm."

"Your head seems to be securely in place, Mrs Meade. Is there anything more to discuss? Everything else seems acceptable, so when can your cleaning woman start?"

"At eight thirty on Tuesday morning. She will need to come every day for a week to clear the place ready for cleaning. Then once a week should be sufficient. Is that acceptable?"

He nodded, and said he would show her out, as he needed to go down to the gate to see Margie. "Lovely person, Margie Turner," he said. "Guards the zoo like a policeman on duty!"

LOIS DROVE SLOWLY THROUGH THE CENTRE OF TOWN, LOOKING for a place to park. The traffic was heavy, and she sat for several minutes at traffic lights outside the police station. A familiar figure walked towards her and tapped on the car window. It was Cowgill, of course.

"Morning, Lois dear. You're looking very lovely, if I may be so bold?"

"Oh Cowgill, not you, too! I'm up to here with lustful old men. Been to see Pettison at the zoo."

"Open up and let me in. I need to tell you things. Quick sharp! The lights are changing."

He sat down swiftly in her passenger seat, and said she should park round the rear of the police station. "I assume that the business suit means you are taking Cameroon Hall on as a client for New Brooms?" His whole demeanour had changed, and he was every inch the policeman.

Lois nodded, and followed him up to his office. She said she had a great many things to do, so she couldn't spare much time. Cowgill immediately got down to the subject at hand.

"I should warn you about the Cameroon Hall zoo; and though it's perfectly fine as far as the animals are concerned, unofficial reports have come to our ears of staff difficulties, burglaries, that kind of thing. On each occasion, Pettison has managed to deal with everything without needing our help. But I strongly suspect that there is far more going on there than we have yet discovered. Can't put my finger on it, but I would say this to you, Lois. Be very careful who you send to clean there. In fact, I would advise you not to take on the job at all. But I suppose you won't agree to that?"

"You suppose right. I intend to send in Dot Nimmo, who is, as you know, a very tough cookie, having been married to a gangland boss in Tresham, and still in touch with useful people."

The telephone rang, and Cowgill answered it with a brisk "I'm busy. Tell them to phone later. What? Where? Right, I'll be there in half an hour. Tell Chris I shall require her to drive me."

"Something urgent?" said Lois.

"Something very nasty," replied Cowgill, getting to his feet. "There's been an accident in Pettison's zoo. His chief worry seems to be that his people are in a state of rigid terror. And for 'people,' read 'monkeys.'"

Fourteen

For Lois, the rest of the weekend had been taken up with a trip with Josie to the nearby shopping centre, newly opened in Tresham, with a tempting number of clothes shops especially dealing in designer fashions. It was Josie's birthday, and Lois had promised her a warm winter coat.

"You'll freeze, gel, come the east winds," Gran had said, critically looking her up and down, and saying that if anyone asked her, a good tweed skirt and lambs' wool twinset would be just the ticket.

"Don't forget the pearls, Gran," Josie had said, laughing.

Although she loved shopping with her daughter, Lois had found her mind repeatedly returning to the woman in the monkey cage. It transpired that the victim was not dead, but badly wounded from a vicious attack. She had been taken to hospital, and the matter referred to the police. According to the news and the local paper, the woman had been a friend of a member of staff. She had—in the owner's words—"trespassed into the monkey people's territory, and paid the price."

Everyone in the zoo, and of course visitors, was warned against trespass as a matter of course. This was apparently the first incident of its kind. One of the keepers had been working in the cage with the door closed when he was interrupted by a woman, who was leaving her cleaning job at the hall, and had come to say goodbye to the keeper. He had opened the door to the cage, and the woman had entered, only to be immediately attacked by a male chimpanzee defending his territory. She had collapsed, but was rescued almost immediately.

So it was probably that Richardson woman, Lois had thought, as Josie emerged from the changing room, in a singing red coat that reached a decent level nearly to her ankles.

On the way home, Josie had accused her mother of having her mind elsewhere. "I can see from your face that you're thinking of something bad. Not another reptile, I hope!" she had said.

Now Lois sat in her office, sorting out the schedules for the midday meeting of New Brooms. All the girls would be present, and Andrew, part-time interior decorator, part-time cleaner when required. Looking at her watch, she saw that there were ten minutes clear until the team turned up. She dialled Cowgill's private number, and was irritated to see that his message service was switched on.

"Ring me, please, as soon as poss. Thanks," she said.

The doorbell rang, and she heard Gran hurrying to get to the door before anyone else. "Come on in, girls," she said. "And one boy, Andrew! You look cold, all of you. Hot coffee any good?"

"Thanks, Gran. We'll have it after the meeting as usual. Where's Dot?" Lois added, and Hazel said she had seen her rushing past the office window, so guessed she would be a little late.

"Not like Dot," Lois said, and began the business of the meeting. Ten minutes later, the doorbell rang again, and Gran ushered in a red-faced Dot. "Sorry, Mrs M. Trouble with the car. My nephew's lent me his spare. Enormous great thing, a black BMW with dark windows. Like driving a hearse. Anyway, what have I missed?"

"Nothing important. We're going through the schedules. Now, here's yours, but there will be a possible change. We have a new client, and I'd like you to take it on. There are a few things to finalise, but then I'll arrange to introduce you. We were to go in today, but there's been a drama there, so we will go tomorrow."

"What kind of a drama?" said Dot, frowning.

"A nasty accident, to be blunt."

Before Lois could elaborate, Dot said, "Oh my Gawd! Not the zoo? I reckon you take your life in your hands working there. My friend's on the gate. Oh no, Mrs M, it's not Margie Turner, is it? They wouldn't give the name on the telly news."

After that, the whole story had to be discussed, and Lois assured Dot that she would only go there to work if it was considered 100 percent safe.

"Don't you worry about that, Mrs M," Dot said, intrigued in spite of her first fears. "My nephew's a mate of old Pettison. I'll get the dirt from him when I take the hearse back. You fix it up for tomorrow, and we'll go and have a snoop," she added. Her face had resumed its normal colour, and her eyes twinkled with excitement. "Now then, what's next?" she said.

* * *

When the team had gone, Lois looked to see if Cowgill had answered her. The red light was winking, and she played a message that was short and to the point. "Need to see you. Please ring back."

She tried at once to call him, and this time he picked up his receiver. "Ah, Lois. I'd like you to meet me at the Cameroon Hall zoo at three o'clock this afternoon. I'll be there with Chris, and I'll warn the gate that you're there with my permission. Needless to say, the zoo is closed today."

So why did he want me to be there? Lois was reluctant for two reasons. She did not like being ordered about by Cowgill. She was not an employee of the police service, and had never received a penny for her help on previous cases. If this *was* a case? The one thing she needed to know for certain, however, was the name of the victim, and the best way of finding out was to meet Cowgill as instructed.

After lunch and a thinking walk with Jemima across the fields, Lois set off for Tresham and the zoo. As she approached the main gates, she saw that they were closed, and a policeman stood by.

"Mrs Meade?" he said, opening the gates. "Drive up to the house, please. The zoo is out of bounds at the moment. Inspector Cowgill is expecting you."

The driveway was now becoming familiar to Lois, and she coasted along, turning over in her mind what Pettison had said to her when she was last here. He had agreed to everything she had stipulated, and made it quite clear that hanky-panky was not in his line. Was he gay? She thought not. Not from the way he looked at her legs! But then that might mean nothing. By now she had reached the house, and drove round the back to park. Cowgill, as if by magic, appeared at the side of her car, and opened the door for her.

"Ah, good. Come with me," he said, and led her into a sitting room, which obviously at some time had done duty as a family library. There were books everywhere, and he moved a couple of piles so that she could sit down.

"Now, Lois, I want your word that you will abandon all thoughts of sending any of your cleaners to this house."

"I'll think about it," said Lois. "Why the urgency? You could have told me that over the phone."

"Because of one very important fact. The victim—you probably know by now—was Pettison's former cleaner. The cause of the attack in the chimps cage is more or less known. The woman trespassed. She had gone into the cage to speak to a keeper, and the sight of an angry old chimp could have given her a heart attack. She certainly collapsed, and was bitten, but only a little. The woman was confirmed as Mrs Richardson, until very recently employed as a cleaner by Robert Pettison at Cameroon Hall."

"Ah. I see. A different kettle of fish altogether. Thanks for telling me, Cowgill. I do see your point, and will certainly think this over very carefully. I have already told Dot Nimmo that she is to work here, and she's really looking forward to it. But this might well change her mind! What have you done with Pettison? He usually shows up if somebody comes up the drive."

"He is answering our questions at the moment. Not always willingly, but we are persisting. Now, if you'll come with me, I'll show you something else you need to see."

"Not another killer reptile!" she said nervously, and followed him out of the room.

THEY WENT THROUGH TO THE MAIN HALL, AND THEN COWGILL indicated the stairs. "Up there, Lois, and I hope you've a strong stomach."

"Not very," she said. "Depends what it is. Is it really necessary for me to see?"

"No, but I'd like you to know what Dot's in for, should you be foolish enough to let her work here."

At the top of the stairs, Cowgill turned right along a corridor until, at the very end, he brought out a key and opened the door. Then he took her hand, and led her gently inside.

"Hey, what are you up to—" She stopped suddenly, gripping Cowgill's hand tightly.

In front of them, hanging from the ceiling, was a very large gorilla, eyes shining from the light in the corridor. It was huge, dark and extremely frightening. Lois tried to back out, but Cowgill held her steady.

"Don't worry, my dear. It is long dead, poor thing. That noose round its neck is meant to be frightening. According to our specialists, it probably died of very old age at least fifty years ago. Moth-eaten, here and there, if you look closely. Now, that's not all. If you've had enough, we'll go, but there is more."

"No, I'm okay. Is the rest as grisly?"

Cowgill nodded, and drew her round the room. The gorilla was a centrepiece, and all around were specimens of the animal kingdom, particularly all sizes of monkeys, some splayed to show their interior workings. Others, like a vast collection of insects, large and small, were laid out in pretty patterns in glass cases.

Lois stared, and then inside felt a rising anger against Pettison. She was not afraid, but furious that he could have made these innocent animals victims of his—his what? Was it some horrid perversion, or a workplace for an amateur 'ologist of some sort?

"This is awful, Cowgill! What the hell has he been up to?"

"He calls it his mausoleum."

"For his *people,* no doubt! My God, if I had him here, I'd . . ." Lois could not think of anything bad enough to do to Pettison.

"Then I'm glad he's not," said Cowgill. "But there is one mitigating fact. He bought this stuff, lock, stock and barrel, from the effects of an eccentric collector who died many years ago. There are some specimens here of creatures that are now extinct, and these are valuable. Anyway," he continued, "now do you see what Dot Nimmo should not come across with a duster in her hand?"

"I noticed you unlocked it. We could tell him to keep it locked at all times when New Brooms is likely to be on the premises."

Cowgill shrugged. "Up to you, Lois. But now you know about it, I trust you will give the whole thing more thought. Now, I must go and find my chaps. Mrs Richardson has been taken to hospital, and we must consider if and when we can allow the zoo to be opened again."

"Are you going to let go of my hand, or do I have to follow you?"

He chuckled, and before she could withdraw her hand, he kissed it, and then marched off along the corridor and down the grand staircase ahead of her.

Fifteen

"So what did you discover from Cowgill about the accident in the chimp cage?" Gran had dished up a steaming stew, full of leftovers from the Sunday roast, and augmented with herbs and her own spicy stock.

"Mm! This smells good." Lois sat down at the table and began to eat.

"Are you going to answer Gran's question?" Derek said.

"Well, best after supper, I think," she said. She had considered whether to tell Gran and Derek about the Pettison mausoleum, and had decided that on balance it would be a good thing to do. Then any extra precautions she had to arrange for Dot would be explained in advance. It was simple, really. She needed Dot to work there to know exactly how things went on, and that would include knowing how the reptile invasion of the shop could have happened. And why!

"Why best after supper?" said Gran. She feared the worst.

Lois had that look about her, one her mother knew so well. Another case of ferretin' was in the offing.

"Well, it's all to do with the zoo, and the chimpanzee attack. The woman apparently went into the cage when she shouldn't have. The animal regarded it as a menacing trespass on his territory. She was a cleaner up at the hall. Oh yes, and that's confidential, but Cowgill didn't say I had to keep secret the details of Pettison's private morgue there. Mind you, I think it's probably best if you do keep it to yourselves."

"Morgue! Lois, you need go no further. I forbid you to have anything more to do with it. An' that's an order!" Derek was sitting bolt upright, looking as stern as he could manage. This, unfortunately, was not enough, and Lois continued as if he hadn't spoken.

"I need to keep in touch with Cowgill to see what they discover about how things go on under the surface. As you know, Dot's keen to take on the cleaning job there, and as yet, I've made no final decision. The important thing is that the zoo is well away from the hall, and there'll be no need for Dot to go anywhere near it. And the woman in the entrance kiosk is an old friend of Dot. Margie Turner, she's called. End of story."

"Of course it's not the end of anything! But I suppose I have to trust in your common sense not to get too involved in something dangerous," said Derek, and getting up, he stalked out of the kitchen and slammed the door.

Gran's eyebrows lifted. "I must say, Lois, I agree with Derek. I'd say it's up to you and Dot Nimmo. She's not my favourite person, but I wouldn't see her come to harm."

Lois sighed. "You were happy to see her eaten by a bear not so long ago. But thanks, Mum. I don't know about you, but I'll not be happy until we find out exactly who put that snake in Josie's stockroom. I'd better go and smooth my husband down, and then it'll be time for Inspector Montalbano on the telly. I might pick up some tips."

Alone in her house in Tresham, Dot Nimmo Looked at the telephone and tried to decide whether to ring her cousin-in-law, Amadeus Mozart Nimmo, Mozzie for short. He was her cousin by marriage, a brother to Dot's late husband, Handel. Handy had been more of a sleeping partner in the dodgy enterprises that the Nimmo patriarch, the late Ludwig, had run successfully in Tresham for many years.

Now she was on her own, outside the dealings of the Nimmo businesses, but she kept in touch, feeling in some way that it kept her closer to her own late husband, of whom she had been extremely fond and proud. Her own son, Haydn, had died in a car crash, and her life had been dark and bereft until Lois Meade came along and recruited her into the New Brooms team.

Yes, now would be a good time, she thought. Mozzie would be in his armchair, with a whiskey at his elbow, asleep and snoring.

"Hello? Is that you, Mozzie? It's Dot here. Long time no see! How're you doin', boy? Good. Now listen, I know you're a friend of that Pettison man. Yeah, the one who comes an' sees to the brassy blonde over the road from me. Well, I need some information. Tomorrow? Yeah, fine. I'll bring the car back. See you then, boy."

She smiled and put down the phone. He was a useful dodger, in his way. Now, when she next spoke to Mrs M, she would have a few interesting things to tell her. A couple of hours later, she was about to go upstairs to bed when a loud rap on her front door caused her to pause. Kids, no doubt. There was a family of no-goods a few doors down the road, and knocking on doors and scarpering was one of their less offensive ways of being a nuisance.

She was halfway up the stairs when there was a second rap. Then she heard the letter box clang, and she turned. Once they had shoved through a lit firework, and if she'd not been there, it could have set the house on fire. She went down and through the hall to the front door. There was something on the mat, with a label attached. She bent down to pick it up, and it moved. She screamed and retreated. Then she could see what it was. A fat and wriggling worm was trying to move across the stiff bristles of her door mat.

"Very amusing," said Dot aloud. She put on rubber gloves, picked up the worm and carefully untied the label. Then she put the twisting body out into her back garden, and was about to screw up the small piece of card, when she saw some writing on it. "*Anima*," she read. "Latin: breath, life, soul."

"Rubbish," said Dot, and threw it into the bin.

Sixteen

Justin Brookes, returned from the fens of Lincolnshire, looked around the meagre room that served as his headquarters. His father had rallied, and after making excuses about important meetings to attend, he had said farewell to his mother.

Justin had taken up residence in the county town of Tresham some years ago, when he had first formed a business relationship with his uncle, Robert Pettison, housing small creatures at the Lincolnshire farm until he could collect them. There were empty barns and stables, so it was no problem.

Justin was getting very fed up now with having to share his room with creepy crawlies. As Robert's valuable consignments grew in number, he had to move. He often had to do a holding job for a day or two, as they had to be kept out of sight. Many were rare, and some nigh on extinction, illegally obtained from the wild, and Robert did not want them examined too closely before moving them on to rich customers. Justin opened the local paper and turned to the houses and flats to see if the one over the Farnden shop was in.

Nothing suitable presented itself at first, so he made himself a coffee and took up the evening paper. Flats to buy and rent. Ah, that should be it! His eye was caught by a name he recognised. There it was: Long Farnden, and the one he meant to take on. The details sounded promising. A one bedroom flat, with parking and a garden. No particulars of rent required, but a telephone number to contact, and he called straightaway to make an appointment to view.

There was no estate agent involved, so no need to leave his name and particulars. It sounded as if the owner had inserted the ad, and so he hoped for a reasonable rent.

"Good morning! Long Farnden village shop. How can I help you?"

Ah! The charming young shopkeeper herself, thought Justin. He announced his interest in the flat, using his old public school voice, and asked if he could come over and take a look.

"Yes, that will be satisfactory," said Josie.

"This morning? I have to be in your area," said Justin.

"No, I'm afraid it will have to be after shop hours. The flat is above the shop, you see. Also, I need the owners, one or other of them, to be present. Perhaps you could come about six o'clock? We are in the high street, and you can't miss the shop!"

Oh, you can be sure I know where the shop is, thought Justin, but he thanked Josie for her information and said he would see her at six o'clock sharp.

"We've got a prospective client for the shop, Mum, so can you be down here at six this evening?"

Lois heard the excitement in Josie's voice, and agreed at once. It was a big step, letting the flat over the shop to someone who could easily be a complete stranger. Derek had said that estate agents did all kinds of financial checks, and wouldn't it be a good idea if they put their flat in agents' hands? But Josie had said she was sure her questions would reveal the kind of character she would be dealing with, and took up Derek's suggestion that either he or Lois should be with her when showing people around.

"Man or woman?" asked Lois now.

"Man. Sounded posh, but nice. Agreed at once to come after shop hours. Said it would suit him better, as he was here and there during the day. Anyway, he is the first, if you don't count Gran, so we may get others. Must go now, Mum. Customer waiting."

Lois put down the phone and went off to the kitchen to find Gran. She needed to make sure her mother had no intention of resorting to her former plan of occupying the shop flat in the future. She was fairly sure the first experience had put her off for good, but she was equally sure that during a long life Gran had maintained a strongly held conviction that she was her own master and quite capable of making impulsive decisions, regardless of the inconvenience to other people.

"It's why you've never been president of the village Women's Institute," Derek had told her jokingly many times. "You can't be trusted to do the right thing."

Gran had retorted that one man's right thing was another man's disaster, and she had every right to make up her own mind. So now Lois told her that a possible tenant for the flat was coming at six o'clock, testing her reaction.

"I hope he's not allergic to creepy crawlies," Gran replied. "Or killer reptiles, for that matter. I trust you'll not tell him about the snake and the toad? Not to mention the rat!"

"So you'd not want to go back there and give it another try?"

"Over my dead body!" she exclaimed. "Which it might very well be, if I was ever fool enough to set up house there again."

"Good, so that's okay. Josie said he sounded posh, and nice with it, so let's hope we've got the right one first time."

"He may be nice and posh, but that don't mean anything. Anyway, what's a posh, well-educated man want with a small flat over a village shop?"

"That's what we intend to find out, Mum. We'll have a list of questions to ask, and Derek's checking out what else we need to do. He's done a job for an estate agent over Waltonby way, and he'll help, Derek says."

"Not likely!" said Gran. "Estate agents are a crafty lot. He'll want to take over the selling, and then you'll be in for percentages, an' all that."

"Yes, Mum," said Lois, and retreated to her office.

Lunch hour in the shop was usually quiet. The morning shoppers had gone, and the big afternoon rush, when the schools turned out, was yet to come. Josie had a quick sandwich in the stockroom, listening to Radio Tresham for any news of the zoo accident. Pettison, being interviewed, was furious that the reporter asked how a visitor could be sure to see the vicious chimp attacker, and was comforted only by the fact that ticket sales, booked ahead for when the zoo opened again, were spiralling up to full capacity.

So he'd been released by the police, thought Josie. They must have been satisfied with his denials of having anything to do with the cleaner's unfortunate accident. He certainly sounded genuinely upset when the interviewer asked him about the victim.

"Listening to the news?" Dot Nimmo had come in, and was grinning at Josie. "I reckon they've got a real problem on their hands. They can't very well take a chimpanzee in for questioning, can they!" She laughed loudly, and then asked if anything new had come up.

"Don't think so," said Josie. "That Pettison man was just being interviewed. He sounded very sorry for himself. Clearly on the side of his monkey person! But a very smooth operator, I reckon."

"You can say that again," said Dot. "If you saw what I saw every week, rain or shine, opposite my front door, you'd see just what a smooth operator he is! Mind you, that woman is a right disgrace. He's not always been the only gentleman caller, I can tell you! But he is now. Must cost him a bit. Ted Brierley—he takes care of her and he's no fool. Clerk at the gasworks don't bring in much. Now, Josie, can I have my raisin loaf and a pound of dairy butter? Thanks, dear. I'm off to see your mother now. I'm hoping to go cleaning at Cameroon Hall as soon as the fuss dies down."

"Bye, Dot," said Josie, returning to her sandwich. Dot Nimmo was her mother's favourite among the team of cleaners, she knew, and hoped that it would be safe to let Dot loose up at Pettison's. After her mug of coffee, she thought it would be a good idea to have a quick look around the flat upstairs to make sure all was tickety-boo, as Gran said. No dead rats or squashed frogs. Or live chimpanzees. She steeled herself, and went upstairs, carrying an old golf club she kept handy, just in case.

Seventeen

At exactly six o'clock, Josie opened the shop door and greeted the prospective tenant.

"Good evening," he said. "So kind of you to allow me to see the flat. I am sure you must be tired after a long day in the shop."

"Not really," said Josie, taken aback by the familiar young man stepping into her shop. "It's not exactly a supermarket."

He laughed. "Well, that's good for a start! I don't think I could manage with a supermarket below me all hours of the day. No, this village looks very tranquil in the evening sunlight. I imagine in summer it is full of children and families?"

"Depends," said Josie, unwilling to let down her guard. "Most of 'em are indoors watching the telly. Anyway, if you don't mind, we'll wait for my Mum to come down from Meade House, up the road. And don't I know you? Aren't you the man with the theatre fliers?"

She watched him closely as he wandered round the shop. When he smiled at her, saying she had a good stock of necessaries, which would be very useful, she saw that his eyes were a deep blue. Cornflower blue, she said to herself, and then felt awkward, as he continued to smile.

The door opened, and she was relieved as Lois came in, breezily apologising for keeping them waiting.

"Not at all, Mrs Meade," said Justin, holding out his hand to shake hers. "Justin Brookes," he introduced himself. "How do you do. Please don't apologise. I am not in a hurry this evening." To Josie, he made it sound as if every other evening he would spend in his club, or dining at the Ritz. She supposed it was because he was an actor.

"You'll know the village from your trips around," she said, as they went upstairs to the flat. "But I don't think you met my mother before."

"Not as far as I am aware. I tend to daydream, so my mother tells me. Do forgive me if we have met."

How lovely, thought Josie. Obviously the apple of his mother's eye.

How reassuring, thought Lois. A calculated mention of his mother?

While Lois took him from the small sitting room into the even smaller bedroom, and then opened the doors of the kitchen and bathroom for him to peer in, Josie took in his beautifully tailored grey-flannel suit and absolutely correct shirt and tie. My, my, she thought. We'll not do better than this, surely? She was aware, however, of her mother's odd attitude. She was giving a discouraging running commentary of the flat's problems, though luckily leaving out the wildlife infestation.

"Charming!" said Justin, after they had inspected Thomas Crapper's lavatory. "Worth a fortune, you know, those lovely flowery bowls!"

"Then I hope you're not planning to run off with it," said Lois. "It weighs a ton, so I'm told. Otherwise we'd have changed it for something more modern. My husband is a very experienced craftsman, Mr Brookes, but even he turned down the job! Anything from lethal security systems to formidable rat traps, Derek can handle them all. But so far, Thomas Crapper has defeated him."

Justin shivered, and hoped they hadn't noticed. This Mrs Meade was certainly living up to her reputation. He laughed, though he knew she hadn't meant it as a joke. "Very useful, I am sure," he said. "Now, shall we look at the garden you mention in the advertisement?"

Downstairs and out into the garden, with Lois leading the way, Justin reckoned he'd be fine with the daughter, but was not at all sure about her mother. Lois was giving off strong signals of suspicion, and he decided to maintain a cool politeness, without too much enthusiasm. After all, uppermost in their minds must surely be the rent, so far not mentioned.

"You could have the use of the shed there," Josie said. "It's a bit scruffy, but it does lock. We don't keep any shop stock there because of the damp. But you might be able to fix that? Or we could get Dad to do it."

"That looks most useful," Justin said. "I am quite happy to damp proof, so long as my handiwork is satisfactory!"

"And over there is the parking place. No garage, I'm afraid, but once the garden gate is locked, it's all quite secure."

"Excellent," said Justin. "Now, perhaps we could go back in and talk about finance. The rent was not mentioned in your advertisement, and I would like to settle everything in advance, if that is satisfactory."

"I'm afraid my husband is not back from work, but he will let you know the rent and the financial side of it," Lois said. "We do have two more applicants coming tomorrow," she lied. "And, of course, we shall need references. My husband will deal with all that, once we have made the necessary checks."

Blast! thought Justin. He had wanted to clinch the deal straightaway. The shop flat would be ideal for his purposes, with the garden shed. Josie had obviously taken to him, so his chances were good. He had no alternative but to agree, and said he would look forward to hearing from them very soon. References could be delivered to them tomorrow.

HE DROVE BACK TO TRESHAM AND HIS CLUTTERED BED-SITTER, changed out of his good suit, and pulled on some jeans and a sweater. There were rehearsals this evening, and he meant to look in. His time at drama school had not been wasted. Although he had not exactly made it to Carnegie Hall, he had a pleasant tenor voice and loved to sing. He often joined the chorus when the troupe put on a pantomime.

After a sausage roll and baked beans, he remembered he had to report to his uncle Robert. He would be much taken up with the drama of the woman in the monkey cage, but he had still found time to send a message to Justin to make sure the shop flat was his, even if it meant offering a little more than the asking price for rent.

"Hello? Uncle Robert, is that you? Can I come over and let you know how I got on with the very lovely Lois Meade and her equally lovely daughter? And I need a couple of references. Just up your street! Splendid. See you in half an hour or so."

"I'M NOT TOO SURE ABOUT HIM," SAID JOSIE. "I THOUGHT HE WAS lovely, though a bit too smooth. What did you think, Mum?"

Gran and Lois sat on one side of the kitchen table, and Josie and her father the other.

Lois frowned. "Perhaps. But that's the way they are these days. And if, as you say, he is an actor, then I suppose he can put it on whenever he likes."

"Well, we'll see what Derek thinks," said Gran. "When are you going to see him, boy?"

"I think I can find time tomorrow afternoon," Derek said. "Now, let's talk about rent, and leases, and references and all of that. Then I shall be well prepared. As for his true identity, we can easily check. Now, Josie, you'd best be off back home. Matthew will be wondering if you've left him for good."

After she had gone and Gran had retired to her bedroom, Lois and Derek sat on at the table for a while, pencilling out figures and deciding on questions to be asked.

At last Lois yawned, and said she was tired and ready for bed. "Derek," she said, "don't you wish we'd never decided to let the flat? It gets more and more complicated. And Josie's not wholly happy about that Justin Brookes."

"The money would be useful, me duck, and although I see your point, I think we should give him a go, provided everything else is in order. After all, what's the worst that could happen?"

"That's what worries me," said Lois.

Eighteen

Pettison's ex-cleaner, Mrs Richardson, lived in one of the many back streets in Tresham, with long rows of redbrick terraced houses in a ribbon of doors and windows from one end to another. The only distinguishing features were variations in front door colours and closed or open curtains.

The Richardson front door was bright red, and what were called the nets were permanently drawn to protect from prying eyes on the pavement, but without shutting out too much light. Mrs Ruth Richardson was a good housewife, and friendly with her neighbours.

Her husband, Tom, was sitting with a neighbour now, talking about his early days. "We met after I came out of the forces. Professional soldier, I was. But then I met Ruth, and fell for her straightaway. We got together, and I came out of the army. Took up gardening, and that's my life now, as you know from my greenhouse next door!"

"And you do a wonderful job at Cameroon Hall. Beautiful gardens there." The neighbour stopped, aware that they were getting dangerously close to talking about the zoo. "What about children?" she asked, and then realised that wasn't very tactful, either. There had never been any young Richardsons in this house, and as far as she knew, there weren't any visiting.

"Less said about that, the better," Tom said. "How about a bit of cake? There's some in the tin. Ruth had a baking session on Sunday morning. Oh my God," he added, his face crumpling. "She won't make no more cakes for a while, will she?"

The neighbour struggled to find another subject to talk about, aside from Tom's damaged wife, still detained in hospital. Rumours were flying up and down the street, and she was longing to ask Tom more pertinent questions. One such rumour was that he had intended to do his wife in, and conceal the body in his wheelbarrow at the hall. This had been elaborated as it went from house to house, and by the time it reached the red front door, the muddled report was that Tom intended to plant her among the wallflowers, but was interrupted by sounds of voices, and in a panic had tipped her out into the zoo's monkey cage, meaning to collect her later. But he'd not been able to do this before she was discovered, so he'd disinfected his wheelbarrow and gone home.

Luckily, before she could ask him any more questions, Tom said that he didn't feel like cake, and he'd have a bit of a rest. So the neighbour went home, saying he was to knock at her door at any time of day or night.

Two streets further along, Dot Nimmo sat by her front window, keeping watch over the fancy woman's house. It was late by the time Dot had finished her New Brooms work for the morning. She made herself a sandwich and resumed her seat. She had noticed Pettison's van when she returned home, and it was still there. She wondered if he was confessing all to the lovely Betsy. As she took her first bite, the front door was flung open, and the little mild husband was ejected with some force. The door was then slammed shut, and Dot saw the poor cuckold pick himself up, dust himself down and attempt a nonchalant air as he walked down the street.

"Poor little devil!" she said to herself, and went back to the kitchen to collect a coffee cooling on the table. By the time she got back to her chair, she saw that Pettison's van, so conspicuous with its snarling tiger, had gone. So he'd made it, after all.

As she washed up the few dishes, she thought about the zoo boss. She prided herself on being able to get on well with all of the New Brooms clients, and she looked forward to meeting him. Mrs M seemed confident, and it surely would not be too long before the zoo reopened to the public.

Her appointment with her cousin was in half an hour's time, and she had to tidy up the BMW before delivering it back to him. When she approached the car, she recoiled with a gasp. A yellow-and-green diamond-patterned snake lay curled up on the roof, and at that instant, it raised its head, looked at her with hooded eyes and then lowered its head again, appearing to go back to sleep. Dot froze. Then she rushed indoors and phoned her cousin.

"Can you come and see to it *now*? I'll watch to see it doesn't get away, though God knows what I shall do if it moves! Come now!"

When her cousin arrived, Dot had remembered the trick with a box and a piece of wood, and had trapped the snake where it still rested on top of the car. With a brick on top, it could not escape, and she said he should come in first and talk to her for a few minutes, then he could tackle it.

Mozzie said he knew Pettison quite well, though Pettison was the kind of bloke who kept himself to himself. Good talker, but when you thought about it afterwards, he had said nothing about himself.

"How did you get to know him then?" Dot asked, and her cousin was frank.

"It was all to do with her over the road," he said, grinning. "Old Pettison rang me up one day, and said straight out that he needed a willing girlfriend. O'course, I'd known her over there for years. Not as a client, o'course, but she had been a prostitute before Ted Brierley took her on. He must have known she wouldn't give up a lucrative business. He was said to have been her pimp, though I don't know the truth of that. Anyway, I suggested contacting her, and she was willing. I don't know whether he became her sole client, but it seems likely. Anyway, after that, Pettison and me met for a drink now and then. Sometimes I can do him a favour; sometimes he can do me one. And don't ask me about that, Auntie Dot! You know better than that, I reckon."

"Gimme a clue," she said.

"This and that, buying and selling, importing and exporting—you know the kind of thing. Uncle Handy was in the same line. Nimmo style, you could say."

"Mm," Dot replied. "So do you think it'd be safe for me to work at Cameroon Hall, cleaning the house?"

"As long as you watch your back, you'll be fine. Anyway, you've had plenty of practice in taking care of yourself, haven't you?"

Dot saw him out, and watched as he gingerly carried the box and piece of wood across the road. There he lifted the snake with a practised hand, and eased it through the fancy woman's letterbox. He was still laughing as he drove off, waving cheerfully to Dot.

THE POLICEMAN ON DUTY OUTSIDE THE ZOO PUT UP A HAND TO stop a smart sports car from going straight through the barrier at the gate.

"Sorry, madam, but the zoo is closed."

"Okay. Then perhaps you'd like to take this and restore it to its rightful place?"

The policeman peered into the box the driver was holding. "Ah, yes. I see, madam. I think we can make an exception for you. Drive on please, and take the turn to the right for the zoo. I will tell them you are coming," he added, putting his phone to his ear. Then he closed the barrier and resumed his place on guard. He looked at his watch. The woman shouldn't take long handing over the snake, and then he'd be off home. What was she doing with the ruddy thing, anyway?

Twenty minutes later, the woman had not returned. He gave her another ten minutes, and then phoned through to check. There was no reply, so he opened the barrier and walked through, heading for the zoo. No doubt he would meet her coming out, but he had to make sure before he left.

Nineteen

Ted Brierley, from the house opposite Dot Nimmo, paused in his pacing up and down his small sitting room. He was worried. Betsy almost never went out without telling him where she was going or what time she would be back. This evening he was furious when he found the door locked on returning from work. He had let himself in the back way, and looked for a note on the kitchen table, where she always left it if she was going out unexpectedly.

As there was no note, he told himself that she would be back at any minute. Probably gone round to the neighbour's for a chat, he thought. She did not have many friends, and he knew that it was because of what she called her home-entertainment business. In the beginning, their relationship was one of convenience. She needed protection, and he could give it to her. Then Pettison came along, and the arrangement with him was ideal. He would continue to visit her, but had said right from the start that he was to be her only lover, and if she strayed to her old game of prostitution, then Pettison would end the deal immediately.

Ted knew that Betsy enjoyed getting to know old Pettison, and they had settled down into a three-cornered relationship. Ted's desires were satisfied elsewhere, and Betsy relaxed when off duty at home. It was a fact that if Betsy had gone back to the old game, they would be financially better off, but Ted had no wish to alienate Pettison, having built up lucrative business contacts with him, and so had agreed to his terms.

He watched the clock until eventually there was a knock at the door, and his fists tightened. She had obviously forgotten her key. He went quickly to open it, and when he saw Dot Nimmo, his anger escalated.

"What's happened to her?" he said in a loud voice.

"Who?"

"The wife, of course. She's not here, and I have no idea where she's gone. Where's she gone?" he shouted. "You keep a close eye on our business, don't you?"

"No need to be unpleasant," said Dot, not in the least offended. "I reckon I can help you there. My cousin's car was outside while he was visiting me, and when he went to go, he found a bloody great snake on top of the BMW. He returned it to sender, Ted Brierley, via your letterbox."

"What on earth are you talking about, Dot? A snake! Betsy hates snakes. Come on, no ridiculous excuses. Where the hell has she gone?"

Occasionally, he and Betsy, along with Justin Brookes, acted as safe houses for new and valuable additions to Pettison's illegal trade. Pettison always laughingly said he was sending them on to good homes, which was not illegal, he assured them. At least, not very.

The snake had been right at hand for Ted Brierley. He considered nosey Dot Nimmo a threat, working for Lois

Meade. It amused him now and then to leave small warnings, in the shape of a worm or, in this case, a snake.

"She'll be back shortly," said Dot soothingly. "I just came over for a flue brush. Me chimney's blocked."

"Mm, well, I suppose you'd better come in. She should've been back hours ago. God knows what she's up to."

After rummaging about in the shed at the back of the house, he found the long-handled brush and handed it to Dot. "There you are, then. D'you want a cuppa? I've been so busy today I've not had time to chat to anybody."

Recognising that he was genuinely worried about his wife, Dot agreed she could stay for a few minutes, and sat down, prepared to listen.

"Good of you to stay," he said, when they were both settled with coffee. "I'm sure she'll ring soon, or turn up, wondering why I'm in such a state!"

"It's because of that accident at the zoo," said Dot, going in with both feet. "We're all a bit nervous, aren't we? So naturally, as she's probably gone to the zoo to get rid of the snake, you're bound to be worried. She'll have gone to see Pettison, I expect, so that'll be okay." She grinned, but he did not return her smile.

"Yeah, s'long as it *is* Pettison," he replied gloomily. He stared into his mug as if his fortune was at the bottom of it.

BETSY BRIERLEY WAS INDEED AT THE ZOO. SHE HAD FOUND A keeper, and he had been delighted when she gave him the snake. Apparently, it was a rare and valuable one, and he had no idea how it could have turned up in Betsy's house. He told her Mr Pettison would be curious to see it. She stayed chatting to him for a few minutes, and then he turned away as his mobile rang.

"Call from my husband?" she said with a laugh. "I bet

he's tracked me down. I forgot to leave a note for him, and he worries."

"No, no, not your husband, Mrs Brierley. It was Mr Pettison, wondering if you'd like to go up for a drink? Seems he recognised your car." He paused. "He said not to take no for an answer."

"So what happens if I say no?"

"I don't advise it. Mr Pettison has automatic control over the main gates."

"Oh, very well," she replied. "Let's go up and get it over with. It's out of office hours for me." She grinned. "So I shall not be more than fifteen minutes; well, perhaps thirty."

"He said I should take you up in my runabout. It's quite comfortable," he added, embarrassed by her brassy smile.

"It may be comfortable," she retorted, "but you look very uncomfortable! Come on, then, lead me to your runabout."

Pettison was waiting under the hall portico. He smiled his usual beaming smile, and handed her out of the vehicle.

"That will do for today, thank you," he said to the keeper. "You can go off home as soon as everything is secure."

"Glad to see you, Betsy," he continued, taking her hand and leading her inside. "Lucky you turned up when I was feeling in need of company. And thanks for bringing back the snake. Careless of Ted to let it loose."

"Company is all I'm offering," she replied. "Can't stay long. Ted will be worrying."

"Oh, Ted will manage. We'll knock back a gin and tonic, and then you can be away home. Give me a couple of minutes to fetch some ice, and then we'll have a chat. I'd be interested to know what you've heard about poor Mrs Richardson."

"Come off it, Petti!" she replied. "You know you couldn't stand the sight of her. Probably arranged for her accident all by yourself!"

He did not smile. "I am sorry you feel like that," he said. "Back in two minutes."

When he returned, he was not carrying an ice bucket, but a small but deadly looking gun in his hand.

"Now, about that snake. You should not have given it to the keeper. My new people do not go anywhere near the zoo."

"Too bad. I'm sure you'll think of something. I had no idea you were at home, and I wanted that thing out of my car as quickly as possible. Ted's furious with me, as it is. Suspects I'm still on the game. But no, you can relax. No such luck for me."

"I see," he said, and frowned. "I think I need to make sure you will do what I say for a little while. Turn around, my sweet, and point your pretty little feet towards the door, and then I will direct you. Don't try anything stupid or brave, because I hate to be disobeyed, as you know. Off we go, then."

The small room at the back of the hall was cold and dark, and Betsy shivered. She was not warmly dressed, having left home in a hurry with the snake. Now she looked around for something to put around her shoulders, but there was nothing. She supposed the room had once been a maid's bedroom, and not been used for years.

"Robert!" she yelled for the umpteenth time, and banged on the door until her knuckles were sore. "Pettison! Let me out of here, or the police will be up here very soon. Let me out!"

"No need to shout, Betsy." He was standing at the other side of the door. "The police, in the shape of one constable guarding the gate barrier, has been up here asking for you. I denied having seen you, of course, and wished him well in his search."

Betsy leaned on the door. "What's the point of all this? Is this some new setup to liven up a jaded appetite? If so, you can stuff it. I'm not available."

"You will be delighted to hear that I am cooking a delicious supper for us both, and I shall be bringing it upstairs in due course."

"Stuff your supper, too!" she yelled. "Let me out of here; otherwise, I'll never allow you to call on me again."

"Oh, I don't think Ted would be pleased about that. I think we can come to some agreement over supper, my dear. Back soon!"

Betsy sat down and thought. She looked around the room for inspiration, and could not believe her eyes. On a rickety bookcase by the door she saw the gun. He had forgotten it! She picked it up gingerly and looked more closely. She was expecting it to be cold and heavy, but it wasn't. It was quite light, and made of plastic. It was a toy gun, and she began to laugh. The man was unhinged, she thought, but harmless.

Twenty

Ted Brierley had doubted Dot's guess that Betsy was with Pettison, and as he heard a car coming up the road, he stood back from the window. No warm welcome from hubby for you, madam, he thought.

Meanwhile, now unashamedly standing staring out of her window, Dot saw the car and nipped out of her front door. The car's headlights dazzled her, and she stepped back onto the pavement. For one moment, she thought it was coming straight at her, but then realised it was slowing to a halt beside her. The lights were switched off, and a woman got out. It was the errant wife, Betsy Brierley, teetering towards her on ridiculously high heels.

"Is that you, Dot Nimmo?" she asked, peering at Dot through the gloom.

"Indeed it is," she said tartly.

"What you doin' out here, then? You need some help?"

"No, it was your husband that needed help. He's exhausted with worry about you."

"And you've been trying to console him, is that it? If so, you're wasting your time, Dottie."

"Don't talk rubbish, woman," said Dot angrily. "And don't judge other people by your own standards!"

"Oh, piss off," said Betsy, unlocking her door and disappearing inside.

"A good spanking for Betsy?" muttered Dot, and she laughed. "She'll get her comeuppance one of these days, and I'll be the first to laugh," she said to her elderly parrot as she went indoors.

"Ha! Ha! Ha!" answered the parrot.

Meanwhile, Betsy confirmed to Ted that she had been with Pettison, omitted to mention that she had delivered the snake to the zookeeper, could not be bothered to tell him about the small servant's room at Cameroon Hall and said she was very tired and was going straight to bed.

Stretched out, Betsy thought about the evening's events. Pettison had been very strange, but then he was always strange, one way or another. He'd laughed when she appeared at the top of the stairs, having let herself out of the cold little room. "Just wanted to let you know the situation," he had said. "And to give you a taste of what might come to be, should you decide to make unilateral decisions or, to put it another way, feel tempted to spill the beans."

She asked which particular beans he wanted kept secret, and then he had turned nasty, ordering her, more or less, not to joke about a very serious situation. He had said she knew very well which particular confidential matters he referred to, concerning the trade with the small animals, and added that if it came to his notice that she had made one more stupid move, as with the snake and the keeper, the gun would be a real one, and the maid's room would be replaced by another, much more unpleasant.

Then he had forced her to drink a couple of glasses of wine, demanded her cooperation upstairs in comfort, and finally changed into his suave, charming self and seen her to her car, still parked by the zoo.

It was a long time before she went to sleep. She wondered if Ted would eventually get fed up with Pettison, and break off all business relations with him, and that would include her. She saw that this was extremely unlikely, and found herself snivelling into her pillow and wishing Robert Pettison was dead.

Next morning, the sun shone brightly into the kitchen at Meade House, where Lois and Derek, with Gran officiating, were finishing their breakfast.

"I'm going to ring Cowgill," Lois said. "It's time they did something about those zoo animals. Poor old Dot sounded quite worried last night. You know she turns most things into a joke, but one of these days, another person is going to be bitten, and end up in hospital. If it's fatal, like it most probably could have been with that Richardson woman, perhaps that'll get them going. Anyway, Derek, are you home for lunch? If Cowgill says the zoo is open again, I might make an appointment to see Pettison about Dot cleaning at the hall."

"You must be mad," said Derek. "After all the rumpus that's gone on there?" He sighed. "I suppose it's no good ordering you to use your common sense, is it?"

"I am using it," she said, "and I'm not mad. I shall make doubly sure that Dot will be okay, and anyway, I'm not putting pressure on her. She's the enthusiastic one."

Gran had said nothing, but her lips were clamped together in disapproval. Now she banged the frying pan down on the draining board, and said she didn't know what her late husband would have said. "Your dad was the only one you took notice of, Lois Weedon. He must be turning in his grave."

"Sorry, Mum," Lois said. She knew that when Gran used her maiden name, she was really serious. "I'll make sure Cowgill knows when Dot starts there, *if* she does. And then Dot can make the decision whether or not to stay. I know I am responsible for her, but I do respect her and her ability to look after herself. If she decides to give it a go, I shall be right behind her."

"I hope not!" said Derek. "One of you up there at Cameroon Hall is more than enough. You stay right here, Lois, else I'll tie you to the table leg."

For once, Lois couldn't think of any reply, and went off to her office to phone Cowgill.

"Good morning, Lois! Lovely to hear from you." He had been sitting glumly at his desk, staring out at the sheets of rain falling on the streets of Tresham. A golf fixture this morning had been cancelled, and he was disappointed, having looked forward to lowering his handicap. Lois's voice had been exactly what was needed to lift his spirits.

"Morning, Cowgill," she said briskly. "What news to report?"

"Um, about what, my dear?"

"The zoo business. I'll fill you in on the latest from this end. Shall I come in and tell you personally, or will you pay my telephone bill?"

"Both! But you know you will never accept any payment from us here. And, yes, it would be best if you came in. About half past ten this morning? I do have one or two more items to report to you."

Almost immediately after she had ended the call, Lois's phone rang, and she picked it up again.

"Mrs M? It's Dot here. Just thought you'd like to know that the scarlet woman returned home late last night. Very stroppy, and more or less told me to mind my own business. Old Ted didn't even meet her at the door, so I expect she got a rocket. Anyway, I'm off now to my Waltonby job. Bye."

At half past ten precisely, Lois walked into the Tresham police station, and said she had an appointment with Inspector Cowgill.

The young policeman jumped to attention, and with a knowing smile accompanied her to the lift.

Cowgill was waiting as she came out, and walked with her to his office. "I'm really glad you came in this morning, Lois," he said. "There's been an important development, and I need your help."

"So what's happened?" Lois said, as she sat down opposite him at his desk. "Found a scorpion in your coffee cup?"

"Not funny, I'm afraid. One of the zookeepers has been bitten by a king cobra, and died on the way to hospital."

"Died? A king cobra! *Now* will you take some action?"

"Yes, of course. You have to believe me when I say we have been busy on this case all along, but not always apparent to the general public."

"I'm not the general public! And a ruddy great snake turned up in my daughter's stockroom. And now this! Surely you could tell *me* exactly what's going on?"

Cowgill nodded. "You are quite right, and I don't forget the considerable help you have given us in the past. But this is dangerous territory, and I am not prepared to risk any damage being done to my Lois."

Lois calmed down, and said that they should get on with

the matter at hand. "Though what with Derek and Gran, and now you, I'm beginning to think I should give it all up, and take up knitting," she said.

"You won't," said Cowgill. "Now, let's begin."

He told her that his men had been called in early this morning, when Pettison had gone down to the zoo and found the keeper. He had been on duty last evening, and was barely alive on the concrete floor outside the cobra's quarters. He had a severe bite on his arm, and although resuscitation was tried, he had died within an hour. Before the poison had taken hold, he had managed to get out of the snake's quarters, and locked the door behind him.

"He was a brave man," Cowgill said, "and was often willing to do night duty when no one else would. He loved the snakes, so Pettison says, and was planning a breeding programme for this particular species, which is under threat from depletion of its natural habitat. I quote. King cobras are deadly, said to be able to kill an elephant, and will eat a female cobra if he doesn't fancy her."

"Now you're making it up to frighten me!" Lois said. "So is the zoo going to stay closed?"

"Until we have arranged for the cobra to be made safe, then we'll go ahead with Pettison and let him open it up again. He's being very cooperative, I must say, and is losing quite a lot of business while it's shut. These two accidents are the only ones I can remember since he first opened the zoo. Could be bad luck."

"Just as a matter of interest, Cowgill, when you say 'made safe,' do you mean killing it?"

"Not sure yet," he said. "It might mean doubling up security. Anyway, keep in touch on that one. Now, what do you have to tell me?"

Lois gave him an account, short and to the point, of Dot's

encounter with Betsy Brierley and her husband. "And then there was their snake, and not a cobra," she said.

Cowgill groaned. "Not another slithering snake?" he asked.

"Yep," she answered. "And this one was returned to the zoo late last evening."

"Tell me the rest," said Cowgill. "And then you and I are going along to Cameroon Hall."

Twenty-One

It was finally agreed that Lois should arrive to see Pettison on her own, so that she could talk to him about Dot coming to work for him, and then Cowgill would arrive about an hour later to do his questioning and observe what was going on at the zoo.

Lois approached the gate, and was surprised to see it was open.

"Morning!" said Margie Turner, smiling from the entry kiosk. "Just the one ticket, is it?"

"No, I'm not going to the zoo. I have an appointment with Mr Pettison. Lois Meade. He is expecting me."

"Oh yes, go on through, and straight up to the hall. You're the lady from New Brooms, aren't you? My friend, Dot Nimmo, works for you."

"That's right," said Lois. "I'm considering sending her to work at the hall for Mr Pettison." She paused, hoping for some useful snippet from Margie.

To her surprise, Margie laughed. "Don't worry, Mrs Meade," she said. "I'll keep an eye on her. And, anyway, our Dot is well able to deal with the likes of Robert Pettison!"

"Do you think she will need to do so?"

"You can never tell with the boss. Lots of rumours fly around, but he's never been anything but a gentleman with me."

"What rumours?"

"Oh, you know. Some say he's gay, and others that he's had every attractive woman in Tresham. Lowlifes, not the upper classes! But as far as I'm concerned, he's a good employer and never put a foot wrong. Off you go then, dear; there's a couple waiting to go in."

Lois walked slowly up the drive to the house, thinking about what Margie had said about Pettison. Lots of rumours, she had said. She thought of his grim mausoleum, and his obsession with rare animals. Obsession? Maybe it was more than that. Collectors became obsessive to the point of breaking the law. A painting, say an old master hanging on the wall of a private mansion. Worth a fortune. Expert burglars employed to steal it, and in some cases, it is never seen again. Some collector somewhere is gloating over his latest acquisition.

She arrived at the front portico, and once more Pettison was standing outside, waiting to greet her.

"Good morning! I hope you are bringing me good news? Come along in, Mrs Meade."

"Thank you," said Lois politely. "As for bringing you good news, I hope we may be able to help you in the house."

They settled in his office, and Lois started the conversation by saying how sorry she was to hear the terrible story of the keeper found dead in the reptile house. "Coming on top of the accident with poor Mrs Richardson?" she said.

"She is fortunately recovering well. But no, the keeper

was a brave fellow, Mrs Meade. I am afraid he was foolhardy, too. Countless times I have had to warn him about being overfriendly with a king cobra. No other keeper is willing to go near it, but he would enter the cage and let it get really close to him, sometimes stroking its neck. He was always very calm and quiet with it, and I believe it trusted him."

"So why did it suddenly turn nasty?" Lois was beginning to feel decidedly queasy. She had had just about enough of snakes.

"We don't know. Something must have frightened it, or him, or he could have forgotten to remain vigilant. A man is no match for a snake of that sort, once it is on the attack."

"But you'd have thought he'd be extra vigilant, after the chimp attack on Mrs Richardson. Anyway, have they been put down, put to sleep, or whatever it is we say? They are clearly a danger to every person who goes into the zoo."

"Not at all. We have very strong security for our visitors. I am afraid it was human error on the part of my keeper. I myself deal with the snakes from time to time, and I am very careful indeed. There is no possibility of visitors being harmed."

"Right, well, we'd better talk about cleaning. I have decided we can take you on as a client of New Brooms, and a very responsible and reliable member of my team, Dot Nimmo, has agreed to do the work."

"Nimmo? Not old Handy Nimmo's wife?"

"She is the widow of Handel Nimmo, yes."

"Well, I'm blowed! Old Handy! One of the best, he was. I'll be very glad to have her working here. We can talk about old times."

"Not too much talking, I hope," said Lois severely. "I expect my girls to work steadily for the time they are allotted, with a break for coffee or tea, but not gossip of any kind, Mr Pettison." A forlorn hope, she said to herself. But that's why I'm sending in Dot, to keep her eyes and ears open.

They then discussed hours and rates of pay, and Pettison confirmed everything as being wonderful, and then Lois said she would be going, as she had other potential clients to see.

"Do you ever do the cleaning work yourself, Mrs Meade? Sometimes I need an emergency blitz on the house at times other than when Dot will be here."

"I can assure you that Mrs Nimmo will never leave a house in a state needing a blitz, Mr Pettison. But if you require extra help, I am sure we can cooperate. Good morning."

Evil old sod, she said to herself as she went off to collect her car and return home. I must remember to wear trousers next time I have to go there. As for Dot, thank goodness she would have drastic remedies for disabling him if he tries any tricks on her!

At the gate, she met Cowgill about to go in.

"How did it go?" he said.

"Fine. I must say he sounded very reasonable."

"Just make sure that if Dot is off sick, you choose carefully who you send instead."

She looked at him, and said lightly that she herself always filled in at such times.

"Lois! Don't—"

"Excuse me," said a belligerent father of four small boys, "but is there any chance I can get into this place? Perhaps you two could make up your minds whether you are going in or out. Thank you." He hustled his boys through, and Lois set off for her car. Cowgill walked towards the hall, looking thoughtful.

Before going home, Lois decided to call on Dot to see if she was back from her morning job. She would break the news to her, and watch her reaction.

* * *

"So when do I start, Mrs M?" Dot had opened the door and spoken before Lois had a chance to begin.

"Tomorrow, if you're sure, Dot. Mr Pettison seemed very pleased to hear it would be you going to clean for him."

"You can leave me to it with a quiet mind, Mrs M. He was an old friend, or should I say colleague, of Handy. Public school, a degree from Oxford, so he says, though some doubted that. He was one of them charmers who could turn nasty in a second if something didn't please him. Don't worry, I shall be fine. Handy taught me a thing or two about self-defence." She laughed, and asked Lois if she would like a ham sandwich. "Fresh from the deli, Mrs M?"

"Thanks, but no, I must get home. Gran will have lunch ready, and Derek's there, too. They'll be waiting with the latest in a campaign to get me to give up taking on Robert Pettison. One thing, Dot," she added firmly. "You are not to go anywhere near the zoo. No call for that. I have made it clear to Pettison that you are not to be sent down with messages, or anything that takes you near those animals. Understand?"

Dot nodded. "You can rely on me, Mrs M. I'll make a really good go of it."

Twenty-Two

"Handy Nimmo's wife? You must be mad, Robert." Justin Brookes was relaxing in Pettison's most comfortable chair, smoking a sweet-smelling cigarette.

"Not at all mad. Better to have Dot Nimmo where I can see her than wondering what tales she's told to all and sundry, especially Mrs Meade, who, as we know, works as a nark with old Cowgill. And he, by the way, came to see me this morning about my latest disaster with the king cobra. That stupid keeper would never listen to me. Always knew better. A very arrogant sort of chap."

"Mm," said Justin. "I'm still waiting to hear from Mrs Meade whether I can have the shop flat. I went there on my very best behaviour."

"And wearing your very best suit, I hope. None of the flamboyant actor with questionable friends?"

"No, of course I was the perfect young executive. You know how well I can perform. If it had been young Josie by herself, I'd have been in there right away. But she said her parents are the landlords, and so I had to talk to them, too."

"She recognised you as the actor delivering fliers, of course?"

"Yes, she did. But I kept up a very sober character."

"Ah well, I very much hope you get it. It could be very useful if you keep your ear to the ground. Literally! The shop on the ground floor could yield very good snippets of information. And you could keep an eye on Lois Meade. I must say I wasn't too sure about the garden shed, but as long as you are careful . . ."

"A perfectly innocent hobby. A lifelong interest in small animals. I made that clear. And they don't use the shed themselves, so there will be no problems. Besides which, Uncle dear, we all know that we don't notice what goes on under our noses."

"We shall see," said Pettison. "But now we have to talk business. I have had policemen wandering all over the place during the last few days, and it's been tricky making sure they don't find anything untoward. First of all, our gardener and his wife. Old Richardson is still spending all hours that God gives in our flowerbeds. Fortunately, the latest on his wife's recovery is good. The police seem to have accepted that for some reason she went into the zoo to say farewell to a keeper."

He paused, and reached for a glass of whiskey at his side. "I can make a guess," he continued. "We had had words up here when she suddenly gave in her notice, and she probably went down to the zoo to stir up trouble. She was a great stirrer, you know, and I am well rid of her."

"Has Mr Richardson given in his notice as well?"

"No! He'd be heartbroken if he had to. No, I reckon her sharp tongue drives him out in all weathers. Still, he's tough as old boots. Must be the fresh air."

"I suppose you'll want us to keep a low profile for a bit? I hope you've warned the Brierleys. Best not to give them any specimens at the moment?"

"I've dealt with that," said Pettison grimly. "To change the subject, how are your parents? I have one special little creature arriving shortly. Your father is so good at keeping them alive until I need them. Good old Brooksey!"

Idiot, thought Justin. He had always suspected that Pettison had some kind of hold over his father, and that's how he'd persuaded him to be part of his "team." I'll wipe the smile off his face one of these days, he thought.

"Dad's had a serious collapse, and Mother is naturally thinking mostly about him. But I come and go to the farm in Lincolnshire as often as I can. The small barn there, where I keep the stuff, is kept heated, so all should be well. And if I can get the shop flat, I should be able to have them in the future nearer to us."

"Good lad," said Pettison.

"It has occurred to me, Uncle Robert," Justin continued slowly, "that you may soon have enough kosher exhibits in your zoo? I know it is dangerous to have them too crowded. You might have mutiny in the colony. And in that case, will you dispense with my services as a middleman?"

"Ah, but you are on the other side of the business, Justin, my boy. As you know, I now have a number of regular clients for my special little people, all very hush-hush, of course, but also very lucrative. They are never on show in the zoo, and there'll always be a need to shelter them temporarily, and that's where you will continue to be a vital member of the team."

Justin sighed. He supposed he must be satisfied that for the moment there was still money to be made from associating with his uncle, and he got to his feet. "Can I sell you a ticket to the play, Uncle?" he said. "Excellent performance from yours truly as a butler. I have one line—'Anyone for tennis?'—but it always raises a laugh."

Pettison waved a dismissive hand. "Away, Justin! I have to make an important call to Africa."

At Meade House, Lois, Derek and Josie were having a conference over a late supper. Lois had been with Josie to the Women's Institute meeting, and Derek had prepared a risotto with prawns, a dish he was particularly proud of.

"Yum, this is good," Josie said. "Are you planning to put Gran on a pension, and take over the housekeeping? Where is she, by the way?"

"She went off with her friend Joan. Something to do with photographs of Joan's new grandchild. She'll be back soon."

"I don't like her being out late on her own," Lois said. "She's not all that steady on her pins, and you know how dark it is in the village. More streetlights might be a good thing, if the council could afford it, which is unlikely. Anyway, are we going to talk about the flat?"

"I think I've decided," Josie said, "but you and Dad must make the decision. The property is yours."

"So what's your suggestion?" said Lois, thinking that she knew Josie's preference already.

There had in fact been only one other applicant, and that was a single mother with two small children. Lois was all for settling for her, but Derek was not keen. He had worried about the rent being paid regularly, and whether having children up there would be storing up trouble.

"My suggestion," said Josie, "is the young executive in the smart suit. Mr Justin Brookes. He seemed ideal to me. I'm not keen on the single mother and two children. The kids are small at the moment, but they were very noisy, and I'm afraid they'd be all over the place. I'm sorry for the mother, but I have to think about security for the shop. How about you, Dad?"

"Much the same as you. The smooth businessman was not altogether to my liking, but we've had no more enquiries. No, I tell a lie, there was one, but she rang back to say she'd heard about the snake, and she couldn't possibly come anywhere near us. I tried to explain it was all safe and tickety-boo, but she put the phone down on me. So I say we should go for Mr Brookes."

"Then it's settled," said Lois. "On balance, I agree with you two, though I did like that young woman. She was very nice and neatly turned out, and the kids were spotless."

"Right, then. I'll ring Brookes, and tell him he can have it, okay?"

"HELLO? OH, IT'S YOU, MR MEADE. NICE TO HEAR FROM YOU. How are the ladies?"

"What ladies?" said Derek, immediately wondering if they had made the right decision.

"Mrs Meade and Josie, of course. I'm afraid I didn't catch your daughter's surname. Vickers? Must have been difficult for her husband when he was at school!"

"Very likely," said Derek. "Now, about the flat. We have talked it over, and decided that you can have it on a six-months lease, to be renewed if all is satisfactory. Does that suit?" He sounded reluctant, and Justin hoped there would be no snags.

"Excellent!" he said, grinning broadly. "May I plan on moving in more or less straightaway? And could I just confirm that I shall find the shed very useful, if that is included in the lease?"

"Yes, that's okay. We'll clean it out a bit for you. It's all rubbish in there, anyway."

"I'll be in tomorrow morning, then, to have a good look at things. Have you a solicitor handling the lease?"

"Yes, that's all in order. You'll be hearing from him."

"Goodbye, then, Mr Meade. I'll look forward to meeting you again. Goodbye."

"Yippee!" he said aloud, and smiled as he thought about the reptiles. He knew Pettison had disapproved, saying it sounded like a boarding-school jape. "Like putting a dead mouse in the head prefect's bed," he had said.

Now Justin reckoned he could tell from Meade's voice that they had had no other applicants. The thought of reptiles reappearing must have done the trick.

Twenty-Three

On Monday morning, at the same time as Justin Brookes was driving over to Long Farnden with the final installment of his belongings, Dot Nimmo made her way cheerfully up the drive to Cameroon Hall. She had had a quick chat with Margie Turner on the gate, and said she would see her again on her way out.

Justin had spent all weekend ferrying the contents of his bed-sitter to the shop flat, and now looked around with pleasure. It was a really pleasant little place, he realised, once he had arranged things to his liking. The sitting-room windows looked over the rooftops to the village hall and playing fields beyond, and if he leaned to one side through an open window, he could just see the front of Meade House, about a hundred yards up the road. Even as he watched, he saw Lois Meade's New Brooms van come out and disappear off towards Tresham. If a spy was needed, he would be Robert's man.

Now for his parents. He would call about visiting, and hope there would be good news about his father.

Meanwhile, Dot Nimmo had arrived at the hall, and after a preliminary chat with Robert Pettison, she had begun work upstairs in the bedrooms.

"I always start at the top and work down," she had said to him. When he replied that he could think of circumstances where that policy could be very pleasurable, she snapped at him that she was a respectable widow and that was quite enough of that.

As she worked steadily from one room to another, she came across a locked door. She went downstairs and found Pettison in the kitchen.

"Can I have the key for that locked bedroom?" she said.

He shook his head. "No, Dot, I'm afraid that is always locked. Not that I've got Miss Havisham shut up in there! No, it's just that we've lost the key. I must get a man to change the lock sometime, but there's only boxes of books I don't want in there, so there's no urgency. Just give it a miss," he said, and changed the subject. "What time do you have coffee? Would half past ten suit you? Then I have to go down to the zoo to check that all is well."

"That's fine by me," said Dot. "And what *about* that zoo? You got another person in trouble in there, I heard. My dear old Handy used to say one death could be explained away, but two was careless."

"I remember Handy well! But in this case there is only one death. My ex-cleaner, Mrs Richardson, fell out with one of my chimp people, but the police are satisfied that there is a good explanation. In the sad case of the keeper attacked by his majesty, the king cobra, my man made a ridiculous error in going into the cobra cage alone and at night when no one else was around."

"Made the front page, though, didn't it," Dot said. "Now,

if you'll excuse me, I'll get on. If you want a handyman to fix that lock, I can recommend one of my nephews."

She disappeared upstairs, and Pettison reflected that he would not allow any of Dot Nimmo's nephews anywhere near the place. A good thing they'd got the mausoleum dealt with straightaway. It would be a disaster if she was confronted with a hanging gorilla and surgical specimens of splayed-out creatures.

By the time Dot had finished her four hours, she was ready for another coffee, and as Pettison had gone out, and had said no need to lock up, as he would be back very shortly, she decided to call in on Margie Turner and see if she had a free lunch hour. They could go to the zoo snack bar and have a gossip. She had not forgotten that Mrs M had expressly forbidden her to do either of these things, and if challenged, would remind her boss that she was in her free time, and could choose whatever she liked to do.

"Yes, okay, Dot. My replacement for the lunch hour should be here in a couple of minutes. You go and get us a seat, and then I'll join you," said Margie.

Dot made her way to the snack bar, passing a roomy cage full of brightly plumaged birds making unfamiliar chattering squawks, and then the famous monkey enclosure, where a tiny wizened face looked slyly at her. She quickened her step and found the snack bar, where she ordered a coffee and a sandwich, and sat down to wait for Margie.

The line to Justin's parents was busy every time he tried to ring them, until he had their phone number checked, and was told the receiver must have been left off the hook. Mother was getting really absentminded. The burden of Dad clinging on to life, and not knowing when the end would come, was becoming too much for her.

Now his phone was ringing, and it was his mother. "Justin? Have you tried to get hold of us. Sorry! I left the phone off. Done it several times lately. How are you, dear? Are you coming up to see your father? He's much the same."

"Yes, I'll come very soon. Glad to hear he's no worse. Now, have you got a pen handy? I've moved into a new flat, and I'll give you the address. I shall get cards printed to send out, but in case you need to know sooner. Ready? Right. The Flat, General Stores, 25 High Street, Long Farnden, Tresham, WZ1 2GB. Yes, that's right. A new phone number, too, but you can easily ring my mobile. That's always with me."

His mother wanted to know all about the new flat, and he gave her a brief description before signing off and saying he'd be in touch very soon. Before he switched off, she said something that bothered him considerably.

"What did you say, Mother?" he asked anxiously. "It escaped while you were feeding it, and you couldn't catch it? It's still in the barn somewhere? Right, well, keep the door firmly shut, and I'll deal with it when I arrive. Thanks a lot, Ma, and don't worry about it."

He turned the radio on to a classical music station to calm his nerves, and sat down to think. He knew it was a rotten trick of Pettison's to ask his father to house Robert's consignments, but the money was good, and though his mother was not keen, his father had seemed quite happy about it. In fact, he had been fascinated by some of the creatures, and had taken it for granted that he mustn't mention them to anyone. Pettison had reminded Justin that he must stress to his parents how valuable they were, and that collectors could break in and do damage if they knew where they were.

Now, to his dismay, he heard his mother's voice breaking into tears as she said how much she was looking forward to seeing him, and he opened his diary to suggest a date.

Loud voices caused him to look down into the street, and

he groaned when he saw Robert Pettison's car. He thought of locking his door and pretending to be out. Then the loud voice was outside on the stairs, and he knew that would be hopeless. Robert would know exactly where he was. Robert had a knack of knowing, and so he crossed to the door and opened it, forcing a smile of welcome.

"Very nice, boy," said Pettison, as he looked around. "I really think that with Dottie coming to clean for me, and you being up here well within earshot of the irritating Lois Meade, we should have that little problem solved. Nip in the bud any forays into enquiring too closely into our activities, won't you?"

"I have already logged in the time she disappeared off to Tresham," Justin said. "But no, only joking. I can see up to her house, though, and who knows, that might be useful."

"Good lad," said Pettison expansively. "Now, when will you be able to receive some very small people? Silent but deadly, as the saying goes."

Twenty-Four

"Morning, Mrs M!" Dot always spoke on the phone as if she had to shout loud enough to cover the distance, however near the unfortunate person taking the call.

Lois held the receiver away from her ear, and said there was no need to bellow. She said this almost every time Dot phoned her, but to no effect.

"Is that better?" yelled Dot.

Lois sighed. She had had a worrying night, after the team meeting yesterday. She dreamt that Justin Brookes had enticed Josie upstairs into the flat, and was about to have his wicked way with her when she drew a knife from her pocket and stuck it in him. She awoke with her heart beating wildly, and it took her a little while to come back to reality.

But now, thank goodness, here was Dot, yelling in her ear that she had nothing but good to report about her first day at Cameroon Hall.

"Well done," Lois said. "Anything at all you'd like me to check on?"

Dot thought about her snack with Margie from the kiosk, and decided to mention it, stressing that it had been in her own free time. She described having seen a small child stick its fingers through a gap in the monkey cage, and she had pulled it free, only to be told by its parents that she should mind her own business. They came to the zoo regularly, they said, and sometimes the little monkey took a piece of bun from the child.

"But apart from that, all went well, Mrs M. There is one room I couldn't get into, but Pettison said they'd lost the key and would get the lock changed. Anyway, it's full of old books, and he said it didn't matter."

Lois thought about the hanging gorilla and the dozens of dissected animals around the room, and shivered. Just as well Pettison had decided not to give Dot the guided tour.

"Right, well, you'll be there again on Thursday. If Pettison has any complaints, which I am sure he hasn't, I'll let you know before then. And don't forget to be vigilant. Ears and eyes open, Dot. You know the form."

JUSTIN BROOKES SET OFF ONCE MORE FOR THE LINCOLNSHIRE fens and his parents' farm. He had not wanted to visit so soon, but his mother's anxious account of the escaped rodent made it imperative that he should catch the wretched thing and return it to captivity. Pettison would be furious if it escaped beyond recall. All his people, as he called them, were valuable specimens. What a man of contrasts his uncle was! On the one hand, he was cold and ruthless, never to be trusted, and on the other, he could be charming, even childishly twee with his ridiculous "people" thing.

The flat fields, soon to be showing the fresh green of

spring, were still drearily devoid of colour, and time went quickly by, as he accelerated the little Fiat to its top speed. A drive through the long, straight roads was soporific, and he was well aware that if he did not have loud music blaring, he could easily drift off and end up in the deep dyke at the edge of the road.

At last he reached the entry to his family farm, and drove slowly down the track towards the house. He was sad to see signs of dereliction. His father had been ill on and off for a year or so now, and the grass edges to the lane had not been cut, nor had the ivy, climbing vigorously over the garden walls. The Virginia creeper, which covered the front of the house, now obscured half the bedroom windows. One or two slates had slipped from the roof, and a gutter hung crazily from the wall beneath. He supposed that when his father died, the farm would be sold and his mother would buy a bungalow in the nearest village. All her friends were there, and he hoped she wouldn't be tempted to move near him.

Now he arrived in the farmyard, and the old dog came to meet him, wagging his tail.

"Hello, Scamp! Where's the missus?"

"I'm here, Justin. Did you have a good journey?" called his mother from the steps into the house. She looked older than when he last came, and he knew that must be because his father was worse.

"How's Dad?"

She shook her head. "Not so great today. He doesn't seem to recognise me anymore. It's quite upsetting, Justin."

Her lip trembled, and she turned away, leading him into the warm kitchen. He glanced back towards the secure barn where the special consignments were kept.

"Did you catch the little rodent?" he asked.

"No, you said not to attempt it until you came, so I

haven't. Why don't you have a cup of tea, and then see what you can do?"

He agreed, and said he would like to see his father first of all. "He might recognise me," he said.

"At least you look more like our Justin in those jeans and sweater. You know he never talks about your acting? No job for a grown man. That's all he says. Anyway, come on in, and I'll take you up."

His father was lying on his side, facing away from the door, and Justin thought how pitiful he looked, a small, skinny figure, and on the back of his bald head one or two strands of white hair sticking damply to his skin. Justin's heart thudded. Surely someone so obviously absent could not still be alive?

His mother leaned over, and tried to tell him that his son had come to see him. "Justin's here, dear," she said, and stroked his brow.

"Help me turn him over," she said to Justin. "I have to do it regularly because of bedsores. The nurse comes morning and night, but I try to do it by myself between times. He weighs almost nothing now, so it isn't too difficult."

The old boy surfaced as they gently turned him onto his back. "Water," he said. "Drink of water."

Justin picked up a glass from the table by the bed and lifted his father into a semi-upright position. He held the water to his lips, and a few drops trickled in. He swallowed, and then moved his head fractionally from side to side.

"Enough. Is that you, Justin, home from school?" His voice was no more than a whisper, and Justin bent closer.

"Yes, it's me, Dad. Home from school. Mum's here, too. Are you warm and comfortable? Time for a little sleep, maybe. I'll come and see you later."

The old man's eyes flickered open for a couple of seconds,

and the ghost of a smile appeared on his face. "Don't forget your homework," he said, and his eyes closed again.

"He'll sleep now," Justin's mother said. "We'll leave him for a bit. Come down with me, and I'll find you something to eat."

Leaving his father's door open so that they would hear him should he shout for help, Justin followed his mother downstairs. She carefully turned away to the cooker as he wiped his eyes and sniffed back tears.

"He's a good age, Justin," she said. "Now, how about that escaped creature? Go and catch it now, while it's still light. I'll have a meal ready when you get back."

Justin approached the barn thoughtfully. He was worried about his mother and her ability to keep things going. They had a farmworker who had been with them for years and years, but he was an old man, too, though still able to be active on the farm.

Anyway, there was nothing to be done until his father had died. The upheaval of selling up and moving house would be quite out of the question at the moment.

He peered in through the barn's darkened windows, but could see nothing. That was intentional, of course. Pettison did not want windows that could be looked through. He sighed. Sometimes he wished his uncle was out of the way for good. Then he could escape, like the little animal, from the bonds that bound him. In even his own thoughts, that sounded overdramatic! But when he was still living here on the farm, he had helped his father with the occasional arrival of strange little animals, and had taken it for granted that in due course he would take over that little job from his father.

He unlocked the barn door and opened it; slipped into the dark, warm interior; and shut the door quickly behind him. He had a torch, and shone it round the room. He could see a cage with the door open, and knew that it must be where the creature had been before making a bid for freedom. He continued examining every corner of the barn, and suddenly came upon a pair of tiny eyes shining at him. There it was!

Moving one foot a fraction caused the eyes to disappear. He remained motionless, and in a few seconds they were back. Now he could see the shape of it, crouching behind a feed sack. He reached into his pocket, and once more the eyes disappeared. Taking a small piece of cheese, deliberately saved from his sandwich lunch, he placed it on the ground about an arm's length away from him, then sat back on his heels and waited.

The trap worked, and Justin held the tiny, warm body in his hand and looked at it before replacing it in its cage. It stared back at him, its whiskers twitching. "Sorry old lad," he whispered. "One day, a great big rat will come along and catch Uncle Pettison by the throat, an' that'll be your revenge."

He put it back gently, and noticed its water dispenser was empty, so he refilled it and then shut the door firmly. He secured the barn, and made his way back to the kitchen, where good smells of rabbit pie were filling the room.

Twenty-Five

"So, have you made sure it won't escape again? Those little people mean big money to me, Justin." Robert Pettison had phoned Justin from his office, where he had been reading about market stalls selling unusual pets being shut down by local councils. All because of loony campaigners for animal rights, he thought, but it was not all bad news, as there would doubtless be increased scarcity of rare specimens and prices would rise.

The line of supply was for the most part well hidden from the authorities, and although now and then one of the couriers was discovered and dealt with by the law, there was always regrouping and a replacement available.

"Are you coming back to Tresham?" he asked.

"Not Tresham, Uncle Robbo. I'm living in Long Farnden now, remember?"

"Of course! With a careful eye kept on the lovely Lois Meade, I hope?"

"Naturally," said Justin. "And, by the way, on closer inspection, she really is a looker. No wonder old Inspector Cowgill is so keen!"

"I should have thought you would prefer the daughter?"

"Not a chance. Do you realise she is married to a policeman, one Matthew Vickers?"

"Ah." Pettison paused for a few moments. "That's different. Even more important that your flat is locked, bolted and barred."

"Must go now," said Justin. "Father has woken up, and Mother's taking me to see him. He is nigh unto, I'm afraid. Back tomorrow. Bye."

Pettison replaced the receiver and sat without moving in his chair for a long time. "Married to a policeman, eh?" he muttered to himself finally. "Then the smoke screen will be essential. But young Justin will cope. I always knew his time at drama school would stand him in good stead, despite what his estimable father said."

Josie had already wondered about Justin Brookes, absent so soon from his new flat. He had said he was off on an urgent trip to Lincolnshire to see his father, who was dying. He would be back tomorrow, he said, and he had seemed very upset. Poor fellow. There was something about him that attracted sympathy. So sure of himself as the young actor and executive, and yet somehow vulnerable at the same time. He could not even have had time to do any food shopping.

Perhaps it would be a kindness to make up a basketful of essentials, with maybe one ready meal for when he returned, and leave them in the flat for him? That would mean using her duplicate key to get in and put the frozen meal in the freezer. But she was sure he wouldn't mind. There could not be any secrets on display. Certainly, he'd had no time for that. She would do it after the shop shut. She glanced at the clock, and saw there was an hour to go.

The door opened and a middle-aged man came in. He smiled, and asked if her vegetables were locally grown. "So nice to find really fresh veg these days," he said, and picked up an avocado pear and squeezed it. "Nearly ripe," he said, and put it back on the shelf.

"I'd be grateful if you wouldn't handle the fruit," she said. "Most of the vegetables and fruit are locally grown, but some things obviously have to be imported."

"I don't know about that, Mrs Vickers. Most things can be grown under glass in this country. In Iceland, you know, they grow bananas in huge greenhouses. Heated by natural hot springs."

"How interesting," Josie said patiently.

He picked up the avocado pear he had squeezed and put it on the counter. "That will be fine for my supper," he said, and looked around the shop. "Nice little shop you have here," he said. "All your own, is it?"

Mind your own business, thought Josie, but she smiled and said, "Anything else I can get for you today?"

"I expect you think I should mind my own business," he said, returning her smile. "But I am looking for a small business for investment purposes. Might you be interested?"

"Not today, thank you," said Josie, as if he was a tiresome seller of clothes pegs.

"Have a nice day," she added, and handed him his avocado in a paper bag.

Him and his heated bananas, she thought, and decided to ring her mother and tell all.

"Hello, Mum, all well?" she said, perching on a high stool behind the counter.

"Fine, but how about you? You don't usually ring me at this time of day. No customers and bored to tears?"

"No," Josie replied, and told Lois about her most recent customer.

"What did he look like? Maybe I would know him," Lois said.

Josie gave her a description, and then remembered that he had called her Mrs Vickers. "Now how did he know my name? He was no stranger, I reckon, though he pretended to be one."

"Did he have a van outside? Did you see him drive off?"

"Yeah, it had a nasty great tiger on one side. Same as the one that came to collect the snake. I think it was from the Tresham Zoo. Oh Lor! Do you think he had anything to do with those reptiles?"

"Very likely," said Lois. "If he comes again, give me a ring, and I'll nip down. Keep the shop door open, and don't let him get near you. I'm sure he's not dangerous, but there's no harm in being careful."

WHEN MATTHEW CAME HOME TO THE COTTAGE, JOSIE TOLD HIM what had happened. He had been interested and said he would report the incident to Inspector Cowgill. "Sounds like Pettison. He's a slimy customer, is Robert Pettison. He wasn't offensive to you, was he?"

Josie shook her head. "But he called me Mrs Vickers—how did he know my name?—and said he was wanting a small business to invest some money in. Asked me questions about the shop. I got rid of him as soon as possible, of course. What about that zoo? Hasn't he been prosecuted for having wild animals in there?"

"Oh, he's too clever for that. Has all the right documents

and valid answers. And anyway, he has spies everywhere, and by the time we get there, it's mostly rabbits and white mice. Except the murderous king cobra, of course, but I haven't heard the latest on that."

"Right. Well, I hope our new tenant will cause us no trouble. He went off to see his dying father in Lincolnshire. I took some food to the flat, including one of our ready meals, which I put in the freezer. A goodwill gesture, I thought."

"I should be careful, Josie. It could be construed as breaking and entering! We shall have to check whether there is a clause in the lease allowing us to have entry under certain conditions, such as fire."

"Oh, stuff the breaking and entering! It was just a nice welcome for a new tenant who must be very sad."

"Has your mother been in today? Cowgill was asking after her, as usual. The man's besotted," said Matthew with a smile.

"Don't tell her that! I talked to her on the phone, after that man had been in. Like you, she reckoned it was the man from the zoo, and told me to watch it."

"Very sensible. When is Brookes due back?"

"Didn't say, except that it would be very soon, as he had business to attend to."

"I might just drift into the shop, if you let me know when he's around. I'd like to take a look at him."

Twenty-Six

Dot Nimmo was still eating toast and marmalade when her phone rang. It was Lois, and after apologies for ringing so early, she asked Dot whether she could give up her Waltonby job to Floss this morning, and do an emergency clean up at Cameroon Hall.

"Pettison has been on the phone, sounding rattled. I don't know what it's all about, but he wants you to go up as soon as poss, to tidy up and generally clean around, as he is expecting a guest. I said that would be okay, and hope you don't mind, Dot?"

Dot said as long as Floss was happy, she would do anything that Mrs M asked. She said she would get ready swiftly, and be up there within half an hour. She felt a frisson of excitement, and wondered who the guest could be. If he was part of the Tresham underworld, it was quite likely that she would know him—or her. But then, why would

Pettison ask so specially for her? He knew her background intimately. Maybe that's *why* he had asked.

She sluiced her face in cold water, and sprayed scent liberally behind her ears and on her wrists. Covers a multitude! she thought. The traffic was heavy in town, and she had to sit at traffic lights for what seemed longer than usual. She listened to her local radio station for news of road congestion, and jerked to attention at the mention of another death from snakebite. This time it was not at the zoo, but at the home of a private owner the other side of the county. She made a mental note of the name, and listened for more information. But it was a brief news item, and other, more cheerful stories followed.

Must make sure Mrs M knows, she thought, and drove up to Cameroon Hall, thinking what she would do if one of the wriggling things escaped up to the house and confronted her on the job. Another thought struck her. Was Pettison's mysterious guest, needing such prompt attention, anything to do with the radio news item?

She parked her car and went quickly up to the back door of the hall. Pettison opened it almost immediately, and welcomed her in.

"Most grateful, Dottie," he said. "And so sorry for the sudden summons! I have my distant cousin coming from Africa, and I would like to be shipshape when he arrives."

"You can't have made it so dirty since yesterday!" said Dot. "But I'll have a go, and leave everything tidy."

She started on the kitchen, and realised why he wanted her services. There were newspapers everywhere, not stacked tidily, but half opened and strewn on the floor. All the crocks from his meals since yesterday were heaped on the draining board, and there was cold greasy water in the washing-up bowl.

His cat, a large evil-looking male tabby, sat next to a half-eaten chicken leg, and glowered at her.

"Shoo, you nasty thing," she said, and pushed it firmly onto the floor, where it yowled and spat at her, then fled rapidly away.

A bin labelled For Compost spilled its contents onto the floor, and she saw that it consisted mainly of a mouldy cabbage and oozing potatoes that had seen better days.

So much for saving the planet, she thought bitterly, and tipped it away. When she reached the sitting room, it was marginally tidier, but the drawers of a music chest had been emptied, and the decorative covers of old Victorian songs had been dumped on the sofa, where they were slowly sliding off onto the carpet.

"What a disgrace!" she said loudly, hoping he would hear. "Those lovely sheets of music are valuable to collectors."

"Would you like them, Dottie?" he said, appearing like a jack-in-the-box at the door.

"No thanks," she said. "But you should sell them, if you don't want them. Where did you get them, anyway? I don't remember seeing that chest before. Is it new?"

"New to me," he said. "Fell off the back of a lorry, as they say. I am keeping it in safe custody until a buyer comes along. Nice piece, that chest. Lovely way of keeping music, with drawers that have a front that lowers like a little shelf."

"Yes, well, I must get on. Coffee at eleven, don't forget."

He nodded, and disappeared. His study was at the back of the house, and she heard the door shut behind him. That was where she preferred him to be, safely shut away from her until it was time to go home. He gave her the shivers when he came too close.

She had been warned by Mrs M, and knew that at any time she would be able to refuse to do the job, and a replacement could be found. But she did not plan on that. She meant to stay until the whole business of trespassing reptiles and sudden deaths was dealt with.

Mrs M was cheerful, but Dot knew that she worried about Josie in the shop. One snake, one toad, one frog and a rat infestation, all more than enough for the girl to dismiss as accidental. They were lucky that a tenant had been found for the flat, as damaging rumours had gone swiftly round the village and beyond.

Pettison appeared again, this time in the guest bedroom, where Dot was dutifully making up the bed with clean sheets and pillowcases.

"Sorry, Dottie!" he said. "Change of plan. Guest is arriving earlier than expected. Called from the station, and is hoping to be here in half an hour or so. Could you finish that, and then leave the rest until Friday? You have worked your magic beautifully downstairs!"

Dot sighed. She picked up her cleaning things, and made for the stairs. As she passed the locked room, she saw there was a key in the door.

"Does he get to see inside the inner sanctum?" she asked.

"Time to go," he replied, and almost pushed her downstairs.

"Just watch it, Pettison!" she said. "You know better than to do anything to harm me. I know too much, so lay off. You look scruffy, if you don't mind my saying so. Best scrub up, and have the kettle on ready to give him coffee."

She put her cleaning things away, and prepared to leave. She was halfway down the drive when a taxi came along towards her. The track was narrow, and it slowed down as it passed. She caught sight of a passenger seated in the back. It was a man, wearing a hat pulled down over his face. In spite of it being a quick glimpse, Dot knew that she had seen the man before.

"I MIGHT BE MISTAKEN," SAID PETTISON'S GUEST, "BUT I COULD HAVE sworn it was old Handy Nimmo's wife passed me on the way here. Going down your drive. What are you up to, Pettison?"

"Up to? Why, nothing at all. And you're wrong about Nimmo's wife. I'm sure I saw a notice of her demise recently in the local press. Now, did you have a good flight? And your luggage got through safe and sound? We must have a glass of hock to celebrate."

His guest sat down in the sagging sofa, and looked around. "Certainly spruced this place up a bit," he said. "Needs repainting right through, of course, but that would cost a bit. A bit short, are you, Robert, old son? Well, I've brought a treat for you this time. Very pretty, very rare. Needs careful handling, but very desirable."

"Only one?" said Pettison. "That's not going to restore the hall to its former glory!"

"Now, now, don't be greedy. More to follow, if all goes well. Things are getting a lot more difficult in this particular market, as you know. Which means, with luck, that lack of availability will cause selling prices to rise. And that's good for you and me. By the bye, the taxi driver had the local radio on in his cab. Something about a woman having been bitten by a snake in this neck of the woods. Anything to do with you, Robert?"

"Of course not," said Pettison.

Instead of going home, Dot drove out to Long Farnden on the off chance of seeing Mrs M. It was raining hard, so hard that Dot could barely see beyond the windscreen. She cut down her speed, and thought about what she had seen at Cameroon Hall. Pettison was possibly involved, maybe disastrously, in the latest reptile accident. She had heard a later bulletin as she drove along, and this had been optimistic. The woman had been taken to hospital, and was said to be doing well. She would definitely recover from the nasty bite.

This particular snake had been a pet, kept by the woman's husband in a shed at the bottom of their garden. Apparently it was handled regularly, and was said to be very gentle and cooperative. He was usually the one of the family who would approach the snake, and on this occasion the wife had gone into the shed, meaning to find a screwdriver and leave swiftly, but the snake had uncoiled rapidly and struck.

A warning against keeping wild animals as pets followed on the news broadcast, and Dottie nodded to herself. Surely the time would come when Pettison would be forced by law to shut down his zoo, and return the animals to their natural habitat. The snake had been obtained locally, so the owner had said.

She drew up outside Meade House, and went in. Lois greeted her at the door, and Gran, forcing a smile, offered cups of coffee, which Lois accepted.

"Come on into my office, Dot," she said. "You've finished very early, haven't you?"

Dot explained what had happened, and said she would like to discuss New Brooms involvement with Pettison and his zoo. "I hope I'm not speaking out of turn, Mrs M, but it's my duty to warn you about that man. When Handy knew him years ago, he used to say he could be very violent, and had once or twice been in a fight. Money talks, and it had all been hushed up."

Lois frowned. "Are you sure you want to go on with this job, Dot? I can get you, and the rest of us, out of it today, if you have any doubts at all."

"Not for myself, Mrs. M. But I wouldn't want you, or the other girls, going up there. I can handle Pettison, and he knows it. So I shall be fine, and useful too, I hope. If all goes well, I'd like to see that devil made to pay the price for all the trouble he's caused."

"Very well. But I don't want you taking any risks. It's not worth it, Dot. Best leave it to the police."

Dot laughed. "You're a fine one to talk, Mrs M, if you don't mind my saying so!"

At this point, Gran came in with coffee. She dumped one mug down in front of Dot, and handed the other to Lois without a smile.

"We're out of biscuits until I go down the shop," she said, and Lois forbore to say that she knew for a fact that there were two packets of chocolate shortbreads in the tin.

"So I'll go up there again tomorrow," Dot said, ignoring Gran's dirty look. "With any luck, I shall see the guest. I was certain I recognised him, though he had his hat pulled down. If it was who I thought it was, then Pettison is a fool."

"How does he convince the inspectors?" Lois asked. She was puzzled. After all, if a dangerous dog bit someone, it was put down immediately. But these creatures of Pettison's lived on. Did he know someone high up in the police who got him off the hook every time?

Dot tapped the side of her nose. "Conspiracy," she said. "Payoffs. Far be it for me to criticise the police force, but there are rumours. Always have been. Some of Handy's friends got away with murder, as they say. Not actual murder, as far as I know. But I wouldn't be surprised. Conspiracy was rife, Mrs M, though I says it as shouldn't."

"Sounds as if we should pull out, then? Please tell me honestly what you think, Dot. We're not conducting a crusade on behalf of wild animals here. I have a cleaning business, and it is my duty to look after my team. And that goes for you, too."

Dot shook her head. "Trust me," she said. "I come from a different world from the other girls, and Andrew, and I know how to look after myself. I promise I'll tell you if it gets too hot."

When Dot had gone, Lois picked up her phone and dialled Inspector Cowgill. When he had heard what she said, he answered seriously.

"I think you should let me make some enquiries and then you come in and we can see what's to be done. I must say Dot Nimmo is probably the best spy we've got!"

"And I'm anxious not to lose her. I'll see you about four o'clock this afternoon."

Twenty-Seven

Justin sped through the flat fens, heading for Spalding, where he planned to stop for a snack, and then on home. Home? For him, home was now the small flat above a village shop, a paradise compared with the flea-infested bed-sitter in Tresham.

His mother had been in tears, and had clung to his hand as he tore himself away. Promising to return soon, and at any time she needed him, he had jumped into the Fiat and waved as he drove off. He had collected two island mice from the barn, put them in a small carrying case in his car, and gone back indoors to say a last goodbye to his father, but the small hump under the bedclothes had not moved, and his eyes had been closed. Surely he could not last much longer? He was taking only liquids, and this morning not even the creamy gruel his mother had prepared had been touched.

As a sudden flurry of rain hit the windscreen, he slowed

down and thought about the farm. He had tried to persuade his mother to sell it, once his father had gone. The idea of a bungalow had seemed to appeal to her, but then she had wept again, and said the Brookeses had owned the land for generations, and she dreaded being the one to hand it over to someone else. She had once more asked him to think about taking it over.

The idea did not please him. A part of him liked a life of action and excitement, walking on the edge of things. Being an actor gave him that kind of life. It was a struggle to make ends meet with the scarcity of good parts to play. The one thing he regretted more than any other, however, was his association with his uncle, Robert Pettison. The man was a monster, and a ruthless one, as well as an affectionate and generous uncle.

Apart from taking over from his father in the animal trade, Justin had got himself into gambling debts as a young layabout, and had helped himself to a small amount of untended cash in his uncle's office. Pettison had discovered it, refused to regard it as a loan, and had held it over him like the sword of Damocles, threatening to inform the police. It had been a small offence, and he had subsequently repaid the amount in full, but it had been a theft, and Pettison let it be known that Justin's parents would be most upset if they heard about it. Perhaps he had thought his way of dealing with it would be good for Justin's character. In any case, here he was, still beholden to his uncle.

Parking by the river in Spalding, he walked along the path beside the flowing muddy water into the centre of town. He found a café for a snack, and sat on a stool by the window, watching the inhabitants going about their business. Lucky people! Living lives of innocent work and family life, he thought, and felt very lonely. He made a decision, one made many times before, that he would cut himself off from his uncle, at least from his illegal pursuits. Then he could build a new life, find a wife, have children, join the rest of the human race.

"He's back," Lois said, coming into the shop. "I saw him getting out of his car round the back. He looked as if he had all the cares of the world on his shoulders."

"He'll be glad of the goodies I left for him, then," said Josie. "I put in a bottle of wine, too. On the house, that'll be. Perhaps his father has died, or is going fast? He's an only child, he said, so it's even worse, carrying the burden of grief, and supporting his mother at the same time. We had a chat before he left, and he's worried about who will carry on the farm."

"Him, maybe? If so, you'll be looking for a new tenant shortly. Now can I have some of that grapefruit marmalade your dad likes?"

"Doesn't Gran have a monopoly on homemade marmalade in Meade House?"

"Yeah, but she only makes orange. A couple of jars, please."

The door opened, and Justin came in. "Hello, I'm back," he said. "I need a few supplies, when you're ready, Josie."

"A good fairy has left a box in your flat," said Lois, and watched his reaction.

"You've been in my flat? I'm not sure—"

"Oh, don't worry," said Josie. "I didn't look around. I just put the box in your kitchen, and a ready meal in the freezer. How was your father? Any improvement?"

Justin shook his head. "Afraid not," he answered. "I'll be going upstairs, then, and thanks for the groceries. I'll settle up later."

Up in his flat, he looked around. Thank heavens he had

tidied up before he left! Nothing incriminating left out. He went into the kitchen and found the box of groceries, and a bottle of red wine. He read the note beside it. "On the house! Welcome back. Josie V."

He looked out of the open window across the houses and to the playing field beyond, where a young boy kicked a ball about with his father. Both were shrieking with laughter that travelled to where he stood, and he could not stop the tears squeezing out from under his eyelids.

AT CAMEROON HALL, DOT WAS CLEANING SILVER, AND ASKED Pettison if his guest was still upstairs, as she didn't want to disturb him with the vacuum if he was asleep. But he had gone, apparently, quite early in the morning.

"He recognised you, Dot," Pettison said. "I told him you had died recently, just in case."

"In case of what?" Dot replied.

"In case you would rather not have been recognised. He is a dangerous person to know, but we get on well together."

"Wasn't he that man from the Far East somewhere, the one that crossed Handy's path once or twice? If so, you'd be far better using someone else. He'd slit your throat as soon as look at you!"

Pettison laughed. "Not if I'm ready for him," he replied. "No, he brought me a very beautiful person to add to my collection. And don't worry; she's put away in a safe place."

AT FOUR THIRTY PRECISELY, LOIS SAT DOWN OPPOSITE COWGILL at his desk, and said that she had one very important question to ask.

"Ask away, my dear Lois. And may I say how lovely you are looking, as always?"

"I can't stop you, but I'd rather you didn't. Now concentrate, Cowgill. It is very simple. I want to know why Pettison has not had his zoo with its dangerous animals closed down by the law, long before this?"

"Good question, Lois. But the answer is not so simple. He has animal-protection organisations inspecting him, and we have been called in on a number of occasions when a visitor has been mildly hurt. Usually a child sticking its fingers in where it shouldn't. We have insisted he tighten up security, and he always obliges. The animals' papers are beyond reproach, all bred in captivity and so legal. Sometimes I wonder if he doesn't have some spy who warns him when we do spot-checks."

"Well, can't you find out?"

"Difficult. Everything points to a bent copper. Now, we arrive at an even more complicated place. The police officer in charge of such checks and inspections is Josie's husband, Matthew Vickers. You see my difficulty? Even more complicated, Pettison occasionally pleads exemption because he has breeding programmes in place, helping to increase the numbers of rare animals."

"But if you're worried about Matthew being a member of my family, why don't you take him off that particular case, and put him elsewhere? Maybe hunting for real criminals. He's a clever fellow, our Matthew, as well as being your nephew and my son-in-law."

"That's just it. Matthew is by far and away the best cop to be communicating with a slippery character like Robert Pettison. And I could swear Matthew is no double agent! No, I shall arrange to monitor Pettison myself, alongside Matthew, and we should be able to trip him up. The surest way of doing this is to catch him in the act of receiving or handing over the wretched animals. Now, we go on to Dot Nimmo's reports from Cameroon Hall. Can you help me out there?"

Lois nodded. "She has already told me some useful things. First, Pettison is very jumpy when she is there. Follows her from room to room, or hides in his study. She has discovered the locked room that I told you about, but doesn't know what's in it. I decided not to tell her, and hope that he doesn't think of showing it to her himself. Dot is quite sensitive in her way, and not fond of creepy crawlies."

"Anything else?"

"Patience, Cowgill. There was another very interesting thing. Pettison had a guest who stayed overnight and then departed early in the morning. Dot was in her car going down the drive on her way home when the taxi carrying the guest passed, going towards the house. She thought she recognised him from the early days when her husband, Handy, was active in the underworld. From Africa or some such. Nasty and dangerous, according to Handy, apparently."

"Name?"

"She couldn't remember, or get near pronouncing it. Anyway, Pettison told Dot the next day that his guest had recognised her, and been sad when told that she was dead. Pettison thought he was doing the right thing, so he said. But the most important thing is that this guest brought "a beautiful person" with him. There was no lady guest, and Pettison said she was put away safely. I suppose you know about his 'people' thing?"

"Thanks, Lois. That confirms our fears that Pettison is actively trading in illegal wild creatures, keeping some out of sight in transit, and selling them on to wealthy collectors and individuals who fancy an unusual pet."

"So what are we going to do about it? Dot is determined to stay cleaning at Cameroon Hall, swearing that she can look after herself."

"Softly, softly catchee monkey, Lois. That's what we shall do. Keep me informed on Dot, and I will let you know what our Matthew can discover. We need to catch Pettison in the act of handing over or receiving an illegally imported animal. He is part of a huge network, and would be a very useful person to talk to. Would you be able to work on that?"

Lois nodded. "We have a secret weapon, you know. Don't forget my friend and colleague, Mrs Tollervey-Jones, late of Farnden Hall, and now living at Stone House in the village. She has done some good work, and has lots of experience with foreign parts. I haven't been able to use her since she arrived back from Japan, full of beans and raring to go, dear old thing. What do you think?"

"Whatever you think best, Lois. I have to warn you that there are dangerous people involved in this trade, and they would think nothing of removing any obstacle that gets in their way. Take care, my dear. You are very important to me. And how is Josie getting on with the new tenant in the shop flat?"

"My daughter is important to me, Cowgill. So far, our new tenant has been fine, but if he puts a foot wrong with Josie, I'll have his guts for garters, so I will."

Twenty-Eight

"I don't see why you're bringing Mrs T-J into whatever nonsense you're up to with Inspector Cowgill!"

Gran stood, hands on hips, by the window after dumping a coffee onto Lois's desk, where she sat working on New Brooms business. The cleaning ladies were all now so familiar with how things went that Lois sometimes thought she could duck out and take up golf. She rather fancied challenging Cowgill to a game! But then something would go wrong with the team. It could be a complaint from one of the clients, a broken vase, or one of the girls unhappy about a predatory male client. Then she would be the one to sort it out.

"All will become clear, Gran," said Derek, coming into the office behind her. "Trust Lois. I am sure the inspector will not allow her to come to harm. And when you think about it, we don't have much alternative but to let her carry on, and say nowt. That's my new policy, and I recommend it."

"Huh, I don't see that lasting long," she said, and stomped back to the kitchen.

"So what can I do for you, Derek," Lois said, smiling, "now you've sent Mum packing?"

"I heard you talking about Mrs T-J, and I thought you'd like to know she's on her way here, full steam ahead." At this point, dead on cue, there was a knock at the door.

"Mrs T-J," chorused Derek and Lois, and she went to answer the door before Gran could frighten her away. Gran did not hold with the old lady being a member of Lois's team. "She should be content to sit back in retirement and sew shirts for sailors, or write her memoirs," she had said.

"Sit down," said Lois. "Thanks for coming in."

"So pleased to get your message!" said Mrs T-J. "Things have been a bit flat since I returned. Now how can I help you? Anything, my dear, except scrubbing front doorsteps!"

Lois explained in detail what she was investigating, and her colleague was doubtful. "Surely you can leave that to the police?" she asked. "I can't see that what goes on at Tresham Zoo in any way threatens your family, Lois, or the business of New Brooms. Am I being stupid here?"

"Of course not. If you've only just returned from Japan, you probably haven't heard about the reptile infestation in the shop. Josie has had to contend with a large snake, a large toad, a squashed frog, and a family of rats. Someone put those things into the shop flat deliberately to harm or frighten my Josie to death. That's why I mean to catch the culprit."

"And that is someone at the zoo? It always seems so clean and tidy, and well managed. What is the man's name at Cameroon Hall? Pettison? That's it. Knew his concubine, poor woman. He nagged her to an early grave. She was a distant relative, you know. Beware, Lois. That is all I can say. Pettison was out in Africa as a young man, and when my father-in-law was a colonial judge, he had some very unflattering things to say about the Pettison family."

"I knew you would be able to help!" said Lois. "Now, let's start at the beginning, and pool what we know and what we intend to do about it."

"First of all," said Mrs T-J, "how is Josie? She must have had a nasty shock."

"Brave, she was. Very brave. And seems to have put it behind her. But I know if something else happened—another snake, or a crawling yellow toad—she would probably flip."

"So it is best to keep her in the dark, until we have cracked the case." Mrs T-J occasionally came out with lovely old-fashioned phrases, and Lois laughed.

"Exactly," she said. "So now, to work."

"Yes, indeed, and I have thought of another thing which may be of help to us."

"Already?" Lois said, smiling.

"This is a personal memory I have of my much-lamented late husband, and not one which I share with anyone except very close friends. At one time he was, I am afraid, something of a philanderer, and one of his ports of call was a house in the back streets of Tresham. One Sallyanne Blickling lived at Number Forty, Hope Street. A very attractive woman, married, with a number of small children, each with a different father. You get my drift, Lois dear?"

"I'm afraid I do, Mrs T-J. But these things happen." Lois was at a loss to know what to say next, but the old lady continued.

"One of those children was the spitting image of my husband. A boy, and he was taken care of, properly educated, and is now a captain of industry in London. One of his sisters—not related to my husband!—lives opposite our team member, Dot Nimmo, and carries on the profession of her mother."

"All this is very interesting, Mrs T-J, but what does it have to do with Robert Pettison? Oh no—I can answer that! This is Pettison's fancy woman! So do you keep in touch with her?"

"As it happens, I do. I was able to help her along when she ran into a spot of trouble. She set up home with a wimp of a man who people said was her pimp, and took his name. Anyway, she is still the major breadwinner. In her line of business there are some pretty disreputable characters, and when I was on the bench, I was able to have one of them put away for a longish stretch."

"Mrs T-J, you are a wonder! What's the shady lady's name? Dot often talks about her."

"Betsy. Betsy Brierley. Pettison is a regular, and, some say, her only client, and she will have useful information. Confidential, of course, but she trusts me. I hope we'll be able to earn her trust."

"Of course. But we may remove her best client from circulation for a while. How do you feel about that?"

"I am sure she will find substitutes. Still a very attractive woman, I would say."

After Mrs T-J had gone, promising to have an early interview with Betsy, Lois relaxed, thinking about what her eccentric assistant had said. This showed a completely new side to the old lady's character. How strong she must have been! A philandering husband, an estate to run, a lifelong justice of the peace, and a lady-of-the-manor image to maintain.

No matter what Mum says, Lois thought, we're lucky to have Mrs T-J aboard.

Justin slept well. He was awoken by the sound of conversation outside his window, and he padded over with bare feet to see who it was. He recognised the top of Josie's head, but the other person was not familiar. Grey hair, cut short, and a stoutish person beneath. Good shoes, looking like a country-woman clothed entirely by Cordings of Piccadilly.

He opened the window, and a blast of frosty air hit him, so he closed it again with a bang. Josie looked up, smiled and waved. Then the other person, a rosy-faced, elderly woman, looked, too. He waved back, and withdrew.

He decided to shower, get dressed, and then have a walk around the village. He knew very little about it, apart from the main street. It would be a nice community to get involved with, especially if he managed to give up his association with his uncle.

Then, suddenly, he was struck by a brilliant idea. He would go solo, obtaining unusual pets from sources which he already knew were legal, and sell them to his own clients for fancy prices, being careful not to tread on Pettison's toes.

So, no time like the present, he thought. I shall wander round, and think about cuddly pets. Such as? He couldn't think of any that were cuddly, unless you counted a cairn terrier puppy he had seen for sale at a recent horse market, and this was hardly a rare animal! He still had the small island mouse in his case, and took it out to look at it. It looked back at him, innocent and appealing. Easy to train, he was sure.

Not cuddly, then. Exotic and fascinating? He had seen a programme on television about a man in Australia who was rearing baby kangaroos, rescued from the pouches of their mothers, who had been killed in road accidents. Appealing and miniature? Just the job! He supposed these would be returned to the wild. But he might make a trip to Australia and run over a few kangaroos of his own. After that, he could go on to snakes, exotic and beautiful. Some people loved to handle them, he knew.

He felt suddenly excited, more cheerful. He could even take over the family farm, and operate from there. In fact, it would be much safer and far enough away from Robert Pettison to be outside his sphere of business. Once he was well established, there would be no end to ways of expanding. Lions and tigers in the cow sheds, a couple of gorillas in the hay barn, swinging from the rafters? He chortled to himself at the immense possibilities. A quick call to a courier right away would sow the seed.

He made the call, and the reply was favourable. He did not commit himself. Merely exploratory, he had said.

What now? He remembered that he had left one or two possessions in his old bed-sitter in Tresham, and decided to drive in and pick them up; then he could deliver the very special mouse to his uncle at the zoo. He clattered down the stairs and walked into the shop.

"Morning, Josie! Thank you so much for the groceries and wine. I can't possibly allow you to give me the delicious Beaujolais. Well, if you're sure, then thanks very much indeed. I slept like a top in your lovely bed. Or perhaps I should rephrase that! The lovely bed in your flat!"

"It snowed in the night," Josie replied, feeling a little embarrassed. "But the sun's shining now and everywhere is sparkling. Are you off out?"

He nodded. "Stuff to collect from Tresham," he said.

"Have a nice day, then," she replied. "See you later."

When he arrived at the bed-sitter, he still had the key and let himself in. It smelt of damp and dirt, and he held his breath while he opened a window. How had he stayed here so long? Well, that was the past, and he had a rosy future before him now.

He began opening cupboards and looking under the

bed, making sure he hadn't left anything, when he heard a sound from the door behind him. He whipped round, and in the dark, unlit room, he saw a tall figure in the doorway.

"Justin, Justin, what are you up to now? My spies have suggested you may be a mole in the organisation. No, don't say anything," he added, as Justin began to bluster. "I refer to a call made not one hour ago, to our mutual friend, my guest overnight, the loyal courier? You know who I mean? You shake your head. Well, a remarkably short memory as well as a stupid brain."

He stepped forward, and Justin was horrified to see he had a gun in his hand.

"Uncle Robert! What on earth are you thinking about? This is me, Justin, your nephew and colleague! And I have the mouse for you!"

"Ex-colleague, possibly," said Pettison. "Get your coat. We're leaving. Give me the key and I'll lock up. You go first, but no silly running away. This gun is right behind you. We need to talk, Justin, and I intend that we do that in the comfort of Cameroon Hall. Now move, fast."

Twenty-Nine

They reached Cameroon Hall after a drive in total silence. Once or twice Justin cleared his throat, as if starting to speak, but his uncle's stony face put him off, and he sat hunched up, his expression blank, as before.

Parking at the rear entrance, Pettison walked round to the passenger door, unlocked it and opened up. "Out!" he said loudly. Justin frowned. This was ridiculous. He knew perfectly well that Pettison's gun was a toy. He used to play with one just like it. But his uncle's evil mood—one with which he was familiar—was not a game. Robert meant business, and Justin searched his mind rapidly for an explanation for his call to the overseas supplier.

"Oh, Uncle Robert," he said wearily, "couldn't we drop the cops-and-robbers bit? I am perfectly willing to explain my telephone call. Obviously, that man misunderstood what I was asking."

"Quiet!" snapped Pettison. He was enjoying himself. He

had no intention of hurting his nephew, of whom he was actually very fond. But subordinates must be corrected, made to understand who was in charge.

"Into my office," he ordered. "Now, while I pour myself a whiskey, you can tell me exactly why you asked a supplier, previously known only to myself, for details of animal people to be delivered direct to you."

"I wouldn't mind a shot of whiskey myself," Justin said mildly, smiling sweetly.

"Oh, very well. You really have been a naughty boy, though. What was it all about? Do you want me to up your percentage? We could discuss it."

"Fine. Now, I have no wish to take business from you, Uncle Robert. You are a very private operator, you know, and I would like to play a bigger part in your operation. I could be a lot more use to you, if you would let me." That should do it, he thought. I shall keep him stalled until I am ready to fly the coop.

Pettison stared at him, as if trying to read his mind. "Is that the truth? If so, I am sure we can come to some new arrangement, Justin. Shall we have another drink and discuss this further?"

"What are you doing this afternoon, love?" Derek finished his plum tart, and asked for a second helping. Gran smiled at him, and cut a generous slice, topped off with a dollop of whipped cream.

"Mum!" said Lois. "Talk about cholesterol! Derek will be a walking tub of lard!"

"Rubbish," said Derek. "I shall work it all off this afternoon. Big job over at Fletching, clambering about in a loft. So what are you doing, Lois? Taking Josie to buy some new clothes? I'd like to cheer her up a bit. You can give the bill to me."

"Hadn't thought," Lois said. "I'd quite like to go over to Farnden Hall. They've opened a new designer-clothes shop in converted stables. Could you do a couple of hours in the shop, Mum? Give Josie a break?"

"Of course I can," Gran said. "It'd be nice to see you with your daughter for a change, instead of tearing about with policemen an' that."

"Your grandson-in-law is a policeman, don't forget," Lois said. "And I don't tear about. But thanks; I'll give her a ring right away."

Farnden Hall, formerly the home of Mrs Tollervey-Jones, was a pleasant, stately home, set in parkland studded with mature chestnut trees, which in spring were ravishing with pink and white blossom candles swaying in the breeze. Josie, in common with other youngsters in the village, had played hide-and-seek there in the spinney at the back of the house, and collected conkers from the chestnut trees in the autumn. They had become adept at avoiding the lady of the manor. Now, as she sat beside her mother in the New Brooms van, she grinned. "A proper visitor, me!" she said. "Not chased out by you know who!"

They found the shop and went in. "Melanie's" was a scented boudoir, with rows of beautiful clothes at astronomical prices, and Lois's heart sank. They couldn't possibly afford them. But Josie had a bargain-hunter's nose, and moved to a rail of last season's models.

"Look, Mum, this would be lovely for the summer." She held up a chiffon dress in pastel shades.

"Perfect for you, Josie," said Melanie, who was a regular customer of the post office in the village shop, and so knew the Meade family well.

"But your father wanted you to have something warm for now," Lois objected.

"Then this will be ideal," said Melanie triumphantly,

holding up a scarlet jacket with a white fluffy collar. "Only really lovely girls can wear this!" she said.

"No need to go over the top, Melanie," said Lois. They were friends from way back, and New Brooms cleaned regularly at the hall and in the developing businesses attached. "But she does look wonderful in it! Will that do, Josie?"

"But look at the price, Mum!"

"No matter. We'll take it, please, Melanie," Lois said.

The door opened, and Lois noticed a change of expression in the shop owner's face.

"Good afternoon. Can I help you?" she said coolly. "I'll be with you in a short while; meanwhile, perhaps you'd like to look around."

The scarlet jacket was now wrapped, and Lois looked at Melanie with eyebrows raised questioningly.

"Old bag!" Melanie mouthed in return. She turned to the new customer. "Now, Mrs Brierley, what are we looking for this afternoon?" she said.

"SO WHAT WAS ALL THAT ABOUT?" JOSIE SAID, AS THEY RETURNED to the van. "And thanks, Mum, and Dad, for this lovely jacket! I shall wear it every day until the summer."

"Not a bad idea to get your money's worth! Anyway, that new customer was, I think, the woman who lives over the road from Dot. A woman of the night, as they used to say. Obviously, not the sort of customer Melanie wants!"

"Her money's as good as anybody else's," said Josie. "Maybe being a pro is what she's good at. Some of them call it sex therapy. You know what Gran says—live and let live! Not that she practises what she preaches. Shall we be off back home, then?"

"In a minute. I just want to look something up in my diary, while I think of it."

Lois shuffled the pages of her diary, keeping an eye on the shop door. When it opened and Mrs Brierley came out, Josie was surprised to see her mother open the car door and go over to speak to her.

Betsy Brierley was also surprised. "Don't I know you?" she said. "Aren't you Dot Nimmo's boss? Anyway, did you want something?"

"Oh, no, not really," said Lois. "I think I've mistaken you for someone else. Please forgive me. I'll be going. Oh, and yes, I do run New Brooms, a cleaning business. Don't forget us, if you ever need any help!"

Useful, thought Lois, as she returned to the van. She knew who I was, quite clearly. We'll see what Mrs T-J does with her. We should get some good stuff on Pettison. Feeling optimistic and cheerful, she drove Josie and the jacket back home in a buoyant mood.

After a pleasant evening with her husband and mother, Lois relaxed on the sofa to watch her favourite detective serial. Then the telephone rang, and she groaned.

"I'll go," said Derek. But he was back after a minute or two, saying it was for Lois. "Mrs T-J, sounding a bit wobbly," he said. "She's been burgled, poor old thing. A masked man, who took some of her silver."

Lois went out immediately and took the telephone from him. "Hello? I'm on my way, so don't worry. Have a strong coffee and wait for me."

After that, Mrs T-J said there was absolutely no need for Lois to turn out, and lightning never strikes the same place twice, and tomorrow morning would be quite soon enough.

Thirty

Next morning, Lois arrived at Stone House to find the police had already been and taken a statement, and would be in touch with the old lady.

"It was one man, last night after dark, theatrically disguised," she said to Lois now. "He made me stand by the door, while he filled his swag bag with the small silver pieces I keep on the table in the drawing room. Then, when I blocked his way out, he laughed and said he had no wish to harm me, but would I kindly step aside! I mean, Lois, I ask you. I thought the days of the gentleman burglar were dead and gone. Then he said I must learn to keep my nose out of other people's business and stick to gardening! Wasn't that stupid? It was all too ridiculously dramatic, my dear! But I know it is best to forget about saving the silver, and just get rid of a burglar as soon as possible. Oh, and he almost forgot to take the silver with him! I had to remind him he'd left it behind. I felt rather sorry for him."

"Mrs T-J! You're not serious?"

"Well, actually, my dear, I am. I suspected at once that he was no professional burglar, but had just been sent to deliver a warning to keep my nose out of the zoo business. I thought I would let him get away with it to see what happened. His voice was familiar, but he did have his face more or less covered, so I'm not sure where I've seen him."

"And the police?"

"Your son-in-law was wonderful, Lois. He was calm and reassuring. Made a list straightaway of the pieces I could remember, and said he hoped and trusted they would all be restored to me. I hadn't the heart to tell him that it was most unlikely I'd ever see them again, and in any case it wasn't very good stuff. Now, we must forget all about this, and return to business. I intend to go into Tresham this afternoon and have a chat with Mrs Brierley. I made an appointment yesterday, to make sure she was there. She will remember me kindly, I hope, and will cough up some interesting info."

"Well, all right, but please be careful, won't you. The likes of Betsy Brierley are not good-hearted girls down on their uppers. They have learned to be ruthless."

"You are teaching your grandmother, Lois, my dear! Dealing with the raffish underworld of Tresham for more years than I care to remember has taught me a thing or two. I shall be perfectly safe, and I'll be in touch."

Lois returned home and stood gazing out of her office window. The snow had turned to slush, and children were out in their wellies, kicking the muddy water at each other and yelling abuse. She saw Josie's new tenant come out and walk away up the road. They'd not talked about him yesterday, but everything seemed to be going well. Josie would have mentioned it, if not.

She was about to leave her office, when the telephone rang announcing Cowgill.

"Lois? Have you heard about Mrs Tollervey-Jones's burglary? Yes, I was sure she would have told you. Well, as you know, Matthew was there straightaway, and I hope sorted it all out. Now, the last thing you told me was that you were bringing the old lady into your investigations at the zoo, and particularly Robert Pettison. Has she acted on your instructions in any way?"

"Not yet. She'd hardly have had any time for that. But yesterday she did say she was going to see Mrs Brierley, whose family she had known through her husband's buccaneering activities."

"Oh my God! Can you stop her, do you think?"

"Not a chance. So you think Betsy was straight on the phone to Pettison?"

"Well, don't forget Mrs Tollervey-Jones was not exactly a hanging judge, but definitely an unforgiving justice of the peace. She'd be well known to the criminal fraternity of Tresham. I think that burglary may have been more a means of frightening her into silence than a straight steal of a few bits of silver."

"She's got some good stuff, Cowgill. Worth quite a bit, I'm sure."

"Mm, well, I have it here in front of me, and I beg to disagree. Most of it is silver plate, and quite modern. I have no doubt she has good stuff tucked away somewhere, but this is not it."

"In front of you!? Do you mean you've got it back already? That must be a record."

"Don't underestimate the long arm of the law, Lois. No, actually, we found it dumped in a rubbish bin outside Waltonby village hall. Can I call and see you later this morning? I have to see Mrs Tollervey-Jones, and then I'll nip up and have a chat."

"I suppose so. I don't know what Derek has planned for today, but unless you hear from me, it'll be all right."

"And please keep a sharp eye around when you're out. I think you may have stumbled on something very lucrative and very nasty. So take care; there's a love."

DEREK, WHEN ASKED, SAID HE WAS SURE THAT WHATEVER HE had planned for this morning would have to take second place to the visit of Detective Inspector Cowgill.

"So what had you planned? A family trip to London? A ride on the old steam train in Fletching?" asked Lois.

"Don't be ridiculous, Lois. Of course none of those things. I am going up to the allotment and shall be home in time for lunch. Gran is going into Tresham this afternoon, and I shall be watching football."

"I see," said Lois. "So having Cowgill here for ten minutes or so won't interfere too much with your day?"

Gran looked round from the Rayburn, where she was stirring a saucepan of soup into slow-moving whorls. "Do shut up, you two!" she said. "If you want to argue, go and do it somewhere else. This kitchen is my territory, and I expect a bit of peace."

"Sorry, Mum," said Lois. "I'm just nipping down to see Josie. Anything we want from the shop?"

"Onions," said Gran.

"And the same to you," said Derek, and all three fell about at the old joke.

THE SHOP WAS BUSY WHEN LOIS ARRIVED, AND SHE HOVERED round the back of shelves, waiting her turn.

"I saw him myself, coming out of Stone House!" said a

woman standing at the counter. "Carrying an old rexine bag, and looking shifty."

"What were you doing, Myrtle, out in the street so late at night?"

"Walking the dog, like I always do, last thing. He didn't see me, I'm sure. Jumped into a car and drove off like a roaring banshee."

Lois walked casually round and approached the woman named Myrtle. "Must have been a bit of a shock, seeing someone suspicious so late at night."

The woman shook her head. "Not really, Mrs Meade," she said. "You'd be surprised what I see when I'm out with the dog. Goings-on of all sorts!"

At that moment, Justin Brookes came into the shop. He was wearing his jeans and jersey, and his hair was attractively tousled. He nodded to the customers, picked up a newspaper and began to read, waiting to be served.

"Look," said Myrtle, "it's here on the front page of the local. 'Local JP gets burgled in Long Farnden. Burglar gets off without a chase.'"

"They'll get him," said her friend. "They always do, in the end. Silly fool must have left loads of prints on that silver. I heard they recovered it already. My friend in Fletching is caretaker at the village hall, and she found a bagful of stuff. Took it straight to the police. All sorts of silver things. She didn't touch none of it, of course, so the police shouldn't have too much trouble identifying the prints."

"Excuse me butting in," said Justin. "Do you happen to know if Mrs Tollervey-Jones is okay? I'd hate to think of the old lady being hurt."

"Oh no, nothing like that. Just one of those collect-and-run merchants. He'll not get far."

"I hope not," said Justin. "We can do without such menaces in our community."

Inside, he was chuckling. It had all been so easy. Pettison had been warned by Betsy Brierley that Mrs Tollervey-Jones was on the warpath, and he wanted her stopped. A quick change into a disguise. Balaclava on the head, scarf wound round half the face, and thick black gloves. It had all been done and dusted in the hour, and he was back in Tresham reporting to Pettison. After that he had returned to his flat over the shop with nobody any the wiser. Mission accomplished! A small dose of the frighteners on Mrs Tollervey-Jones, and back into Pettison's good books.

Thirty-One

Mrs Tollervey-Jones looked at herself in the mirror on her dressing table. Her short grey hair waved naturally, curling pleasantly around her face. Her clear blue eyes had an honest, straightforward expression, and her lips, unadorned by lipstick, lifted at the ends in a half smile.

"Much too pleasant looking for a justice of the peace," she muttered to herself. She had recently retired from the justices' bench, and was restless. Having moved from the hall and its farms and parkland into a substantial stone house in the village, she had simply not enough to do with her time. "Except," she said to her reflection, "when Lois Meade requires help from me, her unofficial assistant."

This thought cheered her up, and she looked in the wardrobe for a warm coat, ready to tackle the suspicious Betsy Brierley. Why suspicious? she asked herself. No reason, really. She just had a feeling about the woman. Something guarded in her voice on the phone.

She left the house, locking up more carefully than usual, and drove off towards Tresham, where she threaded her way through the back streets to where Dot Nimmo lived on one side of the road, and Betsy Brierley on the other. As she reached the top of the street, she was passed by a van and for a moment was startled by a large snarling tiger staring at her from the van's side. Aha! Mr Pettison has been a-visiting, she thought. I must be careful how I tread.

Betsy answered the door, and stared at Mrs T-J. "I don't know you, do I?" she said. "You said your husband had something to do with our family, but I've asked around, and none of 'em remember anything about you."

"Could I come in for a few minutes? I won't keep you long, but I'd like to explain. Thank you, dear."

Huh, thought Betsy, no good soft-soaping me, duckie. It'll have to be a pretty good explanation, after what Pettison has just told me.

Mrs T-J perched on the edge of a chair, nodded a good morning to Mr Brierley, who stood nervously by the fireplace, and began to talk about her husband. She was tactful when mentioning his little weakness, but said he had had several love children around town when he was young.

"One or two of them were, I believe, brought up by your family, Betsy. In fact, one of the boys, a very bright lad, did very well. Ended up as quite a notable chairman of companies, that sort of thing. I'm researching the family history, and wondered if you remember anything about that, or, since you are much younger than my generation, whether you heard this clever son being spoken of?"

Ted Brierley shook his head, but Betsy said that as a matter of fact, she had been to see an old aunt recently, and she had identified a photograph on her wall.

"A very handsome chap, he was, apparently," Betsy said now. "And, as you say, very big in the city. Lord Mayor of

London, even, later on, after a distinguished career. Pity Ted didn't get any such genes from *his* family."

"Thanks for nothing, Betsy!" he protested. "If that's the way the wind's blowing, then I'm off out to the club. I'll watch the racing from there. I'll be back for lunch, so don't stay too long, Mrs Whatever your name is."

"Sorry about him," said Betsy, after he had slammed the front door behind him. "He's always a bit of a misery."

"I am so sorry to have caused unpleasantness," apologised Mrs T-J. Privately, she thought she had never encountered a more unforthcoming couple. However, a job was a job, and Lois would be expecting a report from her.

"Are you working now?" she asked, and Betsy's face hardened.

"And what's it to you if I am?" she said.

"Oh nothing. I was just being polite. Do you know, I thought a tiger was on the loose on my way here? It turned out to be painted on the side of a van. Advertising Tresham Zoo. Do you like zoos, Betsy?"

Betsy said that zoos were all very well in their place, and she could take them or leave them.

"I'm fond of London Zoo, in Regent's Park," Mrs T-J said. "I know my way around there, and can avoid the reptile house! I'm afraid reptiles give me the shivers. As for snakes, I cannot bear even the thought of them. It's something about the way they move. No legs; no wheels! They just slither in the most alarming way. And so swift! I can understand how the poisonous ones can be so deadly."

Betsy said she felt much the same. "I work at the Tresham Zoo, on and off," she said. "Mr Pettison asks me to take over the gate when Margie is off sick."

"Ah, Mr Pettison, yes. Now, I have heard tales told about him. An eccentric gentleman, I believe?"

"Eccentric? He's much the same as any man. You can

take it from me, he's no different from most men. They're usually interested mainly in one thing. Sorry to be very vulgar, Mrs Jones, but it's what's between his legs that he's most concerned with! It's a complaint that I can treat, and he comes to me regular. Nursey, he calls me."

"So he is otherwise a simple, good-living person, do you think?" Mrs Tollervey-Jones was not in the least shocked. She had heard much worse in her time.

This unsettled Betsy, who had hoped to frighten the old tab away, in case of further rich revelations. On the contrary, Mrs T-J settled back in her chair, and enquired if Betsey saw much of him outside the zoo.

"Comes here for his treatment," said Betsy, now with a superior smile. She was beginning to respect this old dear. "Tells me all his worries, an' that. Running a place like that zoo is full of problems. Only recently, there's been two accidents, one of them fatal, associated with it. A cleaning woman injured, and then one of the keepers killed. He's got a lot of rare animals there, you know. Priceless, some of them. Not many left in the world. He gets them from all over and breeds them for posterity."

"I hope he knows how to look after them! Some of the creatures bred in captivity are not so badly off, having known nothing else. But most animals brought in from the wild are lucky to last a year. Sad, isn't it? Myself, I think a good dog and maybe a cat to keep the mice down are all one needs."

"I dunno," said Betsy. "I do fancy having one or two of 'em. He's got some of them spectacled whatsits—like baby crocodiles—caimans, that's it. You can hold them in the palm of your hand, and they're real little darlings. I wouldn't mind one of them."

"But not if they're going to die on you?"

"Oh, Petti can always get me another," she said loftily.

"Now, Mrs Jones, I'm going to turn you out. I've got a client coming in a few minutes, and he'll not want to see I've got company! Bye-bye, dear. Been nice talking to you. Bye!"

MRS TOLLERVEY-JONES DROVE AWAY WITH A SMILE ON HER FACE. She had been much amused by Betsy Brierley, and admired her confidence and lack of embarrassment.

"You could call it a service, I suppose," she said aloud to herself in the driving mirror. What was it Pettison called her? Oh yes, Nursey! Wonderful. She decided to drive straight back to Farnden to report to Lois on her morning's work.

When she drew up outside Meade House, she saw the unmistakable Inspector Cowgill getting into his car. He must have seen her approaching, as he stepped out again and came over to where she had halted.

"Good day, Mrs Tollervey-Jones," he said. "I was hoping to have a word with you, but there was no one at home at Stone House. Are you free, by any chance?"

"So sorry, Inspector. I had an urgent request to visit someone in Tresham. But I could go back home and see you there for a short while. I have promised to have a talk with Mrs Meade, but half an hour would be fine."

Women! thought the inspector. I'm surrounded by scheming women. My beloved Lois twists me round her little finger, and now this old duck is quacking about allowing me half an hour of her precious time. And I'm a famous detective! He laughed, shrugged and drove down to park outside Stone House and wait for Mrs Tollervey-Jones to join him.

"SO WHAT DID HE WANT, LOIS? AND YOUR ILLUSTRIOUS ASSISTANT?" Derek said. He had emerged from the sitting room, where the football match on television had just finished.

"Did they win?" asked Lois.

"Yes, four to one. Walked it. Now, answer my question, please."

"Well, since you ask so nicely, Cowgill wanted to tell me about the dangers of dicing with the likes of Pettison. He also wanted to know all about Josie's new tenant in the flat. Seemed very interested to know if he had been seen with Pettison, or if he mentioned his name. I was cagey, and said I wasn't sure. But if he's suspicious of Justin Brookes, there is every reason for us to be, too. I'm all for sending him packing, straightaway. He's a bit overnice, if you ask me."

"I think that'd be a bit hasty," Derek said. "It may be nothing but gossip. Cowgill has to listen to everything, but we have no reason to suspect Brookes of anything, do we? Josie seems to have quite taken to him. Makes her feel safer when the shop's empty, she says. No, I think we should hold hard for a bit. See what happens. And Mrs T-J?"

"She wanted to fill me in with how her talk with Betsy Brierley had gone. She picked up some useful stuff about Pettison. About his trade in rare animals, an' that."

"And is it time for tea? I'm ready for a cup, and Gran's come home with cream cakes for all," said Derek, contenting himself that Lois had at least shared with him some of what she had been discussing.

Thirty-Two

Josie was up early in the shop sorting the Sunday papers. Two handy schoolboys delivered them, one on his bicycle to outlying farms, and the other walking through the village at a leisurely pace. As she saw them off on their separate ways, she was startled to hear a car engine close behind. It was the Fiat, and as it came out from behind the shop, the window was wound down, and Justin Brookes leaned over to speak to her.

"Morning, Josie," he said. "I'm off to church. I don't suppose you'll accompany me?"

Church was the last place she would have expected him to go, and she shook her head politely, as he had expected. "Sorry, no can do. I have to shut up shop and do some urgent admin this morning. Unfortunately, it won't wait for me!"

He nodded and smiled, wondering what he would have done if she had said yes. He closed the window and drove off with the Ferrari-sounding roar. She watched it go, and laughed. They were jolly little cars. There were quite a few of them now, and often one would pull up outside the shop. Lovely colours, too, and a silvery one appealed to her. Perhaps, when she'd done the books, there would be enough on the right side of the accounts to enable her to buy one. And pigs might fly, she said to herself.

"Church?" said Matthew, when she arrived home for a late breakfast. "That man-about-town going to church?"

"He may be praying for his sick father. The old boy is expected to die anytime now. You can never tell with people, anyway, Matthew. Even you darken the doors of the church at Christmastime!"

Justin pulled up outside the lych-gate and waited. Several cars parked behind him, and the occupants disappeared up the path. Then the one he was waiting for drew up in front of him on a small hillock where the footpath curved round the corner. Its engine was switched off, and then the door opened. A tall girl with a face like a Pre-Raphaelite painting came towards him, swinging a large white carrier bag, a chic dress-designer's name emblazoned on the side.

"Hi, Justin. How's business?"

"It's not likely to improve, sweetie, if you swing the poor things to and fro like that! Enough to make them seasick! You'd better get in, and let me make sure they're still alive. This is a new supplier, and Pettison is very anxious that I should check."

The girl, an old friend of Justin's and recruited by him into the chain of handlers designed to mislead any curious investigators, now explained that she was about to be married, and would not be operating for Pettison anymore. "But I'm sworn to secrecy about the whole thing, and I shall keep my word," she said.

Justin frowned. He quite fancied her, and would be sorry not to see her anymore. At the same time, he envied her. How good it would be not to be any longer under Pettison's control. He looked into the carrier and saw a metal box, like a miniature cage, with airholes and a glass front. Inside, two tiny shrew-like creatures stared at him. They were something out of a Disney film, and belonged somewhere in a forest under dark branches and leaves, where they knew their predators and how to avoid them.

"They're toys!" he said loudly, firmly putting such thoughts to one side. "We've been had!"

Then one of them flicked its tail and crept into the dark corner, quickly followed by the second one.

"Satisfied?" said the girl, as Justin jumped back into his seat. "They're dear little things. You can take them out if you like. They're quite tame. I had fun with them last night. Mind you, I think they are delicate, so take care of them. When are you handing them over to Pettison?"

"Tomorrow. I'm living in a flat now, over Farnden village shop, and there's a place I can keep them hidden."

"Right-o. Now, are we going to church? I quite fancy Holy Communion. Makes me feel good again."

"Not me," said Justin. "I am beyond redemption. Thanks anyway. See you soon."

She left him, and headed up the church path, and he started the engine and drove off.

Outside the shop, Justin saw a police car, and his heart thumped. What the hell?! Only one thing to do, and he accelerated, driving past as fast as he could. Three minutes later, he realised the police car was closing up behind him, its lights flashing. He drew into the side of the road, and opened the window. A police officer came up and looked in.

"Morning, sir," he said. "Just thought I'd introduce myself. I'm Matthew Vickers, husband of Josie in the shop. I understand you've taken on the flat? Nice little place. Used to visit Josie when she lived there. Hope you'll enjoy living in Farnden. Oh yes, and watch your speed through the village. You were going at forty-two miles an hour past the shop! Just a warning, sir. Good morning."

Thank God I flung my jacket over the carrier, Justin thought. Well, that had been a turn-up. But he had been very alarmed, and realised that one careless move could bring the whole of Pettison's house of cards tumbling to the ground. In other words, the zoo would be closed and Uncle Robert arrested and very likely put in prison.

So what to do with the creatures now? He knew Pettison was away for the weekend in a country hotel nearby, for a couple of nights of mad passion with his fancy woman. "A treat for me, dear boy," he had said to Justin. "Work hard; play hard. Not a bad motto for the likes of us!"

So, no good going into Tresham. He would just drive back to Farnden, take the key to the shed from its hiding place, and conceal the carrier in there until tomorrow. He had cleared it out and put an electric convector heater in, and hung a dark cloth over the small window.

The wind was icy when he walked from his car to the shed, and he hurried in. Switching on the heater, he took the box from the bag, and looked around. There were shelves along the back wall, and he put it carefully on the topmost. Then he tore the bag in half, punched a few holes in it with a screwdriver, and upended it over the cage, where the creatures had now reappeared and were following his every move with their button-bright eyes.

"There you are, then, little ones," he said. The girl had given him some stuff for them to eat, and he decided to come back when they had settled down. Perhaps at lunchtime, when nobody was around.

Back inside his flat, he made himself a coffee and looked

for a newspaper. Yesterday's had gone out with the rubbish, and he had nothing to read. Perhaps Josie was still in the shop, and would have a spare.

He walked round into the shop, and found the door still open.

"Hi, Josie?" he shouted. "Okay for me to come in?"

In a couple of seconds she stood there, smiling. "You didn't go to church did you?" she said accusingly. "Mrs Tollervey-Jones called on her way back, and said you were not there. I'm afraid you can't get away with anything in this village," she added.

Justin looked suitably humble. "Afraid I couldn't face it," he said. "All that stuff about descending into hell and rising again, not to mention the sick and the dead. Couldn't get through it, really."

"Of course not," Josie said consolingly. "I quite understand. Have you had any news about your father?"

"No, he's still hanging on. No change. It's very hard for Mother, and I hope to be able to get up to see her again soon. I wish they were nearer, but that's how it goes these days. Years ago, families all stuck together in the same place, especially in the farming community. I've let them down, poor old things."

"You couldn't have been expected to stay in the middle of nowhere, after being sent away to school and university. Anyway, can I help you?"

"Yes, have you got a Sunday paper left? Any one will do. The *Despatch*?" He laughed. A real rag, that one. "Yes, that'll do fine," he said, and retreated back up to the flat.

His coffee was lukewarm, so he put it in a saucepan to heat up, and unfolded the newspaper. A picture of a snake, rising to strike, took up the whole of the top half of the front page. Underneath, a young girl smiled at the camera in a smaller picture. He read the text and discovered that the girl had been playing in a neighbour's house, and ventured into a small, dark room with her friend. Apparently, the door had been left open by accident, and they had encountered the unfriendly creature, which immediately struck the girl on the arm, where she had put it up to shield her face.

She was taken at once to hospital, and was being continuously monitored. The owner of the snake had been taken for questioning, and the snake confiscated by the police. There followed a strong warning by the paper about keeping wild creatures in the home as pets. Alarm was spreading about the increasing numbers of such accidents, and the local Member of Parliament was taking the matter up with the authorities.

"Ye Gods," said Justin aloud. "Not traceable to the honourable Pettison, I hope. His name had not been mentioned, so perhaps this was another case which apparently had nothing to do with him."

A nasty smell of burning coffee sent him running to the kitchen, where he ditched the contents of the saucepan and set about making a fresh lot. He supposed it was a matter of time before the investigations came close to the zoo once more. Then Pettison might find it hard to wriggle free.

"Delicious," said Matthew, patting his stomach. "You'll soon be as good a cook as your grandmother, Josie dear."

"As well as shopkeeper and general skivvy, mister policeman," she replied.

"A wonder of the world! Now, can you tell me, please, where I might find a designer-dress shop called Noelle Noelle?"

"Never heard of it," Josie said. "Why? Are you planning on buying me a present? Mum's just given me a lovely jacket. Must be my birthday."

"No, sadly not. I cautioned your flat tenant this morning. Doing more than forty-two miles an hour through the village. I could have booked him, but had a stern word instead. We had a chat, and I noticed a white bag peeping out from under clothes in the back. 'Noelle Noelle' was written on the side of it, and the strange name caught my eye. Uncle Cowgill's asked me to look out for anything odd about Justin Brookes, so I made a note. I can look it up. Now, what's for pudding?"

Thirty-Three

Dot was up bright and early, and took her breakfast to a little table by her front-room window. She had decided to keep a watch on Betsy Brierley's house for as many hours as she could. There would be the New Brooms weekly meeting at noon, and she hoped maybe she would have something to report.

Yesterday, she had seen the zoo van once more parked outside the Brierleys', and Betsy had emerged out of it looking, in Dot's opinion, like something the cat brought in. Her hair was set in tight little curls, and she had plastered on so much makeup that her face shone like a beacon. False eyelashes, falsies under her tight sweater, and jeans so sculpted to her bottom that she could hardly move, let alone bend down to pick up the front-door key.

So she's been off with the boss, thought Dot, and stood up, half shielded by the curtain. Betsy finally got the door open, and before she could go in, her husband had stepped out onto the pavement, and was having words with Pettison.

"Poor little sod!" muttered Dot. "That zoo man could eat him for breakfast!"

She could see Pettison laughing, and then he got into his van and drove away, leaving Ted Brierley, also laughing, standing on the pavement listening to Betsy, who, as far as Dot could tell, was shrieking at him about not being gentleman enough to pick up the door key from where she had dropped it. Eventually, the pair of them went inside, and the street was quiet.

"I'd not change places with her for all the world," Dot said to her parrot, now so old and mangy that it could hardly move. "Lost all the respect she ever had. Pettison don't respect her, nor does Ted, and nobody in the street will speak to her. She pretends she don't care, but I bet when she's alone in the house, she cries her eyes out."

Dot could not have been more wrong. Betsy Brierley went upstairs, changed into more comfortable clothes, and set about berating her husband for making such a fool of them both. "You're wasting your breath on him, Ted," she said. "He's a stuck-up fool, and one of these days he'll get his comeuppance. Still, his money's good, and I had a good feast for supper last night. A glass of champagne as a starter! That's the life, Ted."

"It may be the life for you, and I know we got together as a cover for your sex therapies, as you like to call them. There's nothing much between us, I know, never has been. But I won't be made to look a fool, Betsy. That man makes me look a fool, and delights in it. People talk, and lately I've been taunted at the club about people whose wives flaunt their wares. We didn't start that way, Betsy. It was all decent and undercover. Better get back to that, before we lose what respect we've got left."

"Long speech, Ted. I'm really scared!" she replied, lighting a cigarette and posing like a second-rate actress by the fireplace. "All I've got to say is, where would we be without Robert Pettison? He pays for me, and for when we hide his little animals. And if you're not happy with that, I reckon we could split and I could blackmail him to marry me! Then where would you be?"

"Don't be ridiculous," said Ted. "And go and take that muck off your face."

Just before Dot was about to leave for Farnden and the New Brooms meeting, there was a knock at her door. To her surprise, when she opened it, there stood Ted from over the road. "What do you want? I'm going out now."

"A couple of minutes, Dot," he said. "I think you'll be interested."

She led him into her front room and turned. "I'm not asking you to sit down, because I really have to get going. What is it, anyway?"

"It's about Pettison, him at the zoo. You know my wife treats him for his rheumatism."

Dot chuckled. "I've never heard it called that," she said.

"Well, she sees him regularly, and has got to know a lot of what goes on there. I know you're in touch with some clever chaps who operate, well, you know, sometimes the wrong side of the law."

Dot said nothing, and he carried on. "The thing is, I need some help. It's confidential, like, an' I need it to be kept that way. Do you know of one of your late husband's colleagues who might be able to help?"

"I can try," said Dot. "But I'll need to know a bit more about it, before I can get them interested."

"Right, well, it's to do with the zoo and the rare animals

he's got there. And about the accidents there. I keep my ear to the ground, and I intend to make use of what I know."

"You mean blackmail?" said Dot bluntly. "Don't even think of it, Ted. And my lot are old friends of Mr Pettison. Now I must fly, else Mrs M will give me the sack!"

He turned and made for the door. "Thanks anyway, Dot," he said. "If you do decide to help, I'll see you right by it. Now to go and play dutiful partner to my lovely girl."

Lois was talking to the rest of the team when Dot arrived, and she ushered her into the office.

"Sorry I'm late, Mrs M," she said. "But I've got something to tell you about Ted Brierley. He just came round wanting help."

The business of the meeting carried on, and Lois sorted out who was going where, who wanted a change of scene, and which, if any, of her clients had complained about a member of the team.

"One funny thing happened this week," said Hazel, who ran the office in Dot's street. "You know that Betsy Brierley, her who keeps open house to deserving customers? Well, she came running down the street once or twice during the week like she was being chased by one of them tigers in the zoo. She works for him up there, doesn't she? Then, the final time, she shot straight into the office and sat down in front of my desk, back to the window."

"So what did you do?" said Lois.

"Asked her if she wanted help in the house. She laughed in a raucous kind of way, and said no, she already had a man."

"And?"

"So I said I was busy, and if she didn't want our help, I'd see her on her way. She looked furtively round at the window, and then got up. 'Thanks for the shelter,' she said, and left before I could tell her that it was not, nor had been, raining."

"Losing her marbles," said Dot. "Caught something from one of her clients, I reckon. They say it softens the brain."

Lois did not know what to make of all this, but hoped that Dot's promised revelation would make all become clear. "Right," she said. "If there's no more business to deal with, let's call Gran in, and have coffee before you go. Thanks, everyone."

"You don't think I should worry, then, Mrs M," said Hazel, not quite satisfied. "They're a rough lot up that end of the street. I do sometimes feel vulnerable, sitting there."

"Not so much of the rough lot!" said Dot. "Don't forget I live up that end. Mind you, come to think of it, there's one or two would risk their all for a couple of quid. Keep the safe locked, dearie," she added. "You can always give me a bell if you're worried, an' I'll come down and rescue you."

"Thanks, Dot," said Hazel. "I'd do the same for you. But do you have any idea what she might have been doing?"

"I reckon the worm has turned in that house. Old Ted has had enough, according to what he told me. He's not much of a man, but even he is finally fed up with being made to look such a fool. Did you see him? Or had he gone back home after chasing her with an axe?"

Hazel's eyes widened. "Do you mean that?" she said.

"No, only joking! But I have seen him push her out and lock the door behind her. Now then, Mrs M, I should be going to Waltonby. Any more instructions?"

"I thought you had something more to tell me," Lois said.

"Yeah, well, coffee first."

After the others had gone, Dot asked if now was a good time to tell about Ted's request.

"Fine. Fire away," said Lois.

"Seems he's planning to blackmail Pettison. At least, I think that's what he meant. Wanted me to ask one of my less-than-reputable family to help him. I told him he was wasting his time, and that my lot were well in with Robert Pettison. I advised against it, but it's obvious he's had enough, poor devil. I said if he was really serious, I might try to help. Did I do right?"

"We shall see, Dot. Thanks, anyway," answered Lois.

Thirty-Four

Robert Pettison was beginning to feel threatened. The police were still circling like vultures, every day turning up with some trumped-up reason to inspect everything, from the house to the zoo to the gardener's shed. Up to now, and with Justin's help, he had managed to conceal animals which could be construed as illegally obtained straight from the wild. He now concentrated on small creatures that were easy to hide, and so far none had been visible to nosy policemen. All such animals he bought for resale, and mostly on commission, with regular customers around the country.

But now there were other people bothering him. Dot Nimmo, for one. It had probably been a mistake employing her, knowing she worked for the celebrated Lois Meade, with the latter's close association with Inspector Cowgill. Dottie was always nosing around, asking about the locked room and announcing that she intended to turn out the cupboards in his office. "Full of rubbish," she had said.

Maybe she would call it rubbish, but those locked cupboards were full of records that were highly incriminating rubbish, going back years. He had forbidden her to touch them, of course, but Dot Nimmo had never obeyed orders and, he suspected, she was not about to change.

Perhaps he would give her the sack. But that would bring him face-to-face with Lois Meade, whose eyes were everywhere, and who would inevitably ask questions he would rather not answer. So, he would have to find a way of dealing with Dottie. He thought of several ways, but the one he liked best was already tested and tried. Several of his animals had poisonous bites, and he could easily arrange for one to escape, blaming it on the keeper, or Margie Turner, when she was filling in.

Then he thought again. No, maybe not poison. One more poisoning would be a death too far. He would have to think of another kind of accident that would not necessarily kill Dot, but render her unable to do any cleaning for the foreseeable future. Yes, that would be best.

Feeling cheered, he got up from his chair by the fire, put out the lights, made sure everywhere was safely locked and bolted, and went upstairs to bed, a glass of whiskey in one hand and a hot-water bottle in the other. Two steps from the top, he tripped on the worn carpet and went flying down the stairs, bumping from one step to another and yelling as he went. His glass of whiskey broke into pieces around him, and the hot-water bottle burst, spraying his face with boiling water.

He reached the floor headfirst, and there was a dreadful cracking sound as bone hit ceramic tile. His last thought before he blacked out was that now he knew how to deal with Dottie Nimmo.

IN THE WARM FLAT ABOVE FARNDEN SHOP, JUSTIN BROOKES HAD fallen asleep in his chair, while the television churned on to a snoring audience. He finally awoke to the sound of the telephone, and fumbled around until he found it.

"Hello? Oh Mum, it's you." His stomach lurched, and he gripped the receiver more tightly. "Mum? Don't cry, Mum; take your time. When was it? Oh, nice that you were with him. It was kindest, really. And he'd had a good innings. Is anyone with you? Oh yes, that nice post lady. Well, I'll leave first thing in the morning, and should be with you in a couple of hours. Then I'll organise everything. Now you're not to worry. Try to get some sleep. Bye-bye, Mum. Love you."

He put the phone down, and was suddenly hit by huge, wrenching sobs. His father was dead. A father who had been steadfast, always defending him against criticism and doing his best to keep a wayward son on the right path. Oh God, please give him rest, and help me to lead—what is it?—a righteous and sober life. In the future. Somehow.

The following morning, Justin was as good as his word, and left Farnden after an early breakfast. He took his good businessman's suit with him, intending to stay in Lincolnshire until after the funeral. He could help around the farm and, in talking to his mother, get some idea of what to do next. He had to face the fact that his uncle and the zoo were going to be closed down in the near future. Uncle Robert thought he was bombproof, but Justin was well aware that the net was drawing tighter. Should he stick by the old idiot, or leave while the going was good?

As the miles sped by, he tried to add up the respective pros and cons. If Pettison should end up in jail, then there would be the perfect opportunity to clean up the zoo, get rid of illegal animal immigrants and run the place as one of the best private zoos in the country. He liked the animals. Not in the stupid "people" way of his uncle. But the chimps and the other captivity-bred monkeys were fun, and he might even build an elephant house, and give kids rides around the grounds. A small elephant, it would need to be.

He laughed. He really knew nothing about keeping animals. But he could learn, and it would be fun doing it.

The other course of action was clear. He could do what his mother dearly wanted, take over the farm, get married and have a family, and they could all live happily ever after. But could he change his present way of life so abruptly? His mother and the farm could tick over for a year or two, to give him time to decide. In any case, now was not the time to worry her with his indecision! He could stay with her for a couple of weeks, and help her to sort out solicitors and all the trappings of the law. He was fairly sure that his father had willed everything to Mum, so it shouldn't be too complicated.

Back in the shop, Josie was opening up when she saw a note put through the letter box. It was from Justin, saying his father had died and he was away to Lincolnshire, and did not know when he would return. He left two telephone numbers, and a cheque for the next installment of rent.

Poor fellow! thought Josie. But perhaps it was all for the best. The old man had been hanging on for so long, in a more or less zombie state, and now Justin and his mother could move forward. She wondered whether to send a card, and then realised that she did not have the address.

Lois appeared, having run down from home to buy milk. "We never seem to have enough," she said. "How's everything, Josie?" she asked, seeing her daughter's solemn face.

Josie explained about Justin's father, and said she was thinking about tidying and cleaning the flat, so it would be nice for him to find on his return. "He didn't mind a bit, last time I went up there. I might tackle the shed, too. I know he cleared one end of it, but there's still a lot of our junk out there."

"Good idea, so long as you're sure he won't mind. I'll give you a hand with the shed, if you want. I'm free this afternoon. Any use?"

Josie said the two pairs of hands were always better than one, and accepted gratefully. She offered Lois a coffee, and was about to go into the stockroom to make it, when her phone rang.

"Shall I get it?" Lois said.

"Better not. It's bound to be some supplier." Josie picked up the receiver and her smile faded. "Oh my God! Hang on; I'll put you on to Mum. Dot Nimmo," she mouthed to Lois and gave her the phone.

After a few minutes, she handed it back to Josie, and shook her head. "I don't know whether it's bad news or good," she said, and explained that when Dot went into Cameroon Hall this morning, she found everything still and quiet, dark because the curtains hadn't been drawn, and all Pettison's dirty dishes from yesterday on the kitchen table.

"And then she found him lying on the floor, surrounded by broken glass and a puddle of whiskey and water mixed, out cold. She thought he was dead, but then saw his leg begin to move. She rushed to call the ambulance, which was there in record time. They took him to the hospital, where they said he had a broken leg and multiple injuries. Poor Dot was sounding nearly hysterical. At least, that's what I thought. But no, not Dot. She was actually making a big effort to stop laughing!"

"Good heavens! It's one thing after another this morning," Josie said. "First Justin's father and now old Pettison out of action."

"I hope there'll not be a third, then," said Lois. "Just watch where you put your feet, Josie love. I'm off now, and I'll see you after lunch."

* * *

It was not until Justin had eaten a sad lunch with his mother, and had returned from taking her on a food-shopping trip to nearby Spalding, that he remembered the cage and the little animals, concealed in the garden shed behind his flat. He swore to himself, and went into the chilly front room, never used except for family Christmases and funeral wakes, and dialled Pettison's number. He would have to explain, ask him to collect and hope that he would understand.

There was no reply, and he finally left a message asking Pettison to ring him, saying it was urgent. He went to join his mother in the kitchen, wondering what to do if his uncle did not ring him back. Should he ask Josie to find them and take them to the zoo? No, the fat would really be in the fire if he did that. He would have to rely on Uncle Robert. There was nobody else. The new keeper had not been in on everything, and in any case, he couldn't think of a good story the man could tell when asking for the key to the shed. Then, of course, there was always Betsy. He had had his own key to the shed copied and left it with her, in case of emergencies. Well, this wasn't an emergency. Not yet, anyway.

Perhaps nobody would find them, and they would die. He saw again the little faces looking at him. Sod it! They were trapped, but then so was he. And he had more to lose. But what more could you lose than your life? If Uncle Robert did not ring him, he would think again, and the hell with it. At least he would not be responsible for animal murder.

Thirty-Five

Greeted with the news of Pettison's accident, Margie Turner stepped in and said she was quite capable of running things from her kiosk for the present, and she would ask her friend Dot Nimmo to help.

"Dot is a cleaner here," she explained to the young policeman, who had turned up to see if there was any help needed. Inspector Cowgill had sent him, he said, and he was obviously dying to do something exciting, like cleaning out the tiger's cage, or swinging around with the chimps.

"We've got a new keeper, and him and me can cope well enough, with Dot Nimmo alongside." Margie had seen the constable's face fall, and took pity on him. She said that he could help her handle the big bales of wood shavings used for bedding. When that was done, she sent him away, saying she would always ring if she needed further help.

"There'll be some others coming from the police station," he said. "Inspector Cowgill will be going up to the house later on."

"That's fine," said Margie. "I know him well. He'll probably have his lady friend in tow."

MARGIE WAS WRONG FOR ONCE, AS LOIS WAS ALREADY DOWN AT the shop when Cowgill rang, and Gran forgot to pass on the message. Josie and her mother had made a start on the shed, and although it was a lot more empty than it had been, there were still a number of things to go into the skip, and others which Josie said she would take home to the cottage.

"Do you think you should check on Gran in the shop?" Lois said now. "Her arithmetic is not what it used to be."

Josie laughed. "I'll just make sure she's okay; then we'll tackle the rest." She disappeared, and Lois looked round at the other items to be dumped. There was a very old pram, probably vintage, left by the previous, elderly owners, and also a ferocious-looking mangle, with a long iron handle and hefty wooden rollers. These things never wore out, thought Josie. Perhaps some collector might be interested in them. She had to wait for Josie to help her move them outside, where Derek could collect them. She took down the piece of cloth over the window. Surely Justin wouldn't want that? It effectively shut out all the light. She threw it in the big bin outside the shed, and went back in.

A white bag on a high shelf at the back caught her eye. It had been torn and looked like rubbish. She put out a hand to grab it, but felt something inside. She removed the cage carefully, and something glinted at her from inside. It disappeared, and she blinked. A result of coming in from the sunlight outside, she thought. But then it happened again, and she moved to look closer.

Two pairs of eyes stared at her, and she saw two little animal bodies, frozen with fear.

"What the hell are these!?" she shouted, and Josie came running. "Oh Lor, Mum," she said. "They must belong to Justin. Maybe he's keeping them as pets? What on earth *are* they?"

"They're not mice," Lois said.

"Not gerbils or hamsters," Josie said.

"They're furry, but smooth with it. And they have tails like mice. And long trunky noses. They're not baby rats, are they?" Lois asked.

"I can't be doing with rats," Josie replied, backing away.

"No, I'm sure they're not rats. Best not tell Gran, or she'll have hysterics. We'll get Derek down to have a look at them after the shop's shut. Have they got food and water?"

They found the foodstuff for them and pushed it through the bars at the back of the cage, and managed to fill up the water bottle upended and attached to the inside. Then they just stood and watched, riveted to the spot, as the creatures began to move, eating so neatly.

"Aren't you finished yet, you two?" yelled Gran from the shop. "I have to go round to Joan's soon. She said to come round and have a cup of tea."

Josie yelled back that they would be finished in five minutes, and then she could leave. Lois put the bag back over the cage, and turned to Josie.

"And then we'll lock up the shed, and ring Gran to ask Derek to come down as soon as he's back from work," Lois said. "Don't worry, Josie dear. We'll sort it all out. Poor Justin must have forgotten all about them, what with his father dying, and all that."

* * *

When Derek came home from work, he was greeted by Gran, saying he was to go straight down to the shop, where Josie and Lois were still tidying up.

"They want you to do something in the shed," she said. "They wouldn't tell me what it was, but they were both excited. By the way, young Justin's gone off to Lincolnshire. His dad's died, and he'll be away for a couple of weeks. Now, do you want to hear the latest tidbit of gossip? Dot Nimmo phoned, and we had a chat. You know that Pettison at the zoo? Him that's the boss, and lives by himself up in the big house? Well, when Dot went in first thing—she goes in to clean most days—she found him at the bottom of the stairs, surrounded by a broken whiskey glass and, to all intents and purposes, dead. Then, guess what happened?"

"Get on with it, Gran. I'm tired and hungry, and don't much care about Pettison, alive or dead."

Gran sniffed. "Oh, very well. I won't tell you any more. You'd better get down to the shop, so that you can all come back and have our tea."

"Gran!"

"Well, he wasn't dead, but had broken a lot of bones and is in Tresham General Hospital. Very serious accident, they said on the news."

Derek stood up from the kitchen chair where he had flopped down, exhausted. "I'll walk down to the shop, then. Five minutes, an' I'll be back. Perhaps we could have supper on the table?"

"Yes, sir; no, sir; three bags full, sir." Gran sniffed again, and turned her back on him.

Lois and Josie were sitting in the stockroom discussing

what they had found when Derek arrived. Lois could see at once that he was in a very bad mood.

"Something wrong?" she said, kissing his cheek.

"I was having hallucinations on the way home," he said. "A warm kitchen, with good smells coming from the Rayburn, and a beautiful wife in a frilly pinny stirring a saucepan, with a happy smile on her face. And what did I get? A mother-in-law with a frown, ordering me to turn round and go out again into the cold night air, to find my wife and daughter with a problem. Oh yes, and something about the zookeeper having had a fall. Apart from that, no, nothing's wrong."

Lois and Josie laughed. "Poor old thing," said Lois. "Well, this won't take long. Come out to the shed. We've got something to show you."

When they put on the light and removed the bag, the little cage was clearly visible, and inside the small occupants once more stared out.

"For God's sake, what the hell are those things?"

"Baby elephants," said Josie.

"They look like shrews to me," Derek said, peering more closely. "But shrews don't have that long snout, do they? Very small anteaters? They're actually quite sweet, aren't they, Josie? Bright little eyes. Not really frightened of us. But I see what you mean by baby elephants! Let's hope they're slow growing. So what d'you think? Is Justin keeping them as pets? Did he say anything about them before he left?"

Lois shook her head. "No, he rushed off up to help his mother, didn't he, Josie?"

They decided to try and find Justin's home number and ring him to see if they needed to do anything with the baby elephants before he returned. Then they shut up the shed and locked it, and made their way back to an irritated Gran.

"So what's so important about a couple of white mice?" she said.

"Good guess," said Lois. "No, not mice, but something rare, I reckon. We're going to get hold of Justin. But supper first! Derek is faint from want of food."

"Oh, and by the way, Lois, Cowgill rang, and Dot Nimmo rang. Cowgill said he'll try again tomorrow, and Dot said to watch the news on the telly. I reckon it's something to do with that Pettison at the zoo. He fell downstairs and Dot found him this morning."

"Dead?" said Lois sharply.

"No, but badly hurt. He's in hospital. Now, please get on with your supper. They're showing a good film in the village hall tonight, and I'm going with Joan. You'll wash up, won't you?"

THIRTY-SIX

"HERE IT IS," SAID GRAN. LOIS AND DEREK WERE EATING hot apple tart and custard, and Gran had relented and offered to call enquiries for Justin's number while they ate.

"What has enquiries found?" Lois asked.

"Very helpful," said Gran, putting down the phone. "Sounded such a nice woman. I reckon she was hoping for a chat."

"Yes, well, what did she say?"

"'Brookes, D. Holly Farm, Longtoft Fen'. That sounds like it, doesn't it? You could try that, anyway."

"Well done, Mum," Lois said. "Right, Derek, will you, or shall I?"

"You do it. I've been thinking. Do you think Justin has anything to do with the zoo? Them creatures looked very unusual. Maybe a rare species? I should ask him outright, if I were you."

Lois dialled the number, and a woman's voice answered.

"Mrs Brookes? Oh good. It's Lois Meade here. We own the shop where Justin has moved into the flat. That's right. Well, we said he could use the shed in the garden to keep some of his stuff. There's something we have to ask him. Is he there, please? Oh, and please accept my condolences on your sad loss."

"Is he there?" said Gran in a stage whisper.

Lois nodded. "She's gone to fetch him. Sounded a nice person, anxious to help. Shame about her husband. Oh, is that you, Justin? Right. It's just that Josie and me were getting rid of some of the junk in the shed, and found these little animals in a cage thing. Yours?" She turned and nodded at Derek. "So would you like us to look after them while you're away?"

She paused, and the others watched, waiting for the answer. Then she nodded and said she hoped everything would go smoothly for the funeral, and hung up.

"So?" said Derek. "Don't keep us in suspense."

"He said he'd be glad if we could make sure they were warm, and give them food and water. He also said that they were a secret present for somebody, and asked us to keep mum on them being here. Or there, in the shop. As long as they were not disturbed, he said, they'd be okay. Fright could kill them, he said."

"Huh!" said Gran. "I reckon there's something funny going on there. If I were you, Lois, I'd inform Inspector Cowgill. He'll know what to do."

"But *we* know what to do," said Lois. "Look after them, and don't let on we know they're there. Simple enough, and the least we can do under the circumstances."

Gran went off to the film, and Lois and Derek turned on the television to catch the news. The item about Robert Pettison was brief. The man had had a serious accident and was in Tresham General. The zoo remained open to the public, and was being run by a team of helpers with the newly trained keeper.

"What about that message from Cowgill?" Derek said.

"It'll keep until tomorrow," said Lois. "Nobody's dead, and there's only the baby elephants to report. And we're not doing that until Justin gets back. I need to think."

"What about?"

"About what Gran said. Something funny going on there. She's a shrewd old dame, my mum, and when you think about it, Derek, who does Justin know who would want a couple of baby elephants for a birthday present?"

"MORNING, LOIS. HOW'S MY FAVOURITE SPY THIS MORNING?"

"Not as chirpy as you, Cowgill," Lois said. "But I got your message. What do you want?"

"You," said the inspector. "But as that is impossible, I'd like a word about that Pettison character."

"Him what fell downstairs in a drunken stupor with a whiskey glass in his hand?"

"Don't forget the hot-water bottle," Cowgill said. "It has not improved his facial features, I'm afraid. Looks very painful. Scalded. He'd just put the boiling water in the bottle. Of course, he should have known never to put boiling water in a rubber hot-water bottle."

"Don't waffle, Cowgill!" said Lois. "Can I come in and see you this morning? There's something I need to ask you. And could we meet at the zoo? I want to look around."

"Fine. I was going there, anyway. See you at half past ten?"

MARGIE WAS ON THE GATE WHEN LOIS ARRIVED, AND AS SHE bought her ticket, she saw Dot Nimmo crossing the drive with a wheelbarrow full of mucky straw.

"Dot! What on earth are you doing? Wait for me. I'm coming in. Thanks, Margie. See you later."

"Morning, Mrs M. I'm not playing truant. Nothing much to do up at the house, with him being in hospital, so I thought I'd help out down here at the zoo. Did I do wrong?"

"No, absolutely right. But dump your smelly load, and come with me for a minute or two."

"Where're we going, then?"

"To the zoo, of course," said Lois, and marched off into the entrance hall, where there was a souvenir shop and directions to the various enclosures.

"Mrs M, I hope you won't mind my asking, but why are we joining the gawpers and going round the zoo like a couple of tourists?"

"Because I'm looking for something. Do you know your way around? Do they have small mammals anywhere?"

"My favourites," said Dot, and led the way. "Look, Mrs M. Those tiny mice—they're from the Isle of Wight. Aren't they dinky? Dear little souls. Then look at these."

Lois looked. Two grey rats stared at her. "Not too keen on these, Dot. I was hoping to see one particular species. Very rare. Perhaps too rare for this small zoo."

"What are they called, Mrs M?"

"Baby elephants," said Lois. "Come on, they're not here. Let's go and have a coffee before Cowgill gets here. I've arranged to meet him. Lead me to the café, Dot. Coffee's on expenses."

WHEN COWGILL ARRIVED, HE AND LOIS WALKED UP TO THE house, where Dot appeared, duster in hand, having got there before them.

"I've unlocked, Inspector," she said. "Mrs M told me you were coming."

"Right. Well, Mrs Nimmo, I'd be glad if you remember that no one is to be admitted to the house at any time."

"Except you and Mrs M?" said Dot.

"Perhaps you'd better give me the key," said Cowgill. "There'll be no need for you to stay. Perhaps get back to muck spreading! Thank you, Mrs Nimmo, very kind of you to help."

"I'm paying her, actually," said Lois, after Dot had gone. "But she's a very useful person to have around. She misses nothing that goes on."

"Talking of which, Lois, my dear, what is it you want to ask me?" He walked through to the hall, where there were still signs of Pettison's fall.

"It's something my mother said, as a matter of fact. Now, if I asked you about endangered species, would you think I was mad?"

"No, never that, Lois. So what are you going to ask me?"

"Gran said she reckoned there was something funny going on. I am sure there is, and it's something to do with baby elephants."

"Now you are mad! There are no elephants here."

"No, but listen. Josie and me were cleaning out the shed at the back of the shop, and found a couple of baby elephants in a cage on a shelf."

Cowgill groaned. "Lois, my dear, *please*!" Lois took pity on him, and told him the whole story, including her call to Justin and his sad family news. "So we're looking after them," she said finally. "But I don't know. They're not the sort of pet you usually have. If they're going to stay on our premises, I need to know if they are kosher, bred in captivity and that, or trapped in the wild and smuggled into this country."

Cowgill was silent. He sighed, and said that Lois was right. There had been suspicions for a long time that Pettison was up to something of the sort. But they'd never managed to catch him at it, or found any endangered species in the zoo.

"We think he has a network of contacts, including places where he can hide the illegal animals until he moves them on. He doesn't keep them in the zoo, as they'd soon be identified. So, shall I pick you up around two this afternoon?" he said. "I'll bring an expert, and we'll have a chat, then go down to the shop and take a look at them. In the meantime, please keep this to yourself, if possible. It could be the very lead we have been looking for."

"Right," said Lois. "Mum was in the shop when Josie found them, and I think she's been snooping, so I reckon you'd better act quickly. Yes, of course I'll be there at two this afternoon. Thanks, Cowgill. See you then." She set off back down the drive, and something made her look round. Cowgill was standing at the top of the portico steps, watching her, so she blew him a kiss and carried on her way.

Thirty-Seven

It was ten to two when Cowgill arrived, parking where Lois could see him from her office window. This time he had a passenger beside him, and it was female. They got out of the car and began to walk up the drive. To her surprise, she saw the woman link arms with Cowgill and look up at him fondly. Who was this then? She went to the door quickly, before Gran could get there, and waited until they knocked.

"Good afternoon, Lois!" said Cowgill cheerily. "May I introduce our species expert, Miss Miranda Cowgill. And yes, we are related! Miranda is my niece, and has helped us out on several occasions where her skills are required. Miranda, this is Mrs Lois Meade, my very good friend and unofficial assistant."

"Please come in," said Lois. "Oh yes, and this is my mother, Mrs Weedon. Could you manage a coffee for us, Mum?"

After this good beginning, things began to deteriorate. Derek appeared, grunted a "How do" and said he hoped Lois wasn't going to be long, as he needed her help out the back. Then Gran tipped up the entire tray-load of coffee in the hall and burst into a series of oaths, blaming it on the dog Jeems, who was crossing her path at the time.

"Right, let's make a start," said Cowgill, when they were all seated. "Could you tell us exactly how the animals came to be here, right from the start?"

Lois told them in as few words as possible how she had found them in the shed, covered with a paper carrier, or half one, up on a high shelf. She and Josie had got hold of Justin, who had been given permission to use the shed as part of his rent on the flat, and he had said they were his.

"Asked us to look after them until he got back," she said finally. "I'd never seen anything like them before, and told Derek, and he thought they were some sort of shrew."

"Did Mr Brookes say exactly what they were?" asked Miranda.

Lois shook her head. "Sorry, no. He was very anxious about them, and told me not to say anything to anybody about them. That's why I called you, Cowgill! I expect he'll never forgive me."

"Very likely. But you may have to do without Justin Brookes for a time, anyway," said Cowgill. "But thanks, Lois. It is a very important matter. Perhaps we could go down to the shop now?"

"And please give our thanks to Mrs Weedon for the coffee, and sympathies about the accident. I do hope she wasn't hurt."

They had reached the door by this time, and Gran appeared behind them. "I'm made of strong stuff, Miss Cowgill," she said. "Takes more than dropping a few crocks to upset me."

* * *

Josie saw them coming from the shop window, and put up a notice saying CLOSED FOR TEN MINUTES. Then she welcomed them in, and they all went out to the shed in the back garden.

"I've got the key, Mum," she said, and began to unlock the shed door.

"We should be very quiet, so as not to alarm them," Miranda said. "They are very sensitive little creatures."

"Not frightened of us, were they, Josie? Not after we'd give them something to eat."

They crept in, and Josie put on the light. Miranda immediately turned it off. "Sorry!" she whispered. "Best to approach them in the dark."

"Over here," said Lois, leading the way. "Up there, look. On the top shelf."

"Where, exactly?" said Cowgill.

Lois felt around on the shelf and then turned to Josie. "Put the light on, dear," she said, and then, blinking in the light, they all stared.

"They've gone," said Lois. "Josie! They've gone! Where on earth—? Who could have got in here?"

"Let's look round," said Cowgill. "Someone might have moved them."

They were nowhere to be found, and Miranda looked at her uncle. "You know what this means, don't you?" she said. "They've been stolen, or retrieved. What a pity."

"Yes, a pity you couldn't see them," said Lois, "but it does mean Mum was right. They were clearly valuable enough for someone to want to steal them. As for retrieving them, I reckon either Justin came back during the night, or he asked someone to collect them for him.

Someone who has another key? There's only one key, isn't there, Josie?"

"Two," said Josie. "I had another one cut for Justin, so he wouldn't have to bother me every time he wanted to go in there. I suppose he could have got a spare cut from his, and given it to somebody."

They returned to the shop, and Josie took down the notice. "Sorry, Inspector. I didn't even suspect anyone would do that. Sorry your journey has been wasted, Miss Cowgill."

"No bother," said Miranda. "Always a pleasure to see Uncle Hunter! But I've just been thinking. Did you get a good look at them? Could you identify them, if I sent you a picture over the internet?"

"Brilliant idea," said Lois. "Send it to me on an email. Then me and Josie can look at it together. Derek's guess was, as I said, a shrew of some sort, and I reckon that's the nearest we've come."

Lois and the two Cowgills walked back up to Meade House, and waved them off, then returned to the house.

"Well, what were they?" said Gran. "They weren't white mice, that's for sure. Are you going to tell me now?"

"Don't know, I'm afraid," said Lois. "They're gone. Lost, stolen or strayed. I felt a right fool, with Cowgill's niece there, an' that."

"What d'you mean, gone? The shed was locked, wasn't it?"

"Yes, it was. I watched Josie unlocking it. So someone got in with a key, or picked the lock, and made away with them. Anyway, all is not lost. Miranda Cowgill is going to send me a photograph of one of those little animals to check out. If it is that one, then Justin is going to be in trouble."

"Such a nice young man, too," said Gran, but her face belied her.

"You don't like him, do you, Mum?" Lois said.

"Too nice," said Gran. "Not like that Miranda Cowgill. Now she's *really* nice."

"Seems fond of her uncle. Nice for him, as he lives alone. Now, where's Derek, or has he given up and gone out?"

In the Brierley house, Betsy was leafing through a magazine, waiting for Ted to come home. She had been late to bed last evening, and had stayed in bed this morning until after he went off to work. Now she had the high tea all ready, table laid and was wearing her sexiest dress, all designed to make a good impression.

She heard the door, and put down her magazine. "Is that you, Ted?" she called.

He came into the room, took one look at her and at the table carefully laid, and said, "What have you been up to now?"

"Nothing, of course! Just thought you might like to have an attractive girl to come home to."

"I see. Well, thanks, but no thanks. Now you can go and take off that ridiculous dress, and come down in something more comfortable. My name's not Pettison."

"Pity it isn't!" Betsy said crossly. "At least he appreciates me. Says I have the figure of a girl. What do you think, Ted?" She knew she was being irritating, but a woman scorned, and all that.

"I think I have had a hard day's work, and all I want is a nice tea and a bit of peace. Is that too much to ask? And while I'm about it, where the hell were you last night? You don't usually work out of hours, except for Pettison, and he's out of action in a hospital ward, with any luck."

"Visiting a sick aunt," she said.

"Rubbish! But forget it. What's for tea?"

* * *

It so happened that last night around midnight, Dot had got out of bed to go for a pee, and had looked out at the street below. The streetlight was still on, and to her surprise, she saw a car draw up outside the Brierleys', and Betsy get out and let herself into the house.

"My God, that woman works hard," she had muttered, and laughed to herself. "Give me a duster and scrubbing brush anytime. You can keep your job, Betsy," she had added. Then she thought that Betsy *was* a real scrubber, in a different sense, and that had made her chuckle again. When she returned to bed, another thought had struck her. Where had Betsy been? Pettison was still in hospital, and surely Ted wouldn't have let her out so late to anyone else?

"Odd little sod, that Ted," she had said, not for the first time, and went straight back to sleep.

Next morning, straight after breakfast, Lois went into her office to check her email. There it was, the one she had been expecting. It was from Miranda Cowgill, and had an attachment. She clicked on it, and up came a photograph, a close-up of a small animal, like a mouse but not like a mouse, she thought.

"Derek! Come and look! I'm in the office."

Derek came in and peered at the screen. "Um, yes. And then again, no."

"Just what I thought," said Lois. "That one has the long nose, okay? But it sort of droops, whereas ours curved upwards. It's got spindly little legs, too, that one. Isn't it a beautiful colour? All goldeny."

"No such word," said Derek. "Well, if you ask me, they are some sort of exotic shrew creature. Not from this country, anyway, else I'd have seen them, excavating behind floor-boards an' that, as I do. What're you going to do, then, gel?"

"I'll see if Josie has had the same email, and ask her what she thinks. She saw them same as me."

At that moment, the phone rang and it was Josie. "Mum? Have you seen it? Isn't it sweet? But I'm not sure it's the same as ours. Our baby elephants' trunks curved up in a happy way, but this one points down. I'd say it was the same, but different."

"Exactly," said Derek. "Clever girl, our Josie."

Thirty-Eight

Halfway down the long straight track, Justin slowed the Fiat down to twenty miles an hour, and looked around him. Nothing, no hedges, no trees. As his father used to say, "Miles and miles of bugger-all!" And now his father was gone, soon to be lowered into the cold, cold ground. No more jokes, no more hair-raising stories of his youth, or romantic, embarrassing accounts of when he courted Justin's mother.

"Poor Mother," he said aloud, and thought to himself that she would miss her husband terribly. After the funeral was over and all the legal stuff sorted, she would be really miserable. He should stay for at least another week. But could he do that? He thought ahead, and realised that he actually could, for once. He had no more assignments to do for Uncle Robert nor was he needed at the local theatre at present. He had checked with the hospital, and they had said Mr Pettison would be at least three or four weeks in their care.

He had been to see the vicar, and arrangements for the funeral were completed. Tomorrow morning, at eleven, his father would be . . . He stopped mid-thought. "My father," he said aloud, "will be buried, and I shall never see him again."

With a sudden burst of anger directed at nobody in particular, he put his foot down on the accelerator, and arrived at the farm with a screech of brakes.

"Justin? Why so fast? You should join me in this very strange mode of transport, slow and careful."

Justin stared. It was Pettison, in a wheelchair and snug in layers of rugs, being lowered from the back of an ambulance, and attended by anxious paramedics.

When they were settled in front of a fire in the farmhouse, Justin's mother explained. "Robert rang soon after you left," she said. "Insisted that he should be at your father's funeral, and asked if we could put him up overnight. Well, as you know, we still have the hoist we got for Dad, and so I said yes, we could certainly manage. Wasn't it wonderful of him? Goodness knows how you persuaded the hospital," she added now, addressing a grinning Pettison.

"Charm, my dear, charm," he said. "Amazing what one can do with a silver tongue. The ambulance will be back for me tomorrow afternoon, after the wake. I shall meet some old friends, I expect, Justin. You see, I had to come and say farewell to a good old friend."

Of course, thought Justin. Brothers-in-law. He thought some more, and then was very sure that he hadn't heard the whole story. With Pettison, there was always an ulterior motive.

"Right," he said. "Well, we'd better get the bedroom ready, Mother. It'll have to be the ground floor quarters, I'm afraid, Robert. We'll never get you upstairs in that wheelchair!"

"Can you spare a moment, Justin, for a little private chat? A matter of business, my dear," he added to Mrs Brookes, who smiled, added another log to the fire and tiptoed out.

"Wonderful mother you have, Justin. I am sure in some ways the death of your father must have come as a relief."

"I don't think we can know that," said Justin coolly. "My parents had a form of silent communication, developed over fifty years of happy marriage. I hope I shall be able to say the same one day."

"Remarkable!" said Pettison. "So now, just reassure me that the little people are still safe and well."

"If you mean the latest consignment of endangered animals, then yes, they are perfectly well, and being looked after until you return. Do you have a customer for them?"

"Oh yes, a very noble customer! Titled aristocracy, no less. He should know better than to keep such people as pets, but who am I to quibble? I run a business, and ask no questions."

"You'll be answering some, one of these days," said Justin gloomily. "I reckon your time is running out. The sooner you get back into harness, the better."

"Ah, now there's the thing. They say I have to stay in hospital, with occasional forays back home, for another three weeks. Even then, I shall still be in a wheelchair, possibly for good. So I wonder, when you get back, whether you could take over for a short while. You know the ropes at the zoo, and with Margie—and, I understand, the dreaded Dottie Nimmo—and the new keeper, things should go on pretty well. What do you think? There'll be suitable rewards, of course."

"What sort of rewards?" asked Justin, suspiciously. He imagined a cage full of rare parrots, or some such.

"Money, my dear chap. What else?"

Justin remembered his dream of running a proper, untarnished zoo, and said that in that case, he would do as his uncle suggested. "You'll have to send a message to say I'm coming. Best send it to Margie. I must stay here for another week, and then I'll return."

"Ah, that brings me to the second thing," said Pettison. "Your mother and I were having a chat, and she confided that she hoped to go away and stay with her old friend in Spalding for a week or two, more or less straight after the funeral. The old boy who works on the farm is quite willing to take over. Not much happening at the moment, he has said. So you can return to Farnden, and take over at the zoo without delay."

They talked for a few more minutes, settling how the latest creatures were to be delivered to the buyer, and then Justin left Pettison to have a snooze by the fire while he helped his mother in the kitchen.

"Watch the milk in that saucepan, will you, Justin. It mustn't boil, so tell me when it is about to."

"How will I know when it is about to?"

"When there's tiny bubbles and a skin forming on the top. Something like that. Anyway, you'll just know. Is Robert all right in the front room? There's not been a fire in there all winter, so it felt a bit damp."

"It's fine, Mother. You must have been surprised to hear from him."

"Yes indeed. And to come all that way in a wheelchair! The ambulance will come and fetch him and take him back to the hospital tomorrow. Don't ask me how he organised it!

All he would say was "Friends in high places," and silly things like that."

"It's boiling. Shall I take it off?"

"Of course! Now, what are you going to do? Supper will be in an hour or so."

"If there's nothing more I can do to help, I think I'll go and make a few phone calls. Check up that all is well back at the flat. Give me a shout when supper's ready."

"Thanks for all you're doing, dear. Oh, and I have decided to go and see my friend Vera after we've settled Father safely . . ." She paused, and wiped her eyes with the corner of her apron. "So you go back, Justin, and get on with things again. I shall be all right, and we'll keep in touch. I might get a computer and one of those things where we can talk face-to-face. Off you go now, dear."

Justin retired to his bedroom, and sat for a while, staring out of the window at the dark, cold fenland. He did not really want to talk to anyone. He felt a stranger in his own home, and realised that the presence of Robert Pettison in the house was disturbing. He fell into a light doze in his chair, and dreamed that his uncle was wheeling himself miraculously upstairs, and finding his way into his bedroom, gun in hand. He awoke with a start, hearing his mother's voice calling him for supper.

BACK IN FARNDEN, LOIS SAT IN HER OFFICE, WAITING FOR DOT Nimmo to call. Gran and Derek were watching television, and she had retired to take the call. There had been a message on the phone, and when she had tried to call back, Dot had been engaged. Lois's thoughts were far away, up in the fens of Lincolnshire, where she had never been, but imagined as looking something like the tulip fields of Holland. Justin would be very out of place there, surely, she thought.

How did the son of a tulip farmer get to be a swinging young actor in the Midlands. She supposed his parents had decided on private education, and then university, in order to give him a broad education, but had succeeded only in producing a smooth young man, like many other smooth young men, with ambitions to make enough money to live in a luxury executive dwelling, somewhere in a leafy suburb.

But was Justin really one of them?

"We know nothing about him," she said aloud, and then continued to remember exactly what they did know. His father had died, and he had a strange preference in his choice of pets. Pets? She stood up suddenly. Of course they were not pets, nor were they Justin's! He was an intermediary and an actor, and of course she knew who was boss.

Her phone rang, and it was Dot. "Thanks for ringing back, Mrs M," she said. "Just checking that it's all right for me to work at the zoo tomorrow."

"As it happens, yes. We've lost a couple of baby elephants and you may be able to help us find them."

Thirty-Nine

Justin padded over to the window to draw his curtains back, and was relieved to see a clear blue sky and a brisk wind blowing the few trees in the farmhouse garden. He had been dreading a wet day for his father's funeral, but now, with any luck, they should be able to smile a little, and welcome guests who had come to mourn the loss of a loved one.

That's what Pettison had said! An old friend, not a distant relative, nor a colleague. No doubt he would want that forgotten. Looking back, Justin remembered that his mother had never shown to him any curiosity about the barn where he had occasionally housed animals in transit. And Pettison had always been around, ever since he was a child. He had taken him for granted, and Father had talked of him as a business associate. Had Mother known all along what his father and Pettison, old school chums, were up to? Father must have told her, years and years ago. She would expect Robert to be here.

An old friend and business associate. Was that it? Justin began to shower and dress, and all the while he was thinking how he could get Pettison to tell him the truth. He reckoned that his father had not become an associate willingly. He had been a strictly law-abiding person in every other respect, and a regular churchgoer. But Pettison had exercised a hold over him in some way. That was his specialty!

"Justin! Breakfast's ready!" His mother's voice brought him back to the present, and he vowed to find out from Pettison exactly what the relationship with his father had been.

The church path was lined with wreaths and floral tributes, and when the coffin, with its spray of white lilies, was taken from the hearse, Justin, with his mother on his arm, followed slowly behind. The organ played some of his father's favourite Mozart, and every pew was full.

"Dad must have been popular," he whispered to his mother, and she nodded, unable to speak.

The service went smoothly, with Father's friends stepping forward and giving short tributes to his loyalty, his kind heart and steadfastness. Justin was the last to speak, and he delivered the encomium in a shaky voice.

Pettison was in his wheelchair at the back of the church, well wrapped up against the cold, and Justin could hear his voice singing hymns in a loud voice. Hypocrite! Just you wait until we're back in Tresham, he thought angrily.

Now it was time to lower the coffin into the grave, and Justin and his mother threw in handfuls of earth with a last prayer. "Rest in peace, Dad," he said to himself. "Rest in peace."

"So when is Justin coming back?" asked Josie, sorting out new stock to go on the shelves.

Lois had arrived early, saying that she needed more porridge oats. "Don't you know, dear?" she replied.

"I've heard nothing, and I'm glad. Sooner or later, we're going to have to tell him we no longer have the shrews. If that's what they were."

"I suppose we could make up a story about them being collected, and leave it at that," said Josie.

"Collected by who?" said Lois. "He's bound to be suspicious."

"Well, that'd be better than having to admit they were stolen. He did ask us to look after them."

"Which we did, to the best of our ability. Not our fault if the shed got broken into."

"It didn't, Mum. Don't you remember? I unlocked it in the usual way with the key. I suppose we should tell the police? I haven't even told Matthew yet. I keep remembering Justin saying we were not to tell anyone."

"But we told Cowgill, and his niece. They know the poor little things have gone."

"Well, let's hope Dot finds them in the zoo. I must say it's the last time Justin uses the shed for his weird pets! It's the funeral today, so he could be back here tomorrow, or even later on today."

Lois paid for her porridge oats, and said they would keep in touch. "And you be careful, my duckie," were her last words as she left the shop.

In Tresham, Betsy Brierley was struggling from the car to her front door, carrying four heavy bags of shopping from the supermarket. As she approached, the door opened and Ted stood there, holding out his arms to help.

"Phew! I don't know, Ted, we seem to get through an awful lot of food. Just dump them in the kitchen, and I'll sort them out later. I'm dying for a coffee, if you've got the kettle on."

When she had taken off her coat and settled down with a hot drink, Ted, who had up to then been silent, began to speak.

"Betsy, we shall have to be a bit careful, you know. My hours at work are being cut. The current economic situation, an' all that. So perhaps we'll give up the luxuries for a bit."

"What luxuries? A bit of cream and a couple of peaches is hardly luxury living, is it."

"No, dear, of course not. But you know what I mean. Oh, and by the way," he said, on his way out to the kitchen, "I found a strange-looking mousetrap in the washhouse, and a couple of dead mice in it. Funny-looking mice, but anyway, as they were very dead, I put the whole thing in the bin. Must have been our neighbour's. They weren't Pettison's were they? He looks after his stuff too well. I know you're not partial to mice so I thought I'd get rid of them. They were rather pathetic, actually, curled up together as if they'd frozen to death."

"Ted Brierley!" said Betsy. "You have just thrown away two and a half thousand pounds! Of course they were Pettison's. I had to collect them from Farnden. Still, if they were dead, they were no use anyway. Make sure you cover 'em up with plenty of rubbish. The bin men come today, don't they? Right. Now, can I have another dollop of cream in this coffee, or would that count as luxury living?"

Forty

THE AMBULANCE HAD ARRIVED IN THE EARLY AFTERNOON to collect Pettison, and Justin waved him off with mixed feelings. A part of him thought it was actually very loyal of his uncle to risk pain and discomfort to come to say farewell to an old friend. At the same time, he was haunted by suspicions that Robert had turned up to make sure no incriminating evidence was left behind. Uncle and his mother had been in close conversation, and had changed the subject as soon as he came into the room.

It had all been so stupid, Justin thought regretfully. Pettison had been ever present in his life, calling in to see his father frequently. There had been a kind of family conspiracy to keep quiet about the endangered animal trade, and for years before he went away to school he had believed that he and his father were actively helping Uncle Robert to do something worthwhile with his breeding programmes. He supposed his parents had assumed that the truth, that his father was colluding with Pettison's illegal trade in rare species, had dawned on him gradually, and they never mentioned it. And he never mentioned it! Good God, how ridiculous! And now, he thought, Mum will continue not to mention it, and so shall I. And if my dream of establishing the zoo comes true, post-Pettison, as legal, with no sidelines, it will be the best in the land.

"All ready for the off, Mum," he said, entering the kitchen for a last snack before he set off in the Fiat. "Are you sure you're going to be all right? I could stay another day or so."

"No need, dear. I'm going to Vera's first thing tomorrow. I'll ring you to make sure you get back safely."

"Fine. Now, is there anything else?"

"No, unless you've got any animals out there in the barn? Don't forget them; otherwise, they'll starve!"

Wow! What an opening! "Nothing there now, Mum," he said. "I took the last lot away. What did you think of them? Did they appeal to you as pets? We've had lots of them over the years, haven't we?"

And then Mum didn't answer, and he had said nothing more, recalled Justin, as he sped through the fens. At last, trees and hedges began to appear and he was ashamed to feel a sense of relief at being away from it all. All the questions he could have asked about the early times of his father and Pettison, all had gone unsaid.

But he could not leave it there. Things had changed, and he intended as a priority to thrash out the exact nature of the link with Pettison. He was sure his father would never have agreed willingly to anything illegal. There must have been some pressure involved. From the beginning. And from his own point of view, he wanted no "from generation unto generation" rubbish from Uncle Robert! Above all, when, as was likely, the trade was uncovered by the police, he wished to make sure his father's name was cleared.

When he reached Farnden, it was six o'clock and dark. The bright overhead light outside the shop lit up his entry to the back of the building, and he coasted in, shutting off his headlights so as not to announce his arrival. He had no appetite for conventional sympathies, and hoped he could creep in and up to the flat without anyone knowing. He saw a light on in the stockroom, and cursed. Josie must be sorting things out in there. But she did not appear, and he shut and locked the flat door with relief. Then he thought of the animals. Oh well, they'd probably been fed this evening. "I'll look at them tomorrow," he muttered, and collapsed on the sofa, where he fell immediately into a dreamless sleep.

NEXT MORNING, JUSTIN AWOKE WITH A PAINFUL NECK WHERE HE had been lying cramped up on the sofa, still in his clothes. He looked at his watch. It was half past nine, and he would have barely enough time to shower, and put on his good suit, and speed into Tresham in time for a meeting with the solicitor who was helping with his father's affairs.

He was on the road, clean and fresh, when he remembered the shrews. "Damn!" he said aloud, and slowed down. Should he go back and feed them? But no, Josie would have realised what had happened, and looked after them. He quickened up, and arrived outside the solicitors' offices on the dot of half past ten.

The loose ends of his father's financial affairs were soon tied up, and when he went out to the Fiat, he noticed the petrol gauge was low, but not alarmingly so, and he decided to risk it.

He was beginning to feel anxious now, with a vague suspicion that something was wrong. He had waved to Josie as he left Farnden earlier, and she had not smiled in reply. Pettison had said he was to hang on to the little animals or, in an emergency, get them to Betsy Brierley, who would know what to do with them.

He put his foot on the accelerator and pushed the little car to its top speed. The straight stretch of road whizzed by, and as he slowed down to drive through Fletching, he heard the unmistakable sound of a police siren. Damn and blast!

"So sorry, officer," he said, as the policeman came up to his open window. "Not concentrating, I'm afraid."

"Very dangerous, sir, particularly at that speed. I'm afraid it'll be a ticket this time. You know what to do, I expect."

"Thank you," replied Justin, and managed to refrain from committing himself further.

When he rushed into the shop, he found Josie sitting on her high stool, reading a newspaper.

"Hi, Justin," she said. "Good journey?"

"So-so," he said. "Animals okay?"

Josie took a deep breath. "I am afraid they're not there. Somebody either collected them or stole them, and the odd thing is, the door was not broken into. So sorry! I didn't want to have bad news for you when you must be feeling sad. Did the funeral go smoothly?"

Justin did not answer. Why had Pettison insisted on him giving Betsy a copy of the shed key? In case of emergencies, he had said. Well, now they had an emergency, and he knew who to ring immediately.

"Excuse me, Josie," he said. "I must make a quick call."

At this point, Mrs T-J came through the door. "Good morning! Lovely morning, though cold."

"Hello, Mrs T-J," said Josie. "Afraid it's not such a lovely morning here. I've just had to confess to Justin that I've lost his elephant shrews."

"My dear, how awful! Justin, your new tenant? Well, I wonder what he was doing with them."

"They were special," replied Josie. "Elephant shrews are special apparently. Golden rumped ones are very rare, and an endangered species. Not indigenous to this country. Bred in captivity, this lot, I think Justin said."

"Dear little things, actually, with their goldy-coloured bottoms," said Mrs T-J. "Used to see lots of them on travels with my husband. Forests being cut down or burned low, you know. Natural habitat for lots of rare animals being lost. Such a shame."

"BETSY? JUSTIN BROOKES HERE. WHAT HAVE YOU DONE WITH them?"

"Done with what?"

"You know perfectly well. Those shrews. I had to go to my father's funeral, and found them gone when I returned. I gave you the copy of the shed key, so don't waste my time. Where are they? I need to hand them over today."

"Sorry about your dad. Don't bother about the animals." Betsy put her hand over the receiver and hissed at Ted, "What did you say you did with them?"

"They were stone-cold dead, Betsy dear, and I wrapped them tenderly in newspaper and put them in the bin. You can tell him that with my compliments."

Betsy scowled at him, and uncovered the receiver. "I'll hand them over, Justin," she said. "Got to go down to the zoo anyway, this afternoon. So I can go up to the house and meet the customer."

"And take your share of the loot? Always handed over in cash, isn't it? No flies on you, Betsy. Well, it'll be between you and Uncle Robert when you next see him. But don't upset him too much. He's still a bit frail. And watch out for yourself. Some of uncle's customers can be very unforgiving."

"Don't you worry, dear. And thanks for the advice. Anytime you want a favour, just you let me know."

What me? Oh Lord, save me from the weaker sex, thought Justin. He made himself a cup of coffee and sat down on his sofa to think.

"WHO WAS THAT, DEAR?" SAID TED SUSPICIOUSLY.

"Justin, wanting his animals. But I fixed him. I said I'd take them to the rendezvous myself. Being helpful, see. The poor soul just back from his father's funeral. Now, we'll have a quick lunch and then I have to go into town again. Forgot to get some moisturising cream from Boots. I used the last this morning. I'll get some crumpets for tea. I don't know," she added. "My head will never save my legs!"

Driving back into town, Betsy planned what she would do. It was extremely unlikely that the pet shop would have elephant shrews. She hoped there would be something like them, about the same size, that could be wrapped up and passed off as the real thing, at least until she had the cash safely in her pocket. Of course, she should never have left them in the cold washhouse. Poor little things. But it was really Pettison's fault for importing little animals into the climate of this country.

It'll be risky, but as long as the man who comes to collect doesn't ask for a close look, all should be well. For the moment, anyway.

"SORRY, LOVE, WE'D NEVER EVER SEE ANY OF THOSE," SAID THE pet shop assistant. "Probably a protected species, I'm afraid. Can I suggest an alternative? I've got a pair of lovely piebald mice. Very pretty, and tame. Bred in captivity, and will eat from your hand."

Ugh! thought Betsy, but she said they would be fine, and

please could she buy a carrying case as well. "And wrap them up well," she said. "It's really bitter out there today."

She was nervous as she placed them in the boot of her car. Suppose they escaped and ran around her legs when she was driving! Telling herself not to be silly, she drove out of town and approached the zoo. Margie Turner saw her coming and waved her through the gates. She drove swiftly up to the house, and in the yard behind, she saw a black car, not one that she recognised, with a figure sitting in it.

Parking next to it, she waved at the man, and got out. He joined her, his hat pulled well down over his face.

"How d'you do," said Betsy. "Very cold today, isn't it?"

"We might have some snow," replied the man.

"Well, we got that out of the way, didn't we. Very James Bond, don't you think? Anyway, here's the consignment. Hand over the cash, and then we can be away from here. You never know when you might bump into a policeman, since that nasty accident in the zoo."

"I should take a look in the bag first," he said.

"Not if you want the creatures alive when you hand them over," said Betsy. "They're well wrapped, and this cold wind could see the end of them."

"Well, if you say so," said the man, handing over a fat package. "Here's the cash. They'd better be all right, else you'll be hearing from us. When's Pettison coming back? The boss sent his best wishes for a speedy recovery."

"I'll tell him," said Betsy, getting into her car. "Bye. Drive carefully."

WHEN SHE ARRIVED HOME, TED SAID THERE HAD BEEN A MESsage for her from the hospital. He sounded curious when he told her, and said quickly that she was to go in to see the boss as soon as possible.

"Huh, well, he can wait," Betsy said, flopping down into a chair. "I'm staying here for the rest of the day. Whatever it is, it'll keep until tomorrow. And I'm sorry, Ted, I forgot to get the crumpets."

"Typical," Ted replied sourly. "I suppose it'll have to be toast and honey again."

"Very good for you, honey," said Betsy.

"Maybe we should keep bees, then," Ted said. "My dad used to keep a hive, but Mum was dead scared and so he got rid of them."

Forty-One

"Have you discovered where the shrews went?" said Josie to Justin as he came into the shop.

"Oh yes, I'm sorry about that. I gave my key to a friend to use in an emergency while I was away, and she panicked, thinking they'd be better off in the zoo. I'm glad to say they're now with a very caring customer. But thank you, anyway, for feeding them and making sure they were all right. I hope there'll be no more animals to leave in the shed! Have a nice day, Josie. Bye."

And I hope I have a nice day too, he thought, as he went to collect the Fiat. I am certainly due for one. I suppose I shall have to visit Pettison and keep him up to date, although Betsy will no doubt have been in touch with him. I could shop her to Pettison for disobeying orders, but I can't be bothered. Anyway, I expect she has a hold over him, their relationship being what it is.

He laughed. "Good luck to them!" he said, and drove into the hospital car park feeling cheerful.

Pettison soon changed his mood. He greeted him with the news that the shrews had turned out to be piebald mice, and he wanted an explanation. The noble lord had been furious, saying he did not intend to put mice into his menagerie of rare and beautiful animals. He required an explanation, and without it, there would be no more orders from him. All this had been conveyed by an intermediary, of course. The noble lord was too fly to be directly involved.

"Menagerie?" said Justin. "What the hell is that? I thought they went out of fashion years ago."

"A very respectable pedigree," said Pettison. "Sometime in the eighteenth century, when exploration was bringing back all kinds of strange plants and animals, every man of power and influence with a country estate had a menagerie, housed often in wonderful buildings, and far enough away from the main house to lessen the sound of tigers roaring and monkeys screaming. I tell no lie, Justin. You can read about them. That's why I call my collection at the hall my menagerie. Only difference is that my animals in the menagerie are dead, and have been for a long, long time. Most of them. Now, my turn to ask the questions. Why did the elephant shrews turn into piebald mice?"

"Don't know, Uncle. They were locked up safely in the shed behind the shop, and when I came back from the funeral, they had gone. Josie Vickers knew nothing about their disappearance. But, as you probably know by now, I guessed and checked with Betsy. You had told me to give her a key, and she said yes, she had them, and would pass them on. My guess is that they died being transported from place to place, and Betsy, the silly woman, handed over substitutes."

"Very annoying," said Pettison. "Between you two dolts, you have lost me a very valuable customer."

"Can't you get some more elephant shrews?"

Pettison shook his head. "No, that line of supply has been busted. This particular business is becoming more and more difficult, with all the ridiculous laws on importing supposedly rare animals. And self-righteous busybodies interfering."

"They have a point," said Justin. "I read that ninety percent of animals imported from the wild, not bred in captivity, like you always say, die within the first year. I couldn't sleep at night if I was as involved as you are."

"Oh, I think you are very involved, my boy," said Pettison. "If, God forbid, I am ever required to take seriously the law of the land, I shall see that you come down with me. I shall need some congenial company."

"Let's hope you can keep out of harm's way, then. Now, I must be off. Last bits of paperwork at the solicitors to do with Father's will." He paused, and looked back. "That reminds me," he said. "I want to talk to you about how my father had the bad luck to get drawn into your activities."

"What would you like me to say, Justin? You must know by now that from the start he knew all about it, was quite happy for his barn to be used for transit purposes, and agreed not to say a word to anyone. Is that good enough for you?"

Justin had paled, and his hand trembled as he reached for his coat. "No, it is not. What did you use against him, to blackmail him into silence?"

"Harsh words, Justin," Pettison said, and shook his head. "It's all a long time ago. Are you sure you want to know all such irrelevant details? We got along well together, your father and I. That's all you need to know."

"No, it isn't! My father was a God-fearing man, and I

know for sure he would never willingly have done anything against the law."

"Oh well, if you insist. To begin at the beginning, we went to the same boarding school and were in cahoots with various schemes there. We delighted in lifting things from other boys who we considered could afford to lose them!" He laughed at the memory, but Justin's scowl deepened.

"Unfortunately, the school authorities took a serious view, and we were sent packing," continued Pettison.

"But that was when you were quite young boys, and I expect you bullied him."

"Perhaps, but the thing was, Justin old chap, your father's family were as poor as church mice, and they were giving up everything to send him to a good school. They were heart-broken when we got the sack, and I helped your father out with finances for a while. We kept in touch, as you know, from then on. He was grateful, and when I needed his help, he was only too pleased to oblige."

Pettison closed his eyes and subsided onto his pillows. "There were other schemes, too, dear boy, but now, off you go," he said in a weak voice. "I need some sleep. Easily tired, you know. Tell the nurse I need her, on your way out."

Justin was still shaking with rage when he got back into the Fiat. For a long while he sat and stared out of the window at the brick wall of the hospital. His misguided father had kept Pettison's lousy secrets to the end! No wonder he had always seemed so worried when Justin asked awkward questions.

And now look at us! Justin caught a glimpse of himself in the driving mirror and shivered. My father is dead, no doubt comforted with the thought that his secrets would die with him. But Pettison had revived them, and Justin could be in the same soup as his father, unless he could think of a way out.

"I'll make you pay, Robert bloody Pettison!" he shouted to the empty car. "See if I don't, you old fool!"

He put the Fiat into gear, moved out of the car park, and turned in the direction of the zoo.

LOIS WAS ON HER WAY TO SEE DOT NIMMO. SHE HAD GIVEN HER permission to help out when required at the zoo, and she intended to add the cost to Pettison's bill. She saw the Fiat driving off up to the hall, and wondered why Justin should be heading that way when his uncle was in hospital. It could have been someone else, of course. Those little cars were very popular now. She waved to Margie Turner and drove on into the zoo park. There she got out of her car to find a familiar figure waiting for her.

"Morning, Lois. I didn't expect to see you here." It was Inspector Cowgill, smiling fondly at her. "Are you well, my dear? And how's the new flat tenant doing?"

"I'm fine, thanks. And wasn't that Justin Brookes on his way to the hall? I need to see him," she improvised, "about a matter of access to the garden behind the shop. Are you hanging around here for a purpose, or have you developed a fondness for snakes?"

"Something like that," said Cowgill. "Shall we have a coffee when you've finished with Brookes? I'll meet you in the café."

"Is it urgent?" said Lois. "I do have to get back to the office. Things I have to see to with Hazel."

"Um, let me see. Shall we say in half an hour? Be there, please, Lois."

Lois frowned. That was very unlike Hunter Cowgill. Definitely not so pliable this morning. Maybe it is something important.

She found Dot measuring out feed for the chimpanzees and asked her if she could spare a minute.

"Yes, but only a minute. I've been told the chimps can get very nasty if they're hungry. What is it, Mrs M?"

"Can you come and see me this afternoon, then? I need to discuss something with you. Are you going up to the hall later?"

"No, not today. I'll probably go up and have a dust around tomorrow, if that's okay."

"Yep, but we do need to get you back to our usual schedules, Dot. It doesn't look as if Pettison is coming home soon, and the girls, and Andrew, are anxious to get back to their usual routines. They appreciate that things are a bit difficult at the moment, but I said I was sure you would understand."

"Right. You're the boss, Mrs M. Can we discuss it this afternoon? I need to get this stuff to those gibbering idiots before they wrench my arm off."

"Chimps? Yeah, well, they don't all dress up in frilly pinafores and serve afternoon tea. Like on the telly. They can be rough, I know."

"I was exaggerating a bit, as usual. The keeper's shut them up until I've finished, thank God! The fully grown ones can be really violent. And they're very strong! That cleaning woman who got savaged by this lot is a lot better, so they say here. She's lucky to be alive, if you ask me. So off I go, bravely into the lion's den! See you this afternoon, Mrs M."

Thinking that Dot Nimmo would be equal to any chimpanzee, however strong, Lois turned to leave. Then, as planned, she decided to go up to the hall and have a nose around while she was there. She would make a list of things for Dot to concentrate on, and then be off home.

The Fiat was there, round the back of the building, and Lois parked nearby. She went through the unlocked back door into the kitchen, and yelled, "Yoo-hoo! Justin! Are you there? It's only me, Lois Meade. Just checking on jobs for Dot."

There was no reply, and she guessed he must be out of earshot. Fine. She'd come across him sooner or later back in the village. She made her way around the ground floor, making notes. It was surprising how dusty and unattractive a place could look when nobody was living there. She came to Pettison's office and stopped. The door was closed. *He* couldn't be in there, since he was safely tucked up in hospital. She gently pushed open the door.

She stopped at once, seeing a figure kneeling by an open drawer in the filing cabinet. The figure turned in alarm, and she saw that it was Justin, with piles of letters of all kinds stacked around in little heaps on the floor.

"What the hell do you want?" he said in a scared voice. "Get out! This room is private."

"I know it is, but private for Pettison, surely. And since you ask, I'm making notes for when Dot Nimmo comes back to work. It's already dirty and dusty everywhere."

Justin scrambled to his feet, and she began to feel nervous, and turned to leave the room.

"Come back here, Mrs Meade," he said. "I do need to explain to you. Perhaps you should get on with your work and forget you've seen me here, and we could talk later."

Lois stopped. "I'll do no such thing," she said. "Unless you give me a good explanation *now* why I should do so."

He walked towards her nodding, and she retreated.

"I guess I owe you an apology," he said. "I didn't mean to be rude. It's just that riffling through Uncle's papers is not something I wanted to be caught at. The fact is, I'm looking for letters between him and my father. Things were not good for my dad, and I'm hoping to put it right. Sorry, Mrs Meade. Could we sit down for a moment, and I'll try to explain? It is quite a long story."

They sat down on the sagging sofa, and he told her as briefly as he could how his father had been blackmailed by Pettison, and now he was in the same situation. When he finally stopped talking, she stood up and said she would have to think about everything. "I'll give you a call later," she said, and walked towards the door. He was choking, near to tears, and as she looked back at him, she tripped, cracking her head on a stone step as she fell.

Justin stooped over her, frantically checking that she was still alive, and then lifted her up with difficulty. He staggered back into the drawing room, where he almost dropped her onto the sagging sofa. Then he sat down on a nearby chair, breathing heavily, pulled out his mobile and dialled emergency.

He grabbed a moth-eaten rug from a pile by the fireplace, and covered her with it, looking anxiously into her face for signs of movement. Her colour was definitely improving. She's very pretty in repose, he thought abstractedly. He wondered what his uncle Pettison thought of her. Probably all he could see was a dangerous enemy. He had plenty of those, the old fool. "Now, I *must* make a plan, and carry it out," he muttered.

He checked Lois's breathing, and looked at his watch. Could it be only five minutes since he called the ambulance? An unpleasant thought struck him. After this, he would no doubt have to look for another place to live.

Forty-Two

Hunter Cowgill sat in the Zoo Café, looking at his watch. It was unlike Lois to be late. Still, she had been reluctant to meet him, saying she was busy. Probably a very small act of rebellion! She had probably gone back home.

He got to his feet, thinking he would see her later. He had a couple of snippets of information for her, but they could wait. Waving to Margie as he went out, he headed for the centre of town.

Meanwhile, in the kitchen at Meade House, Gran was also checking the clock. It was long past the time Lois should have returned, and she now heard Derek's van arriving. He would likely know what had happened to Lois. Maybe something wrong with her van, and she'd got a lift home with him.

But when he came into the kitchen, apologising for being late, he knew nothing about Lois's absence. "Have you tried Hazel in the Tresham office?" he said now.

"No, I didn't think of that. You know how she hates to be checked up on."

Derek dialled the number, and after a few words with Hazel shook his head, and said to Gran that she hadn't showed up there. Due to do so, but she hadn't even popped in.

"It's possible she's broken down somewhere and forgotten her mobile." He went upstairs to their bedroom and, sure enough, found the phone lying on the dressing table. Odd, he thought. Her mind must have been on other things. He returned to the kitchen, and said they might as well have lunch, and then he'd do some more enquiring if she hadn't turned up.

Conversation limped along as they ate shepherd's pie and peas, and in the end, Derek said he couldn't fancy any pudding, and went off into Lois's office to look for clues to where she might be.

IN THE DRAWING ROOM AT THE HALL, JUSTIN STARED AT LOIS. Her colour was definitely better, and her breathing regular. He willed her to wake up. It was after lunchtime, and someone would be bound to be looking for her. He went over to take a closer look. Although she looked much better, her eyes were still closed. Perhaps he should take her into hospital himself?

He went outside to check on the Fiat. He'd never be able to manhandle her into that! Her own van was still there, and the key dangling from the door. Obviously not worried about car thieves. But now he could cancel the ambulance and take her in her own van with not too much trouble, and straight to the emergency department. He could then leave her there, and scoot off out before they asked him any questions. Feeling more optimistic, he once more lifted her up.

God, she was heavy! He struggled out to the car, where he had left the door open. With great difficulty, he heaved her into the passenger seat, and stood back to take a few deep breaths. Then he went back to the kitchen door and went inside and checked that he had put his uncle's office back into good order. He called the ambulance service, had a last look inside, and closed and locked the kitchen door. In the intervening few minutes, Lois had opened her eyes, slid across to the driving seat, started the engine and was well away down the drive before Justin could recover from his astonishment and chase after her.

Now, happily on the way home, Lois laughed aloud. That was easy! All she had to do was pretend to be still out cold, and then wait for a suitable opportunity. Her head ached, and when she put her hand up, her fingers came back stained with blood. Soon fixed, she thought. She had already cooked up a story for Gran and Derek, who, if he knew the truth, would probably explode, and steam off into Tresham to teach Justin a lesson he wouldn't forget. She drove into Meade House yard, switched off the car engine and got out.

She could see Gran and Derek inside the kitchen, and, feeling a little dizzy, she opened the door and managed a greeting, before her head spun, and she fell straight into Derek's arms.

"Lois! What on earth has happened to you?" Gran rushed round to help him, and together they got her onto a kitchen chair, where she rubbed her eyes and said she was perfectly okay.

"For God's sake, woman," said Derek, "what's this? You've got a ruddy great graze on your head. A real mess! You shouldn't have been driving home!"

"I fell over," she said. "Nothing much. It'll soon mend."

"Meanwhile," said Gran sternly, "you'll sit there while I

get some stuff from the bathroom to clean you up. Derek, don't let her move."

"You okay, me duck?" said Derek.

"Not really," whispered Lois. "Didn't want to alarm Mum. I really did just fall over up at Cameroon Hall, and hit my head on a stone step."

"What were you doing there?"

"Making notes for Dot for tomorrow. The floor was slippery in the kitchen. I feel a right fool. I'd been talking to Justin Brookes, and he told me some interesting details about his father and Pettison. It's all a bit fuzzy at the moment, but I expect it'll come clearer."

"You're not a fool, not you, my love. But I expect you were in a hurry, as usual. You are much later than we expected."

"I think I was out cold for a bit. Then I came to, and took my time until it was safe to drive. Poor old Justin must have been very worried. I suppose I should have waited before driving off, but he'd gone to lock up, and I wanted to get home as quickly as possible. I think he'd rung for an ambulance. Don't know what happened to that. Derek, could you put the kettle on? I'm dying for a hot drink."

Gran arrived back in the kitchen, armed with the first aid box and clean towels. "Now then, young lady," she said, "let's get you cleaned up. Derek, you go and light the fire in the sitting room, and when I've finished, we'll help Lois in there to watch television for a bit. There's a good antiques auction programme. And there you will stay, Lois Weedon, until it's supper time. Orders, my lady."

By the time Gran had finished and Lois was safely tucked up in a rug on the sofa, she acquiesced gratefully. She was feeling dizzy again after walking through the hall, and leaned back against the cushions, closing her eyes. "Might have a little sleep," she said. "Put the telly on, and then I'll have something to look at if I wake."

Derek and Gran left quietly, and said they would be in the kitchen, if she needed any help. "Now then," said Gran, as she made a cup of tea for the two of them, "do you think we had the whole truth?"

Derek shook his head. "Lois wouldn't lie to us, but she is very good at editing what really happened. It wouldn't have taken that long to make a few notes, would it? The interesting things Justin told her must have been quite important."

At that moment, a figure passed the window, and Gran went to open the door.

"Hello, Mrs Weedon. I wonder if Lois is at home?" It was Mrs Tollervey-Jones, and Gran drew herself up straight.

"She is, but she's having a rest. Is there anything I can do for you?"

"Well, maybe you can, but perhaps I could come into your warm kitchen for a moment. It is very cold standing here."

Derek came up behind Gran, and said of course she must come in. "We're having a cuppa. Would you like one?"

"Thank you so much. That would be lovely. I can warm my hands round the cup."

Gran was looking daggers at Derek. She did not hold with Mrs T-J. She was now unofficial assistant to Lois in her foolish ferretin', and encouraged her to take on dangerous missions.

"The thing is," the old lady said, "I think I recognised the man who stole the silver. I was in the cattle market in Tresham. I go there most weeks. I love to look at the cattle and sheep, you know. The thing I most miss after selling up the estate. I used to visit our farms, and have talks with the tenants. Looked round the herds and helped out when the vet arrived. So now I just go and stare at the beautiful animals and meet old friends."

"And the burglar?" said Gran.

"Well, he was near the auctioneer, so I could see him clearly. He was with another man, and I could swear he was the new tenant at Josie's shop flat. Young, fair-haired. Very nice looking. You couldn't miss him, really. He stood out among all the beady-eyed farmers and stockmen."

"Well, I suppose it could have been him," Derek said. "We don't know much about him, but he claims to be an actor/businessman in Tresham. Don't know what kind of business, but it could be connected with his uncle's zoo. He kept some rare animals in our back shed. Strange fellow."

"There's a lot that's strange about him, if you ask me," Gran said. "Deals in rare animals, I reckon. Like Derek said, he kept a couple in Josie's shed. Could explain him being at the market. Maybe does his dodgy deals there."

"Of course, I had forgotten the elephant shrews. Did they turn up?"

"Dunno," said Derek. "Lois might know. She may be awake now, so shall I go and tell her you're here?"

"Only if she's feeling well enough. Not like Lois to be resting during the day!"

"She had a fall. Not too serious," said Gran. "It's only a surface graze, but enough to give her a nasty turn. Shouldn't have driven home, silly girl."

"Then don't trouble her, thank you," said Mrs T-J. "I'll see her tomorrow, perhaps in the morning. Give her my love, and tell her to be sensible and rest."

"Some hopes!" said Derek.

"WHO WAS THAT?" ASKED LOIS, WHEN GRAN BROUGHT HER A CUP of tea. "Someone came in, and then left again, walking down the drive. I could hear footsteps and I thought it might be Dot. I've just remembered I was going to see her this afternoon."

"Brilliant, my dear Watson," said Derek, following on behind. "Except that it was Mrs T-J, and she'll give you a call tomorrow morning. Nothing urgent, she said."

Gran sat down in a comfortable armchair and looked at Lois. "Did you sleep?" she said.

Lois nodded. "Drifted off for a few minutes. You can turn up the telly now if you like. I'll stay here and watch with you."

"More like I'll stay here and watch that you don't stir," answered Gran. "Derek's decided not to go to work. So he'll take Jeems for her walk, after he's rung Dot Nimmo and told her you're not free this afternoon."

AT HALF PAST FIVE, LOIS FINALLY WOKE UP FROM A DEEP SLEEP. The sound of the telephone woke her, and Gran got to her feet. "I'll get it," she said, and went out into the hall. A couple of minutes later she was back. "Josie would like a word," she said, holding the extension.

"Hello, dear? What's new?"

"It's very strange, Mum. Justin's just been in. He's collected all his things, put them in the Fiat, and then came in again and said he was very sorry, but he wouldn't be coming back. He said the rent was paid up to date. Nothing wrong with the flat, he said, but after his father's death he had had to make other plans. He seemed in a hurry, Mum, so I didn't delay him. I just think it was very strange."

"Mm, very strange," said Lois. "Done a runner, has he? Never mind, Josie dear. I think I know the answer. He was rather rude to me this morning, and probably thinks he'll go before he's pushed! Don't worry, we'll get a nice middle-aged couple next time. Thanks for letting me know, anyway. See you tomorrow. Bye-ee."

Forty-Three

First call next morning was from Hunter Cowgill. At nine o'clock, when Lois was already busy with the cleaning schedules, the phone rang.

"Ah, there you are," he said coolly. "Something happen yesterday? I was expecting you to join me for a coffee."

"Sorry. Something came up. I'm coming into town this morning so can I call and see you? It is quite important, but best told face-to-face."

"Very well. Would ten thirty suit?"

"Fine. See you then."

The second caller was Mrs T-J, and as Lois had been filled in by Gran about the man in the cattle market, they agreed to meet for a cup of tea around three.

Thirdly, there was a call from Justin. When she heard his voice, Lois sat back in her chair and was silent for a moment, collecting her thoughts.

"Mrs Meade? Are you there? I do have to speak to you. Please!"

"Yes, I'm here. What do you want? I know you've left the flat. Probably because you were very rude to me yesterday! I can't remember all you said, but I know you're trying to clear your father's name, should the illegal animal trade become known publicly. However, let's forget about that for a moment. What do you want?" she repeated.

"To offer my apologies, and an explanation. I'm afraid I panicked, and then you ran away and fell down. I didn't know what to do, and was about to take you to the accident and emergency department at the hospital when you came round and drove off. I was really shocked and felt terrible afterwards, not knowing where you had gone. You looked so dreadfully ill at first. Are you feeling better now?"

"Yes, I do feel better. But I have a nasty wound on my head where I fell in the kitchen. And I can't remember much of what you told me before I fell."

"Can I tell you again? I was, as you saw, looking through Uncle's files. I was hoping to find some evidence of him blackmailing my father for many years. I need to know how much my father was involved in Uncle Robert's little schemes. It was enough to keep him under a financial obligation to Uncle; I do know that. I loved my father and looked up to him. I am very anxious to clear his name."

"Justin, this is all very interesting, but I fail to see what it has to do with me. An apology from you is all I need. I've told nobody else about your stupidity, just that I fell over and banged my head."

"Oh thanks! That's a huge relief. And the other thing is, do you think I could come back to the flat? Would Josie think I was completely mad?"

"Very likely, I should think. Up to you, Justin, to turn on the old charm. One thing, though. Leave me out of it. I shall be in touch with her this evening, so unless she mentions it, I'll keep quiet. Bye. Oh, and there's a matter of the police. I'm afraid I shall have to tell Inspector Cowgill most of what you told me. I'll do my best for you."

COWGILL GREETED HER WITH AN ANXIOUS FACE. "ARE YOU ILL, Lois? Not hiding something from me? And why have you got your hair done up that way? It suits you, but makes you look more forbidding."

"Good," said Lois, and explained about Justin and her fall, giving him an edited version. She had no wish to drop the lad into trouble at the moment, and now believed firmly in his explanation. In any case, he was more useful on the spot, than if he moved away, maybe to an unknown destination.

"I just hope you haven't left anything out of that explanation, Lois," said Cowgill. "What I have to say is much less worrying, and I hope helpful. You remember our main aim is to catch Pettison at the time of handover, or at least in possession of animals illegally imported. I think this time we may have a chance to succeed. Because he's in hospital, and out of action for a while, he'll need to keep in touch with his so-called colleagues. We are now sure we know at least one of them, confirmed by what he told you." He looked closely at her. "Are you sure you're feeling perfectly all right, my love? I was extremely worried, you know."

"I'm fine, really," she said. "Carry on. It all sounds pretty exciting to me."

"Not so sure about that, but we do know that Betsy Brierley is, as well as being Pettison's mistress, an occasional handler, with her Ted. Now she has been reported by the owner of a pet shop in town, asking for some kind of shrews. He knew they were rare, and smelled something fishy. In a manner of speaking, you understand. So he called us." He was glad to see her smile.

"Ah, the poor little shrews," said Lois. "I thought they wouldn't survive in this weather."

"How would Betsy have retrieved them from your shed, do you think?"

"Dunno," said Lois. "It was safely locked, as you know. But if she had got a key from somewhere, she could have waited until the shop was closed and nobody was around, and then let herself in and lifted the animals. Then locked up again when she left. Not difficult. Justin could have lent her his key. Josie still has one, of course."

Cowgill nodded, and soldiered on. "So, definitely Brookes is one of them. Now, if there are more animals arriving in this country before Pettison is discharged, I suspect he will find a way for the courier to visit him first. In these transactions, cash is always used. And he will already have worked out that Betsy is on the make and would probably have siphoned off a chunk of cash for herself before handing over the rest to him."

"So how will we know which of his visitors is the suspect one? Look for a cobra disguised as a bunch of flowers?" Lois said, and laughed. "I think you'll find Betsy Brierley has taken over the whole job until he gets out. Maybe you should pull her in? No doubt she takes her cut, but that's something he'll have to deal with. No hospital is going to allow animals, deadly or otherwise, into its wards."

"I don't want Betsy, not at the moment," said Cowgill. "I mean to get the head of this particularly nasty setup. The head of the snake, you might say. And since all of them, including slippery Pettison, are born liars, I'll still have to wait patiently, and catch him in the act."

Forty-Four

Lois looked at her watch. It was too early to find Mrs Tollervey-Jones, so she had spent a happy half hour looking in the library for details of elephant shrews. It was too late for rescuing them, but in case more turned up, she wanted to know what Josie would be dealing with. After finding shrews, and learning more about them, she turned to chimpanzees. She had been struck by Dot saying they could be violent. The general image was of an intelligent, friendly animal. But then, you could say that about dogs, and yet small children had been savaged by pet dogs. As she trawled through the websites, it was obvious that there was a huge and lucrative network of quite legal suppliers, and mostly the animals were sold with a full supply of documents from health authorities and vets. There were also fraudsters, more difficult to trace, and dangerous to know. Wild animals should be in their natural environment, the law said, not treated as amusement for human beings. No wonder Pettison called them his people. She believed he genuinely thought of them as equals. How ridiculous and pathetic! Perhaps he should be expending his energies on saving forests and jungles and the planet in general. Or maybe he thought that was what he was actually doing?

She returned to her car, and drove slowly back to Farnden. She was early, and hoped that Mrs T-J was at home. Luckily, she spotted the old lady in her back garden, sweeping up leaves and debris from particularly hard frosts, and greeted Lois with a big smile.

"Wonderful! You could not have arrived at a better time, my dear! I've done quite enough for a woman of my great age. Come along in now, and we'll have a nice hot cup of tea."

As advertised by chimps, thought Lois, and, with a sudden feeling of hopelessness at the thought of the huge and shady trade they were up against, she followed her into the house.

"You're looking a bit down, Lois. Are you sure you're feeling better? Shock can be quite difficult to recover from. You must give it time, my dear. Anyway, here's tea, and I've baked old-fashioned currant buns for us. To hell with slimming, I say!"

Lois laughed. "I think you're fine as you are, Mrs T-J. What was it that nice Japanese friend of yours called you? A lovely English gentlewoman. And quite right, too. Now, you did say you had something to tell me? Was it about possibly spotting your burglar in the cattle market?"

"Yes, it was that. But there was more to it than I said on the phone. After the auction had finished, I made my way round to the auctioneer's office. An old friend, you know. I asked him about the man I saw, and he remembered him, but couldn't tell me his name. He's often there, at the auctions, and sometimes has a woman with him. Doesn't bid for anything. But Sam Downing, the auctioneer, said he'd seen him afterwards, when he went to get his car, in a huddle with a couple of other people. So is he the charming Justin Brookes? Or am I mistaken?"

Lois brightened, and said she was sure it could have been. "Did you notice anything unusual about the burglar, anything you might recognise again about the man at the market?"

"I'll give it some careful thought. He was quite a pleasant burglar, in his way."

"Mm, well, we shall see. These buns are delicious! May I have another, please?"

In a private ward in Tresham General Hospital, Robert Pettison stared out of the window at the wintry scene. He was bored. Each day, his condition had improved, until he had no tubes or monitors attached to him, and was able to walk with a stick around in his room, holding on to the furniture. Daytime television was appalling, and he hadn't sufficient concentration to read a book. The newspapers were full of bad news. A magazine brought to him by a kindly nurse, full of pictures of the royal family and their relations, had bored him further. He knew one or two of the distant ones, and had thought perhaps he could make a few pounds telling a more juicy story than the one in the magazine. But blackmail was a dicey business. He had no interest in it, except where it had become vital, such as with Justin's father, and that was hardly blackmail!

Who would have thought that the young Desmond Brookes, so promising a pupil at their school, until they were summarily dismissed, would have thought it beholden on him to go back to the dreary fenlands and take over the family farm? A first at Oxford, and offers of good jobs galore. That could have been his future.

And now his son, Justin! Nothing like his father, who had grown into a mild man with a dread of trouble, dating back, no doubt, to his bullied days at school. Justin was for years a biddable young chap, and he, Pettison, had made use of this. Now he had changed, with the death of his father.

A nurse knocked at the door and came in. "You have a visitor, Mr Pettison. May he come in? Ah, I see you're sitting out in a chair. Well done, my dear!"

"Who is it?"

"A Mr Smith. Says he is an old friend."

"Smith? Unlikely. But let him in," said Pettison. "And turn him out again in ten minutes' time, please."

The nurse showed him where the alarm button was, and then opened the door wider. A strange-looking man came in quickly. He was small and thin and had dark brown hair and a moustache. He wore cotton gloves and a black jacket and trousers.

"Who the hell are you?" said Pettison.

"Never you mind," the man said in a muffled voice. He seemed to be having trouble with his moustache. "Put your arms above your head and keep them there, now!" he added, and before Pettison could reach for the bell to summon a nurse, the man produced a gun from his pocket, and pulled the trigger. Red paint squirted out and hit Pettison on the side of his face, and then directed downwards, until his whole visible body was covered. He spluttered, touched his bell to summon help, and then slumped to one side

The visitor ran, like a shadow, out of the hospital and away. The whole episode had taken no more than five minutes.

Forty-Five

"WHO WAS THAT MAN?" SAID THE HOSPITAL RECEPTIONIST, as a dark figure ran by the desk and out of sight.

"Goodness knows," said her colleague sitting next to her. She was a volunteer worker who helped visitors find their way around the vast hospital complex.

"He looked in a hurry! Maybe he was late for meeting somebody. Hey, listen, there's alarm bells ringing somewhere. Do you think it could be him?"

"I don't remember him coming in, though he could have, while I went to the shop for tissues. I expect you were busy with someone else."

They then had a conversation about security in general, and agreed that they should stay at their post, in case someone else tried to get out unseen. "Doesn't matter however many measures are put in by the authorities, there'll always be ways of getting in and out without being noticed," said one.

"Like that man over there, walking straight past us! Hi! Come back here."

She stood up and gestured to the man, who returned to the desk.

"So sorry, sir," said the first receptionist. "My colleague obviously did not recognise you. Please carry on."

"So what was that all about? I thought we agreed—"

"It was the new consultant, you dope! Don't tell me you've never seen him before? He's famous."

"Not to me, he's not. It would have been polite, at least, to check in with us at the desk."

IT WAS GETTING DARK, AND JUSTIN WALKED ROUND TO THE entrance to his flat, but then thought that before he went up, he should check there were no lingering telltale signs of the shrews' occupancy. It had been dark when Betsy collected them. The shed key was on his ring, and he unlocked and looked around. He could see that much of it had been cleared. No signs of a cage or food. Betsy must have taken them all.

He looked around, and wondered what he could do with the space, now he had decided not to handle any more illegal animals. Derek had obviously taken what he wanted to keep, and stored it in the old pigsty at the bottom of the vegetable garden. And recently Josie had said Justin could do what he liked with the neglected patch. She had grown things there when she lived over the shop, but now had no spare time, and so it was not used.

He quite fancied growing a few things there. It would make him feel more rooted to something permanent, with a few gooseberry bushes and maybe cabbages and lettuces. It would be good exercise, too, digging over the plot, ready to do some planting.

He began to whistle, and went upstairs to the flat feeling

much more cheerful. He would ask to borrow some gardening tools this afternoon and make a start.

As he unpacked all the things he had so recently taken away, he felt a fool. He really would like to go and have a word with Josie, but she had said that her mother had told her about his rudeness, and she wanted no more to do with him on a personal level. He must use his own entrance, and as long as he paid the rent on time, and kept no wild animals—or tame ones, for that matter—he could stay.

He dialled his mother's mobile, and sat down in a comfortable chair. "Hi, Mother. How are you? And how's Vera? Hope you're not getting up to mischief, the pair of you. No, of course I'm not! I'm still in the flat. Planning to do some gardening soon. Yes, fine, thank you. Now you take care, and I'll be up to see you as soon as possible."

The kettle was boiling, and he made himself a cup of coffee. Then he unwrapped the sandwich he had bought in Tresham, and began to eat.

In town, Dot Nimmo came out of her house and locked the door. She was about to get into the car when she saw Betsy Brierley come out into the street. She looks a bit wild, thought Dot, and waited to see what would happen next. She enjoyed a good marital punch-up, as a viewer of course, and was pleased to see Ted Brierley follow Betsy along the pavement. He caught up with her after a few yards, and grabbed her arm. This was going to be good, thought Dot.

Ted pulled Betsy to a halt, and she turned on him. "What the hell do you think you're doing!?" she shouted, slapping him round the face. He recoiled, and then went in again on the attack. But Betsy had had enough. "Get back indoors, and I'll explain one more time!!" she shouted, and then turned to look at Dot. "And you can mind your own business, Dottie Nimmo!" she yelled. "There's a thing or two I could teach you, you boring old fart!"

Dot roared with laughter. "Very good, Betsy," she called. "Couldn't have said it better myself. Come and have a cuppa with me when I get back. Shouldn't be more than an hour."

In a couple of minutes, it was all quiet again. Derek pulled up outside the New Brooms office at the other end of the street, went inside and greeted Hazel, who said he had missed a good sideshow. "I could hear every word, right down here," she said. "Betsy and Ted were at it again, with Dot joining in."

"Women!" said Derek. "At least you're a rational person, Hazel. I don't often come in here, but it's always calm and pleasant. You're a good girl, and Lois is lucky to have you."

"Thanks," said Hazel. "How can I help? I guess you don't want a cleaner for your office!"

"No, we've got Gran, who is a law unto herself. No, I've been working in town, and wondered if you'd got an evening paper? I like to check the football results, and the man on the corner has sold out."

Hazel reached across her desk, and produced the paper. "It is delivered every day," she said. "Half the time nobody looks at it. You take it, Derek. You're welcome."

By the time he reached home, tea was laid on the kitchen table, and he eyed the chocolate sponge set in pride of place.

"Lois in?" he asked Gran. She nodded, and said her daughter was at last being sensible and was reading the evening paper in the front room by the fire.

"Ah, well that makes two evening papers. I got one from Hazel. I'll tell Lois tea's ready, shall I?"

The chocolate sponge was a shadow of its former self by the time tea was finished, and Gran said she'd be surprised if any of them could eat supper. "You'd better go and sit by the fire and let it sink," she said, and Lois and Derek dutifully went through.

They had been settled only a few minutes when Lois said with a chuckle, "Oh my God, Derek, have you seen this?"

He looked over the top of his paper, and saw Lois's smiling face. "What are you talking about, me duck? Oh, that paint job. If it was meant to be a practical joke, it's not funny. I didn't read all of it."

Lois shook her head dumbly, choking with suppressed laughter. Then she spluttered, "Page four, halfway down. The report about goings-on at the Tresham General Hospital," she said. "I expect this'll cause some trouble. It's not funny really, but, well, read it . . ."

Derek found the page, and read on. "Nasty," he said, unamused. "But it could have been worse. Sounds like a bit of a revenge prank, harmless but nasty. Could've happened to you, what with your ferretin' an' that."

Lois got to her feet. "Don't be ridiculous, Derek. That unkind joke was only possible because Pettison was helpless and couldn't fight back. Anyway, I have to make a telephone call. Back in a minute, and don't worry. Nothing's going to happen to me."

Forty-Six

Early in the morning, the telephone at Meade House had begun to ring, and it had gone on intermittently until well after breakfast.

"I reckon the whole world read yesterday's evening paper!" said Lois, after an amusing talk with Mrs T-J, who said she felt ashamed to find the Pettison story funny, but that he really had it coming to him. "Strange, isn't it, how wide he had cast his net," she said. "Lots of people have come out of the woodwork, apparently, claiming to have been tricked by him into parting with sums of money, small and large."

"Have you heard from Cowgill?" Derek asked Lois now. "He'll have something to say, you bet."

"No, but I'm giving him a call later, on a different matter entirely."

"Not that different," said Gran.

Lois said nothing. She had to admit that she had no real

need to ring Cowgill, but she was curious to have more details about Pettison. It would affect what else had to be done in identifying his suppliers. Would the business of importing poor little animals continue? Without his presence, would Justin or Betsy take over? And how important was he, anyway, in the dangerous network of dealers?

She wondered how the red-paint story, in considerable detail, had got out from the hospital, which would surely be anxious to make as little as possible of it. That a man with evil intent had got into the private wing of the new hospital extension was bad enough. But that he had got out again without being challenged was a very serious matter.

Now, in her office and busy with New Brooms business, the thought came back to her. Who had given the story to the newspaper? She picked it up again, and looked for a byline. No name. At the start of the story, it was anonymously "by our reporter."

She looked up the number, dialled, and asked for a girl who was one of her son Jamie's girlfriends. "Diana in the newsroom, please," she said.

"Hello? Lois Meade here. New Brooms. Is that you, Diana? Ah, nice to hear your voice again. Yes, we're all well. Have you heard from Jamie? Oh good. Now, dear, I have a request. I wonder if you could tell me who wrote the story about Robert Pettison? No, it's not idle curiosity! I do have a good reason for wanting to know. Ring me back? Fine. I'll be here for at least another hour."

The call came back after twenty minutes.

"Hi, Diana, nice of you to ring back. Yes, I'm all ears. Anonymous call, did you say? But surely you don't print all anonymous stories from people wanting to cause trouble? Oh, verified by the hospital. Good heavens, what a mess. Oh, would you? That would be really helpful. Hear from you soon, then. Bye."

Lois sat for another half hour, doodling on the back of an envelope and thinking. Then she put on her jacket and set out for the shop.

"Morning, Josie. All well? Has Matthew got rid of that cough?"

"Almost," said Josie. "You look like the cat's got the cream. What's new?"

"Nothing, really. Not yet. Is the wicked Justin back in the flat?"

"Yeah, I think so. I told him I don't want to see anything more of him than is necessary. He actually had the cheek to come in and ask to borrow gardening tools! Apparently, he intends putting the patch at the back down to vegetables, with a bit of lawn down the bottom near the pigsty."

"Sounds like he means to stay."

"I wouldn't bank on it, Mum. I couldn't trust him now, not after messing us about with the flat."

"Ah, well, there could have been a good reason, I suppose. Still, as long as all is well now, and you make sure you remember to lock up out the back, so you're safe in here."

"Yep. Anyway, did you want a word with him? I'm pretty sure he's in. Sometimes I think he's got hobnailed boots, the row he makes!"

"Something to do with settling in, I suppose. I'll not bother him. A clause in the tenancy document about security needs rewording. Just in case."

But as she left the shop, she saw the nose of the Fiat edging out into the road. Justin saw her and immediately got out. "Mrs Meade, how are you? Looking a lot better than the last time I saw you! Can you ever forgive me?"

"No," said Lois. "But, to change the subject, I need to see you sometime about the tenancy agreement. Needs rewording."

"Right. Shall I give you a ring? Oh, and by the way, what

do you think of the news? About Uncle Robert, I mean. It's the talk of the town!"

"It could have been worse, I suppose. The hospital must be really furious. It puts them in a really bad light! They are being very cagey about it, but your uncle is said to have had a relapse. "

"Shame," he said, and then smiled at her. "Must fly! Late already. Bye, and take care." He revved up the engine and started off with a squeal of tires.

"What a dope," muttered Lois. "He'll come a real cropper one of these days."

Justin was heading into Tresham. He passed the New Brooms office, and pulled up opposite Dot Nimmo's house. After knocking at the Brierleys' front door, he looked at his watch. Not lunchtime yet, so Ted should be safely down at his club. He knocked again, and it was immediately opened by Betsy.

"No need to knock the house down!" she said. "You'd better come in, I suppose."

Dot, up in her bedroom getting ready to go over to her next job, saw the car, which she recognised, and made a note to have another look to see if it was still there when she went out. She strongly disapproved of Justin having the Farnden shop flat, and had said so forcibly to Lois. "Him being Pettison's nephew is enough to have nothing to do with him," she had said.

Inside the Brierley house, Justin sat down on a stool in the tiny kitchen, watching Betsy, as she continued hand washing a pile of frillies while he talked.

"I bet you don't remember good sensible knickers required for handstands in the school gym?" he said.

"Blimey, I'm not that old!" she said. "And if knickers are on your mind, I'm not available at the moment."

"No, certainly not," he said. "I'm here on business. We need to decide what to do now the network is very likely to break down. God knows how much they'll find out. You got any plans?"

"Oh, I shall have to carry on, if I'm able. There'll be a lot of work to do, but it is lucrative, and we need the money. Whether Pettison will be well enough to get back into it is another matter. Also, there will be a lot of personal stuff to face. I must say I don't look forward to it. But, as you know, it is difficult to see a way out without us incriminating ourselves. We're in a bit of a limbo at the moment."

"What does Ted think of it all?"

"He hasn't said much. But on the whole he's sticking by me, much the same as ever. He ain't got much alternative, really."

"So, we'd better keep in touch, Betsy. It'll be up to us. I do have some thoughts about how we could carry on in the future, once Pettison is out of the picture. And I can't see him ever taking over again. That episode in the hospital must have set him back quite a bit."

"So what are you suggesting? I do sometimes think it'd be nice to keep the zoo going without all that illegal stuff. The two of us, and Ted, could carry on with the zoo and any animals we introduce should be aboveboard an' all that?"

"Yes. If we could make the transition without being incriminated with Pettison's past, it would be a much better way for the future. You know how to handle the animals, and I've a reasonable head for business."

Betsy looked him up and down, as if sizing up his chances. "Do you really think we're going to get away with it? All that we've done over the years, I mean? Because I don't. If you ask me, the fuzz are biding their time. They know most of what goes on at the zoo. Cowgill will strike when he's ready. And it don't matter how good we are now; our past history will do for us, but especially Pettison, with any luck. We'll just have to wait and see. The best thing you could do would be to go back to Lincolnshire to be a farmer. How's your mum, by the way?"

"Bearing up. She's more or less decided to sell the farm and buy a bungalow. Her friend Vera is willing to go in with her and be a sort of companion. I reckon that's the most sensible solution, though I'm haunted by my late father's hopes that I would take it over."

"Well, he's gone now, so you'll have to make your own decisions. Anyway, I'm busy, so if that's all, I'll see you out."

Opposite, Dot watched them talking as they came out of the door, and then Justin drove off with the usual high-pitched roar.

"What ho, Betsy!" she shouted across the street. "That was a quick one and no mistake! Doing all right?"

Betsy laughed. "Nosy parker!" she called back. "Come in for cuppa this afternoon? See you then."

Forty-Seven

Saturday was usually the busiest day of the week, but the zoo was nevertheless quiet. It was eleven o'clock, and Margie looked around to see if anyone could take over while she stretched her legs and had a coffee. There was certainly no rush of customers to deal with

She stepped out of the ticket booth, and called to the keeper, who was walking through the yard on his way to the animals.

"Hi, Dan! Are you busy? You couldn't take over for ten minutes, could you? I need a little break. My legs are older than my brain, and they seize up if I don't walk about a bit."

He agreed readily, and, armed with the daily paper, he took up residence in her little quarters. There was just room enough to open the right pages, and he settled happily.

"Hi, Margie!" Betsy was already sitting in the café, coffee and a large iced bun in front of her. "I shouldn't, but I weakened," she said.

"I expect you have to keep in shape, in your business," Margie said, with a knowing smile.

"Yeah, well, I may not have to do it for much longer," Betsy replied. "Things are bound to change around here."

"How's Pettison, then? Last I heard was that he was stable, and with a good chance of a complete recovery. We've been assured that everything will go on the same meantime, and our jobs are secure," said Margie. "I should have thought you could say the same?"

"We shall see," said Betsy mysteriously, and got up to go. "I have to check a few things up in the hall," she said. "The gossips are busy, as you can imagine. I shall have to see that everything's okay if he's coming home soon."

"You got a key, then?"

"Oh yes," said Betsy loftily. "Had one for years. I'd best go up and see to the post, an' that."

"You're private secretary now, as well, are you?" said Margie, smiling.

"I do my best," said Betsy, and walked off.

She was somewhat daunted when she let herself into the hall, and saw a large pile of letters on the doormat. Sorting through them, and discarding all the rubbish, she came across one with a foreign stamp. "Oh blimey," she said. "Better open this."

It was from Africa, and the message was blunt. "Dear Sir, your consignment has been dispatched and will arrive soon. Notice of exact time and place of arrival will follow. Yours faithfully," and the rest was an unreadable squiggle. There were no contact details, and no clues to where exactly it might have come from.

Now what? She read the message again, and made a decision. Taking out her mobile, she dialled a number. "Justin? Can we meet? It's urgent. Yes, I suppose that will be all right. Your flat, around six o'clock? See you then."

She stuffed the rest of the post into a bag, and returned to her car. There was nobody around, and she suddenly felt a shiver. It was a creepy old place, she thought, and if any of the animals escaped they'd have a hell of a job finding them. Safely in her car, she drove off down the drive and out into the comforting traffic jam, full of real people going home to lunch.

Back in her ticket booth, Margie Turner settled down for afternoon chats with families coming into the zoo. She liked to have a few words of welcome with each lot, and then direct them to where they should start. Most of them chose the chimps, and after that the sadly lonely tiger. He was a mangy old thing, and no one could remember where Pettison had got him from. Most of the time he slept, but occasionally padded over to the visitors and yawned, showing his crumbling old teeth. Only very rarely did he oblige with a roar, and that was when children poked sticks at him, until reprimanded by the keeper.

Before he went into hospital, Pettison had taken delivery of a new, fully grown chimpanzee, bred in captivity and trained to be mild and friendly. So the keeper had said. But today he was clearly depressed. He sat on a branch of dead wood, his head in his hands, looking gloomy.

"Cheer up!" said the father of a visiting family. "It may never happen!"

His wife laughed. "Perhaps that's why he's worried," she said. Suddenly the chimp bounded down off the branch, and came to the front of his enclosure. He banged his huge fists on the bars, and chattered angrily.

"Come away, children!" said the visitor. "Let's go and look at some little rabbits."

"Missing his master," said the keeper, when the incident

was reported to him. "Old Pettison had got fond of him, and brought him treats to eat. I expect the poor thing is wondering where he's gone."

"He'll have to get used to somebody else for a while, won't he?" said Margie Turner, who had heard about it from a visitor leaving the zoo. "If you ask me, it's a bad idea to get too friendly with animals. You never know what they'll do next."

Forty-Eight

The bells of St. Martin's church, around the corner from Dot Nimmo's house, began their loud pealing for morning service, and Dot paused from her weekly chores, wondering whether she should go. She couldn't remember the last time she went, and doubted if she could remember when to stand up and sit down. Never mind, she told herself, God won't mind if I get it wrong. I don't like them modern hymns, but maybe there'll be one or two of the old favourites.

"Shut up, parrot," she said, passing his perch. "I'm going to church, and I'll say a prayer for the good Lord to take you sooner rather than later."

There was a trickle of worshippers entering the church, and Dot was surprised to see Betsy and Ted among them. She fell in beside them, and together they sat in a pew suitably near the back of the church. Dot wondered if Betsy confessed her sins? Since she regarded her work as a service to mankind, she probably didn't.

After the service, when some of the parishioners were collecting at the back of the church for a gossip, Dot and the Brierleys stood at the top of the steps outside, watching two strong men lifting a wheelchair bodily down to a specially adapted car. The occupant of the chair was well wrapped up from head to toe in thick rugs to keep out the cold.

"Must be a devout Christian," said Dot, "to venture out in this icy wind."

"Mm," said Betsy, and she and Ted exchanged a furtive look.

"What?" said Dot.

"What nothing," said Betsy. "Come and have a sherry, and we'll have a gossip of our own."

When they were safely out of the cold and into Brierleys' warm sitting room, Dot began again. "Okay, what's up? Is it to do with that man in the wheelchair—oh God, no! It wasn't him, was it? He's not in circulation again, is he?" She laughed at the ridiculousness of the idea.

"Depends what you're talking about, Dottie," said Ted.

"I'm talking about Pettison, of course. We all know there was a dreadful thing happened to him, but nobody knows the whole story, for some God-knows-what reason."

"If we tell you, will you promise God's honour not to tell anyone?"

"Natch," said Dot. "Cross my heart and hope to die."

"No need to go to that extreme," laughed Ted. "Over to you, Betsy," he said, and with a full glass in her hand, Betsy began.

SUNDAY LUNCH WAS ALWAYS A SPECIAL MEAL IN MEADE HOUSE, when Josie and Matthew came over, and sometimes Lois's eldest son, Douglas, with his small family. Jamie, her youngest, was a concert pianist and spent most of his time flying round the world, performing at concerts. He visited his family about four or five times a year, on average.

Today, Gran had cooked a large free-range chicken, with all the trimmings, and five of them sat round the table, appreciating the warmth of the Rayburn and the good red wine poured out by Matthew with a sure hand.

"Good health," said Derek, holding up his glass.

"And so say all of us," chanted the others.

"What are we all doing this afternoon?" said Lois. "I'm walking Jeems. A short walk today, and a quick one to work off this magnificent lunch. I'd be glad of company."

"I'm watching the sport on telly," said Derek.

"Me too," chorused the others, including Matthew, who was a renowned football player in police circles.

"And you Gran? One thing you're not doing, and that's the washing up."

"Thanks, Josie. No, I shall retire to my bedroom, put my feet up and read a book."

"And I shall have a nice snooze, like Gran," said Josie. "Mum, looks like you're walking on your own today."

The meal over, Lois went to fetch Jeems's lead, and the little dog was dancing about everyone's feet in her excitement at the mention of a walk.

Then the phone rang. "Blast!" said Derek. "Who can that possibly be? I'll answer it."

He disappeared, and a few seconds later was back, saying it was for Lois. "An old friend," he said, and then, making sure Gran could not hear, he whispered in her ear that it was Dot Nimmo. "Said she's sorry to bother you, but was sure you'd want to hear."

"Hear what?"

Derek shrugged his shoulders. "Better go and find out," he said, and Lois went quickly to her office, closing the door behind her. Dot would never ring her on a Sunday, unless it was really important.

"Hello, Dot? Something wrong? Oh gosh, if it's really a matter of life or death, you'd better come over straightaway. See you in about half an hour?"

She returned to the kitchen to find them all except Gran staring at her. Gran had already gone upstairs to her room, shutting her door with a bang that everyone could hear. She was mildly offended by Josie suggesting that she intended to have a snooze. She picked up her book, a racy novel about Regency folk, read two pages, and fell asleep.

"So who was that?" said Josie. "Are you going to tell us, or is it a secret to do with ferretin'?"

"I'll tell you later, when I've talked to her. It was Dot Nimmo, and she says it's red-hot news."

"You bet it's nothing that couldn't keep until tomorrow," said Matthew. "I guess she's bursting to tell somebody."

"COME ON INTO MY OFFICE, DOT," LOIS SAID, A SHORT WHILE later. "We shan't be disturbed, with any luck. Gran's safely asleep upstairs. Now, what is it all about?"

"Well, it's like this. I went to church this morning, and no, the whole place didn't fall down in surprise. Then, even more surprising, I saw Betsy Brierley, with Ted, and went to sit with them. Afterwards, she asked me in, and then she filled me in on what we had just seen."

"Which was?" Lois settled comfortably in her chair. This looked like it would take some time.

"A man in a wheelchair, who'd been in the church, was being carried down the steps by a couple of strong blokes, and stowed away in a special vehicle. The man was wrapped up against the cold, and you couldn't even see his face.

Then, when I was having a sherry with Betsy, she told me who he was."

Lois sat up straight, and her eyes opened wide. "Not him? Not Pettison? But isn't he very poorly?"

"Yes, I know that's what we all thought after that story in the newspaper. But he isn't that bad. He's still suffering, but it's more in mind than in body. They got the paint off very quickly, and he hadn't swallowed any, or anything like that. He's back in his own room. You know the phrase? 'Responding well to treatment'?"

"What do you mean, 'in mind than in body'? We all know the red-paint details. That story was an anonymous one, given to the newspapers by someone who didn't want his name mentioned. Tell me again what happened. Your paper probably gave a different report!"

"Well, this man got into the hospital without being spotted, and made his way to Pettison's private room. A nurse saw him and let him in. She shouldn't have, but he convinced her he was family. He was there for only about five minutes, they reckon. Pettison had asked the nurse to get rid of him after ten minutes, but luckily he was able to reach the bell before that, and she came running. Too late to catch the intruder, though." Dot began to laugh. "Oh, sorry, Mrs M," she continued. "It's just the thought of it. What if he was wearing one of them little shorty hospital nightshirts?"

"Dot! Get on with it, gel," said Lois. "Most of that I can read in the newspapers."

"No, there's more. Now, we all know that the nurse ran for help, and they got him cleaned up and back into bed. His face was red and sore, and he was very cold. But mostly he'd lost the power of speech. He wasn't damaged, but it was the trauma and humiliation, Betsy said."

"And it was him in church?" Lois said thoughtfully. "He

must think he's going to die in mortal sin. But knowing Pettison, he probably had some ulterior motive. So what else did Betsy say?"

"Well, apparently her and that Justin Brookes, who's Pettison's nephew, are keeping things going, and have plans for the future of the zoo."

"How are they going to keep it going? Pettison may recover, I suppose, and then it'll be business as usual."

Dot shook her head. "No, Brookes and Betsy mean to make some changes. There's no possibility of Pettison recovering immediately, and maybe never as good as he was before, so it seems."

"This'll take some thinking about," said Lois. "Thanks for coming over, Dot. I do appreciate it. On your day off, as well. I'm just about to take the dog for a walk. Do you want to come?"

Dot shook her head. "Gracious no, Mrs M. I'm going home to a good fire and a film on the telly. I'll say cheerio, then, and see you at the New Brooms meeting tomorrow."

Forty-Nine

"So what did she want, gel?" Derek said, as they sat side by side on the sofa, the telly finally switched off, Josie and Matthew waved off to the cottage, and Jeems safely in her basket in the kitchen.

"You mean Dot? Well, I'm sworn to secrecy, I'm afraid."

"Oh dear, not again," he said. "Couldn't you make up a story, not necessarily true, and then I can be happy?"

"That's a bit devious, isn't it?"

Derek shrugged. "Please yourself," he said.

Lois took a deep breath, and began. "Once upon a time, there was a nosy old man who lived in a nice village in the English Midlands. He couldn't bear for his wife to have secrets from him, so he attached her by the wrists to a picture hook on the wall. It'd have been a very strong hook, as she was seriously overweight." At this, Lois collapsed into laughter. "Oh Derek, this is ridiculous. No, I'll tell you a serious story, and you can decide how much I am making up."

When she had finished, they both sat in silence. Then Derek spoke in a whisper. "Was it really all over him?" he said.

She nodded. "He was covered with it, everywhere," she said.

"And the nurse found him like that?" Derek put his arm round her shoulders.

She nodded again. "But he didn't swallow any paint, or anything like that."

"No wonder he's lost the power of speech, poor old fool."

"I think it's time for bed," Lois said. "It's been quite a day." She kissed him fondly, and he gallantly stood up and pulled her to her feet. Then he picked her up, moved two steps and put her down again.

"You're right," he said. "She was seriously overweight."

NEXT MORNING, LOIS WAS IN HER OFFICE PREPARING FOR THE team meeting when her phone rang. It was Diana, and she had news. "Hi, Mrs Meade. Jamie's been in touch. Apparently he heard the story in Australia! No, that wasn't the reason I'm ringing. This morning we've had a handout from Tresham Zoo," she said. "I thought you might be interested."

"What does it say?"

"It says that owing to local rumours about the zoo closing, they want to assure all visitors that although it is under temporary new management, they are open as usual, and there will be more interactive opportunities, as well as upgrading the café."

Justin and Betsy haven't wasted any time, Lois thought. I hope they've consulted Pettison. He is still the boss, after all.

"That café could certainly do with an overhaul," she said. "Coffee tastes like dishwater, and the cakes are always stale."

"I don't know what the interactive bit means. I can't think that visitors are going to be encouraged to hug a tiger!"

Lois laughed. "Thanks for ringing, anyway, Diana. I'll keep you posted if there are any juicy developments; then you can have a scoop!"

As soon as she signed off, the phone rang again. This time it was Inspector Cowgill, and his tone was brisk. "Morning Lois," he said. "Perhaps you'd like to come and see me this afternoon? I have to go up to Cameroon Hall first, but perhaps we could say half past three?"

"I presume it's important?" said Lois.

"Could be," he answered, and that was the end of the conversation.

Dot Nimmo was first for the New Brooms meeting at midday, and she was in a very good mood. "Guess what, Mrs M," she said.

"What?"

"The zoo van, the one with the tiger draped all over it, drew up outside the Brierleys' this morning, and guess who got out of it?"

Lois shook her head. "Tell me, Dot," she said patiently.

"Justin Brookes, followed by Ted Brierley. How unlikely is that!"

"Certainly is," said Lois. "I wouldn't have put Justin down as one of Ted's bosom pals. Justin's altogether too public school, don't you think?"

"Yeah, well," said Dot. "That whole business with the red paint smacks of stupid public school goings-on, d'you reckon?"

"You may be right," said Lois, who had come to the same conclusion. "Oh, there's the others at the door. Could you let them in, Dot?"

*   *   *

In the staff room at the zoo, Betsy and Justin were sorting through another pile of post that Betsy had collected. She was keeping the one she had opened until the end, and after junking most of the rest into a plastic sack, she handed the delivery note to him.

"It doesn't say what the consignment is," she said. "What are we going to do about it?"

Justin groaned. "I had hoped that there wouldn't be any more of these," he said, "but I suppose there could be several orders outstanding. I see they'll let us know exactly when and what in due course. Have you found a later letter from them?"

They looked again at the small pile of envelopes that were not junk, and Betsy pulled out another with a foreign stamp. "This is the same," she said. "Here, you open it."

Justin duly opened the envelope and extracted a single sheet of paper. "It's brief and to the point," he said. "A consignment of bees bees! will be delivered to Cameroon Hall on Tuesday. That's Tuesday of this week!"

"In other words, tomorrow," said Betsy.

They stared at each other. Finally Justin said that until they could find out some more about them, he would transport them—safely, he hoped—to Farnden. "I've taken over the garden at the back of the shop, and they can go down the far end. Maybe in the pigsty, if they're coming from tropical parts."

"Bees!" said Betsy again. "I cannot bear them, Justin. Ted will tell you. I run screaming if one gets in the house. Are you sure about this?"

"We don't have much option, do we?" he said flatly. "There's no contact name, address or anything else. We have to accept them, and that's that."

"We could refuse to accept them?"

"And then what? We'd have officials from sundry authorities crawling all over the zoo. And probably another damaging story in the paper."

"Did you put that other one in? Was it you what done it?" Betsy said.

"Of course not," said Justin. "If it had been me, I'd have thought of something a bit more sophisticated to do to him."

Betsy looked at his frowning face, dark with what she thought must be extreme dislike.

"So what did he ever do to you?" she said. "He was one of my best customers."

"All water under the bridge," Justin replied. "Best forgotten."

"But not forgiven?"

"No, not forgiven," he said. "Now we'd better arrange who's going to be up at the house ready to receive the bees. Not you, obviously!"

"No, it'll have to be you. Perhaps Dot Nimmo might take a turn. I believe she's up there cleaning on a Tuesday."

"I'll ask Josie in the shop. Her mother will know. She's New Brooms' boss, isn't she? Okay, Betsy, let's get on with it."

FIFTY

"MORNING, MUM," SAID JOSIE, AS LOIS CAME THROUGH the shop door. "You missed a call. It was Justin. He's in Tresham already, and wanted to know if Dot will be cleaning up at Cameroon Hall, and if so, would she be prepared to take in a parcel?"

"Yes, she is, and it's up to her whether she accepts a parcel or not. I'll ring her on her mobile. Did Justin say where he would be?"

"Yes, he phoned from the hall, and said he would be there all morning. I think he wants Dot for an hour or so in the afternoon."

"Right. I'll do it now."

After her call, she said to Josie that Dot had been intrigued, naturally, and agreed to take in the parcel, if it had not arrived when Justin was there. She said he'd not given her any idea of what was in it, except that it mustn't go astray. Postmen often left parcels on the doorstep, he had said.

"Not if they're parcels needing a signature before delivery," said Lois. "Anyway, no doubt Dot will report. Now," she said, fishing a shopping list from her pocket, "can you get these together, and I'll collect later on? I have to go into Tresham this afternoon. Cowgill has summoned me. Your Matthew has no doubt acted as go-between again."

"Mum! He's very discreet! It's not easy for him, you know."

"No, sorry. I know he's really tactful. And a good policeman, thank goodness. I always feel safe, now you're both living in the cottage."

UP AT CAMEROON HALL, JUSTIN WAITED IN SOME TREPIDATION, hoping in a way that the parcel would not arrive until Dot had come to take over. But quite soon the bell rang at the back door. He rushed to open it, and was greeted by a deliveryman with a white van with no contact details on it. He carried no parcel.

"You can come and get 'em out, mate," he said. "I'll be damned glad to get them out of my van. The cold weather is supposed to send them to sleep, but they're buzzing about like mad. I should leave them outside, if I was you. The warmth inside the depot has probably woken them up."

"I was wondering if we could transfer them from your van straight into mine? I've got a really safe place to put them. No good leaving them here to terrorise the neighbourhood!" Justin said.

"Do what you like with them, but sign this, please, to say they arrived alive and buzzing when I handed them over."

Between them, they managed to transfer the hive, safely protected, into the zoo van, and Justin returned to the house. He made himself a coffee, and settled down to think until Dot Nimmo arrived. But before that, he reminded himself, he had to call Josie, and ask her if it was okay to put the hive down at the end of the garden, well out of the way. He had meant to do some mugging up on beekeeping on the internet, but had no time, and reckoned he could master the basics from asking around friends.

Where had Pettison intended to keep them? And why had he ordered them? Surely bees were bees, full stop. Nothing rare about bees. Maybe he just fancied keeping them. The estate was large enough to put them well out of harm's way, provided he was here to keep an eye on them. But now, with nobody in residence, it would not be possible, in case they decided to fly off to pastures new, stinging a few dozen citizens on their way.

The more he thought about it, the more he became convinced that Pettison would not be in the business of making honey, or even keeping them as a new hobby. They must have been intended for a client. Perhaps someone would be getting in touch, and then they would be able to get rid of them.

When Dot arrived, soon after lunch, she was horrified. "I'm not staying here unless you get rid of them bees," she said to Justin. "And have you asked Mrs M if she's willing to have them there at the back of the shop?"

"Well, actually, I spoke to Josie, and she said she'd think about it, and ask her mum and Derek. But I haven't got time to wait for that. She didn't sound too bothered, and I can always take them away again."

"Best get going then," said Dot. "I shan't settle until you've gone."

All the way to Farnden, Justin was aware of the bees. The buzzing seemed to have died down a bit. It was certainly freezing in the van, and he wondered if they would die of the cold. If they did, they did, and maybe a good thing, he decided.

"Oh hello," said Josie, as he came into the shop. "Mum said to tell you it would be all right, so long as you know how to look after them. And so long as she can have the first pot of honey! I said it was in direct competition with the shop, but she pointed out I could sell your honey, too."

"Thanks a lot," he said. "I'll get them unloaded and down to the end of the garden. I might put them in the pigsty overnight, and then take a look at them tomorrow."

"What sort are they?"

"Are there different sorts?" he asked. "I know they're not bumblebees. And they've come from Africa. That's about all I know."

"There's mason bees and honeybees and also killer bees," said Josie, "but I think those ones come from Africa, so it might be them! Anyway, they're not an endangered species, as far as I know."

IN THE BRIERLEY HOUSE, THEY HAD BEEN TALKING ABOUT Pettison. "Poor old sod hasn't got any relations that I know of," said Betsy. "I suppose I'd better go over to the hospital and pop in for a few minutes. Last time I went, they said they weren't sure that he knew a visitor was there. He's deep in a sort of coma, or trauma, I suppose. He's good at pretending, mind. Still, I shall have him on my conscience unless I go."

"Rum sort of conscience you've got! Anyway, make sure you don't get involved. With his future, like," said Ted. "I don't want to have to take responsibility for him, no way. And anyway," he said as an afterthought, "I'll not be surprised if this silent act isn't all put on. It's easy to pretend, and not speak. You can bet he's busily thinking out some new scam."

"You're right, Ted. We have to be careful. It's quite

enough taking over running the zoo for the time being. Though I must say Justin has turned up trumps. It's given him something serious to do, I reckon. He was a bit of a drifter before. Cagey about his past, although he let slip his dad, who's just died, wanted him to run the family farm. I really think now, having seen him in action, that he could do it perfectly well. As for the zoo animals, he's wary, but is learning how to handle them. Farmer's instinct, I think, more than anything else."

"Well, you do what you like," answered Ted. "You always do, anyway. But don't drag me into it. As far as I'm concerned, I'd be happy to see that place closed down tomorrow, and him with it."

Betsy did not reply. She was well aware of Ted's feelings about Pettison. He naturally couldn't stand the sight of him. But, as she occasionally reminded him, he was happy enough to spend his money. He had asked her pertinent questions about Justin lately. Perhaps he was thinking about setting up a new client for her, now Pettison was out of action. But there was nothing doing there. Not that Justin was gay. She was sure of that. But he was not the sort to take up her offers. Not yet, anyway. She liked working with him at the zoo, and that was that.

"Bye, Ted. Should be back in an hour at the most. And, by the way, Justin phoned to say the latest addition to the zoo is a hive of bees! Arrived today, not exactly by post. He's keeping them behind the Farnden shop until he knows what to do with them. So, off to Pettison. Shall I give him your love?"

"Buzz off!" said Ted, and she set off, still laughing.

Betsy joined the queue of visitors in the waiting room at the hospital, and walked with them through the maze of corridors until she came to the private wing. The receptionist said it was fine to go straight in to Pettison's room. "Not sure if you'll get anything out of him," she said, "but he may know you're there. Just talk about things he might recognise."

The room was warm and quiet, and smelt strongly of a pleasant flowery perfume. Was it a spray, or had he had a visitor with an expensive scent? The latter, she decided, and wondered who it could have been?

She leaned over and kissed his forehead, now revealed from the mass of wrappings.

"Hi, Petti," she whispered. "It's Betsy come to see you."

His eyes were closed, and apart from an occasional flicker of one eyelid, there was no visible reaction.

She settled down in a chair, and began to chat about things going on in the zoo, and what she and Justin were doing to keep it up and running. "He's really helpful, Petti," she said. "He got stuck into it straightaway, and we're working well together."

Still no reaction, though she could have sworn there was a fleeting change of expression. Continuing to chat about nothing very much, she came to the latest consignment of animals. "Or insects, to be truthful. A hive of bees! And Justin's taken charge of them at his flat. When you feel up to telling us who they're for, we'll move them on to the client. I'm not keen on bees, I must say!"

Pettison stirred, moving his legs very slightly, and then appearing to lift one arm. To Betsy's surprise and horror, he moaned, and then appeared to whisper something. She put her ear to his mouth, and was sure of one word only.

"Killers," he said, quite clearly.

Fifty-One

"JUSTIN? I'VE GOT A MESSAGE, OF A SORT." BETSY TOOK A DEEP breath. "I've been over to see Pettison, and he seemed much the same. But then I mentioned the bees, and he kind of moved, and then whispered something. I could only get one word, but he repeated it once, and then relapsed into his usual nothingness. I told the nurse, and she was really excited. Said it was definitely a step forward, and asked if I could visit again tomorrow. I'm home now, and had to ring you. He said 'killers.' That's all."

"I suppose it's good news," he said. "But what do you think he meant?"

"It's obvious! He meant the bees, and was telling us they're killer bees. Ted's looked them up in our encyclopaedia. They come from Africa, and they're deadly if they sting you! All you can do is run, and even then they can follow you!"

"Oh my God, what do we do now?"

"I should leave them in the pigsty until we find out who they're for; then whoever it is will have to collect. As long as they're shut in, we're all right."

"Well, the pigsty has only got the bottom half of a door, and that's bolted. But the top half must have gone years ago. It is really cold tonight, so I'm sure they're either dead or fast asleep. Anyway, I've fixed a tarpaulin tacked down temporarily over the open top half, and I'll see what I can do tomorrow to fix it properly."

"We could ask the pest control people to help."

"They'd just take them away. There's probably a lot of money resting on this consignment."

"Oh for heaven's sake, Justin! They're killer bees. We don't want a death on our hands, do we?"

He did not answer. Then he coughed, and said he had to go, but he'd be in touch tomorrow to reassure her. She said goodbye, but felt that somehow the danger was still lurking.

NEXT MORNING, LOIS WAS AWAKE EARLY. SHE HAD HAD A nightmare about Josie held in the hand of a large gorilla standing on top of St. Martin's steeple. Unable to free herself from a sea of treacle covering the ground beneath, she had fought her way out of sleep and lay awake sweating and trembling. The terror had remained with her, and she decided the only thing to do was to go down to the shop and make sure Josie was fine.

"I'll not be long, Mum," she said. "If Derek rings, tell him where I am. He's gone into Tresham for supplies."

"I don't know why you have to go traipsing down to the shop so early, getting in Josie's way?"

"I shan't be long," Lois repeated. "I'll take Jeems, and then carry on for a bit to give her some exercise."

Josie was at her usual chore, sorting out the newspapers, and was surprised to see her mother so early.

"Nice to see you, Mum," she said. "Though I hope it doesn't mean there's something wrong."

"No, no. Just getting some fresh air and exercise with my dog. Everything all right with you? Are the bees safely buzzing?"

"Dunno, really. I haven't had time to have a look. I know Justin went down there with a piece of tarpaulin Derek found for him to cover the top half of the door. Apparently he wants to keep them shut in until he gets some instructions from the zoo."

"Right-o then. I'll be on my way. So long as you're all right."

After she had gone, Josie was puzzled. Her mother did not usually pay early morning calls without some good reason for doing so. And why did she keep on asking if I was all right? "Does she know something I don't?" she said aloud. "If so, what?"

The next customer was even more of a surprise. A woman who announced herself as Betsy Brierley came in, and asked if Josie knew where Justin was. Apparently he was not answering his phone or his mobile.

"I expect he's still asleep," Josie said, trying to remember what she had heard about Betsy Brierley. "He was out the back, working on the pigsty door last evening. My gran walked by on her way back from seeing her friend Joan, and heard him banging away down there! Can I help at all?" Like selling you an expensive box of chocolates, she thought. I'm not here as an unpaid assistant to my tenant.

Betsy shook her head. "No thanks. Sorry to trouble you. I'll catch up with him later. I'm on my way to the hospital. They asked me to go in urgently, and I need to tell Justin. Thanks, anyway."

Josie shook her head, trying to make some sense of this. She remembered Betsy's association with Robert Pettison, who was still in hospital after a humiliating shock. Everybody knew that, from the local papers.

A van drew up outside, with deliveries for the shop, and Josie put all else from her mind as they unloaded the heavy boxes.

Meanwhile, Betsy drove into town and circled round and round trying to find a place to park near the private wing. It was a bad time of day, she supposed, all part of the morning rush. Finally, she parked under a tree, which dripped heavily onto her car roof. Not a good start, she decided, and made her way to reception, where she was directed to the private wing. She was greeted by a woman washing the corridor with mop and pail. "He's not up yet, dear," she said. "Ask at the office this end. They'll help. Most of the nurses will be in the office doing the changeover. Night staff going off; day lot coming in. Busy time of day. Do they know you're here? It's not visiting time."

"I was phoned," Betsy said crossly. "Urgent, they said."

"You go and knock on the office door. They'll send someone."

Finally, Betsy found the office, braved the scowling staff as she knocked at the door, and explained.

"Oh yes, that'll be Nurse Brown. I'll tell her. Wait there." The door was closed, and Betsy was about to walk away and go straight home, when it opened again and a familiar nurse came out.

"Ah, Mrs Brierley," she said. "It was concerning Mr Pettison. Earlier on, he seemed restless, and we caught some sounds from him. The only thing we could make out was 'killers,' and as this seemed to upset him, we thought perhaps you could shed some light? Perhaps have another session and hope he explains? It's an odd word, isn't it, under the circumstances?"

Betsy sighed, and said yes, very odd. But she had an idea what he meant. She would go and sit with him for a bit, and see if he said anything else. "And you couldn't rustle up a coffee for me, could you?" she added.

"There's a machine in reception," the nurse said unhelpfully, and returned to the office, shutting the door firmly in Betsy's face.

"Sod that for a bunch of soldiers," Betsy said, and marched off, her high heels clacking noisily along the empty corridor leading to the private rooms. She sat with Pettison for half an hour, and he didn't move. Nor did he say anything more, and Betsy finally gave up and left.

When she reached home, Ted was still there, and had not yet gone to work at the gas company's showrooms.

"What's the matter with you?" she said grumpily.

"Got the morning off. Not required. It's the beginning of the end, probably. There's not enough orders to keep us all busy. Short time, and then the chop. That'll be me. Helping at the occasional funeral doesn't make enough to buy a couple of pints. And you're not in work yourself at the moment. There was a call for you, by the way. From one of your old regulars. We might need some of them if Pettison doesn't make the grade. Mind you, if he no longer wants you, we can get back to the old days with plenty of customers. More lucrative in the long run. It's not all bad news, Betsy. Meanwhile, I think I'll go down into the shed and eat worms."

He pretended to lick his lips. Betsy frowned and turned away from him.

"Oh, and talking of worms," he continued, "I suppose I might do a bit more for the undertakers. They were on to me lately, to do more hours, heaving coffins and escorting them into the church an' that. I've got the gear, so might have a go. The pay is rotten, but they're advertising for suitable men, and it'd be better than eating worms, don't you think?"

"Oh, for God's sake!" said Betsy. "I've had about enough this morning, and it's only half past ten. *Please* leave me be. No, make me a coffee, and then leave me be."

By eleven, at the Farnden Shop, Josie had had a stream of customers. Apparently the word had got round that a hive of bees had been delivered, and the neighbours were either worried or curious. Several other villagers had honeybees, and they all belonged to a society with its headquarters in Tresham. The people who lived right next door to the shop were very worried.

"My Sid is allergic to bee stings," a neighbour had said to Josie. "I do hope you know how to handle them," she had insisted. Josie had replied that they belonged to the tenant in the flat, and he had assured her that they would not be there for long, and, in any case, he knew all about bees.

The day passed quickly, and Lois had rung Josie several times, ostensibly for good reasons, but really because she could not shake off the nightmare. Finally, she rang the shop once more and asked if Justin was there, and if so, could Josie give her his number as she wanted to ask him something important.

"To do with bees?" Josie said. "Because if so, I can tell you what I've told everyone else. They're not here for long, and he knows how to deal with them. Will that do?"

"No. I'd like his mobile number, please. I expect you gave it to me before, but I've lost it."

Josie sighed, looked up the number, and gave it to her

mother. "I'm shutting up shop soon, so if you need me, I'll be back at the cottage. Bye, Mum. And I really am all right," she said. "Give my love to Dad."

After a minute or two, she heard the phone ringing in the flat above. It rang for quite some time, and then stopped. Josie went out to the back of the shop and looked for the Fiat. It wasn't there, so Justin must be out somewhere. She looked down to the end of the garden and hesitated. Then she shook her head, went back into the shop and locked up.

LATER, WHEN IT WAS COMPLETELY DARK, A VEHICLE DREW UP outside the shop, stopping under the security light. Justin, back upstairs and dozing in front of the television, heard the engine, pulled his curtain back a little and looked out. There was a long, dark shape and a man had lowered a ramp at the back. He was slowly bringing out a wheelchair with a figure completely wrapped in rugs. Justin let the curtain fall back, quickly switched off all his lights, and checked that his door was locked. He had no need to guess who was in the wheelchair, and he had no wish for a conversation with Pettison at the moment. He was too tired, and the fact that the scheming old sod had arrived in the dark did not bode well. He would wait to see what would happen next.

Fifty-Two

MAKING VERY LITTLE NOISE, THE MAN AND WHEELCHAIR disappeared through the side gate, and then Justin could hear crunching on the gravel path that led to the back of the building. He must have left the gate unlocked, he realised with dismay, and grabbing a warm jacket and a large torch, he went silently down his stairs and out into the backyard. He could see from a light carried by the figure in the chair that they were approaching the pigsty.

"Stop! Stop at once!" he shouted, switching on his own torch. They stopped, and he made his way down over the wet grass to where they stood.

"Uncle Robert!" he shouted, as if the man in the chair was deaf. "What the hell do you think you're doing?"

"Good evening, Justin my boy," said a sepulchral voice from inside the wrappings. "We are paying a social visit, but with a purpose. How are you? And how's my Betsy?"

"Glad to hear you've regained the power of speech, you old fraud," Justin said crossly.

The wheelchair attendant, warmly wrapped in scarves and an all-embracing overcoat, leaned forward and whispered something in Pettison's ear.

Pettison laughed. "Later," he said. "Now I must take a look at the new consignment of goodies. I believe you have them safely in here? I would like to take them back with me to the hall. I have now discharged myself from hospital care, and I am not too ready to trust leaving them in your care. From what I hear from my spies, you have been changing things at the zoo. Without my permission, unfortunately. It suited me to remain what you unkindly called a fraud, and I am now much improved."

"I thought as much," said Justin. "Now, Uncle, this is madness! We can't move bees in the middle of the night. That tarpaulin at the top is only tacked down. Supposing we drop the hive?"

"My friend here is very strong, though he doesn't look it. Open up, please, and then we'll make an inspection. Of course, if they're all dead, you're welcome to keep them!"

Justin was beginning to shiver, in spite of his warm coat, and stepped forward. "If you insist," he said. "And if I let you have a look, will you agree to go back to wherever you belong, and come along another day and do this sensibly?"

"Open up!" Pettison said, in a suddenly harsh voice. "At once!"

"Can't you get out of the chair? Your legs are probably as miraculously restored as your voice! It would be so much safer," said Justin anxiously. He had a feeling that everything was being taken out of his hands.

"Of course not! I truly lost the use of my legs in that

bloody fall! Now, will you open up, or will my friend here make sure you do?"

Justin sighed. "No need to threaten, Uncle. And honestly, I can't believe a word you say. The tarpaulin's nailed down. But I can open the bottom half door, and Tarzan here can push you in, if you're determined to do it. You'll see the hive in the corner. I advise you to make it a short inspection."

In great trepidation, he opened the padlock, drew back the bolt and opened the lower door. The tarpaulin flapped in a sudden gust of wind, making a loud noise. One corner of it came free, but the rest remained fixed in place. The attendant, bending over, pushed Pettison inside.

Justin waited for a few seconds, and then heard a shout, two loud shouts, and then the attendant reappeared, pushing the tarpaulin completely free of the doorway and waving his arms around his head. "Bloody hive fell over," he yelled.

Justin stepped forward to rescue his uncle, but the well-wrapped attendant shoved him hard to one side, pulled the half gate shut and secured the bolt and padlock. Justin grabbed his sleeve, but he wrenched himself free. "Run for your life, Brookes!" he shouted, but the scarves muffled his voice. He sprinted up the grass and disappeared into the darkness.

Justin could hear the buzzing now, growing louder. "Uncle Robert!" he shouted, and, galvanised into action, he wrestled with the door. Though he could have sworn he left the key in the padlock, he couldn't put his hand on it. There was no way out for the wheelchair.

"Uncle Robert!" he yelled. "Cover yourself up!" He couldn't hear whether Pettison replied, and, making a reckless decision, he vaulted through the black cloud of bees to where the wheelchair stood. His uncle raised one weary arm, and was then quite still. Justin knew if he didn't leave at once, he could be fatally attacked, and so dragged off his coat, completely covering the motionless Pettison. He pulled the wheelchair to the door, and shouted for help. But nothing happened, and he finally climbed out. Then he rushed back into the house, where he phoned for an ambulance and the police.

Once more covering himself with coats and scarves, and though he could see the bees were no longer flying around, he returned to work away fruitlessly at the bolt. Then Derek appeared armed with a metal file and had freed it by the time they heard the wail of the ambulance approaching the shop.

By now, of course, alerted by the shouts and the siren, neighbours and others had formed a throng outside the shop. The local bee man arrived, and Justin insisted on accompanying him down to the garden. He watched as a policeman and the expert, completely shrouded, with not an inch of flesh showing, extricated the wheelchair from the pigsty.

"The padlock," Justin said. "I'm sure I left the key in it. I always do, to make sure I don't lose it. Did you find it?"

The policeman shook his head. "No key, I'm afraid. Lucky Mr Meade here got it open. Doesn't look as if he was in time, though," he added quietly.

One of the paramedics wheeled the chair up the garden, and under the light of a torch, Justin looked at his uncle. His face was decently covered, but he could see his hands, swollen and an ugly purple colour, still gripping the wheels, as if he had tried to move the chair.

"Is he—?" he asked the paramedic, who nodded and said he was sorry, but no person could have survived that kind of attack. "It's usually quick," he added. "Collapse brought on by anaprophylactic shock to the system of all those stings."

It was not until after the police and the ambulance had

gone, and the onlookers drifted away to their beds, that Justin began to feel pain from the odd sting on his own neck and hands. His bathroom light was the brightest, and he extracted the stingers as he had been told how.

Finally, after a stiff drink, he thought again of the bolted half door. He was absolutely sure he had shut it in the afternoon, and left the key still in the padlock, as usual. Unless it was found in the garden in daylight, the key must have been taken away. There was only one person who could have done it, and that was the wheelchair attendant, who had done a runner and disappeared off in his vehicle.

"Justin? Are you all right?" He recognised Derek Meade's voice, calling to him from the foot of his stairs.

"Yes and no, thanks. Come up, if you want to. I could do with someone to talk to." Two sets of footsteps came up the stairs, and Lois and Derek appeared.

"Let me look at those stings," Lois said, producing antihistamine ointment and soothing balm.

"Yoo-hoo!?" Another voice from below produced Mrs Tollervey-Jones, who had heard the commotion and come to help. "I'll not stay, if you'd prefer to be left alone," she said to Justin.

"No, no. You're welcome. I dread being alone, to tell the truth. There's been a real tragedy here tonight."

Mrs T-J busied herself in the kitchen making mugs of hot, sweet tea, saying they were all suffering from shock, though not as much as Justin, of course.

"Uncle was completely helpless," said Justin. "He couldn't get out of the chair. His legs were really damaged when he fell downstairs. Do you know if his death was instantaneous?"

"Oh yes," said Mrs T-J, who did not actually know for sure, but *did* know the answer Justin needed. "And I've remembered a very curious thing," she added.

"I hope it's not bad," said Lois. "We don't need no more shocks tonight."

"No, but very interesting, in the circumstances. I have been thinking about your uncle, Justin. As I told you, Lois, I knew the Pettison family a long time ago, and a similar event came back to me. They were having a garden party—people did in those days—when a swarm of bees arrived and lodged in a mulberry tree. One of the young Pettisons tried to move them out of the garden, and got terribly stung as a result. Apparently he was allergic to bee stings, and lost his life as a result. It might run in families, Justin, so I hope you'll be careful in the future."

"Thanks," he said, though still overcome at the thought of what his uncle had suffered. "I'm really glad the experts have taken over, and will have moved them out by early tomorrow. So with luck, I should be free of bees for good."

Mrs T-J made her excuses and left shortly after this, and Derek said they must be getting back.

"You go, Derek," Lois said. "I'll stay here until morning, to make sure Justin is all right. There could be aftereffects, I'm sure."

"Well, all right, but where will you sleep?"

Justin butted in immediately. "It's so kind of you, Mrs Meade. You can have my bed, and I'll wrap up with a rug on the sofa. I feel an absolute weed, but I would be glad to have you nearby until tomorrow. Then I can go to the hospital and make sure I've done the right things. I suppose the police will want to see me, and I have some serious thinking to do. I think I'm Uncle's only living close relative, except for my mother, of course. She's his sister. So goodnight, Mr Meade, and many thanks."

After Derek had gone, Lois said another cup of hot tea would be a good idea for both of them. Justin broke into a pause in the conversation, and said, "Something's not right, Mrs Meade. Not right at all."

"Not right with what?" said Lois. Justin was very pale, and she wondered if he was having a relapse. "Best tell me what you mean," she said.

"It's the half door of the pigsty," he said. "You know, the padlock holds the bolt in place. The key was definitely in it when I opened the door to let Pettison and his helper go in, and I'm sure I left it there. But when I tried again to pull it open to get Uncle out, there was no key. In the end I tried to get him out of his chair, but he was not responding by that time. That's why I climbed over the door to get out."

"I don't think he could've got out, anyway, Justin. Somebody said he'd lost the use of his legs in the accident."

"Yes, that's what he told me. And I didn't know what to believe. I thought he could have been using that in order to carry out some plan or other. He always had plans, did Uncle Robert. Some good, some bad." He covered his face with his hands.

"Were those bees part of a plan?" asked Lois.

Justin took his hands away, and looked at her. "We all know the bees were probably the latest in a long line of mostly successful scams," he said. "I could give you details."

"I remember what you told me about your father, but if you want to tell me more, carry on," said Lois, and fetching a bottle from the kitchen, poured a slug of whiskey into their mugs of tea.

Fifty-Three

"So you're back," said Gran, as Lois came through the door, looking tired and miserable. "And a fine time to come back, I must say."

"Oh, give it a rest, Mum. I'm sure Derek has told you what happened."

"Yes, he has. And I can't think of any reason why you should have stayed down there all night long, with only a young man for company."

"He was a very sick and unhappy young man," Lois said, irritation rising. "He had been stung by killer bees, seen his uncle killed by bees of some sort, and was having a bit of a reaction to his own stings. Naturally, I stayed with him. He was better this morning, but I suggested he should go to the hospital to check all was well. Okay?"

"All right, all right. No need to shout. There was a message earlier for you from your friend Cowgill. He wants to see you at the police station as soon as possible."

Derek appeared, and put his arms around Lois. "He can wait," he said. "This young lady is going straight upstairs to bed with a hot water bottle and a milky drink, and she's staying there until lunchtime."

Gran shrugged. "I'm only the messenger," she said, "so there's no need for you to be sharp with me."

It was early afternoon by the time Lois drove into Tresham and parked her car behind the police station.

"I owe you an apology for bothering you so early in the day," Cowgill said, as soon as she entered his office. "I hadn't realised you spent the night with an attractive young man."

"Not you, too!" said Lois. "Do you want a sensible conversation or not? If not, I've got plenty of work to do."

"Sorry, my dear. Very unfeeling of me. And, as you know, I wouldn't upset you for the world. Now, sit down, and we'll have a chat, if you're not too tired."

"And even if I am, I suspect," said Lois. "There's an awful lot I've got to tell you. There was plenty of time for Justin to unburden himself."

"Right, let's begin at the beginning," he said.

It was a long tale Lois had to tell, and nobody came out of it very well. Justin had admitted his own involvement in the illegal trade in rare species, but had only touched on that of his father. With luck, he had said, he could rest in peace. He trusted Lois to keep silent, and his mother had spent most of her life keeping silent. "It's up to you, Cowgill. I expect you knew all about that, anyway?"

Cowgill nodded. "Of course, in our investigations, we discovered Brookes senior's part in what had been set up by Pettison, but perhaps on compassionate grounds we shall have no need to make that public, except in our own records. I'm afraid Justin's part in the whole thing is different. He handled the rare animals and sheltered them until they were passed on. Pettison gave him a cut of his profits. Justin Brookes has broken the law, and will have to go to trial and accept his punishment."

"Oh dear, that means Josie will have to find another tenant."

"Not difficult, I'm sure. It is a nice little flat, if you don't know about the reptiles."

"Is that a joke? Not funny. Shall I carry on?"

"Sorry! Yes, please, carry on."

"Right. First, Pettison had made a lot of money. It was a lucrative business, and he had built up his private zoo as a result. Everything aboveboard there. Regular inspections found nothing wrong, and in fact it was considered a well-run place, and an asset to the locality. Second, Pettison knew quite well what he was doing in the illegal side of his business. Justin was paid to keep quiet, and only animals that were not rare, or had been bred in captivity, were on show in the zoo. The others were kept out of sight and passed on to customers as quickly as possible. He had quite a mailing list of clients and worked on orders only."

"What about the Brierleys? They were both involved, weren't they? Certainly, they were in contact with Justin. And she was responsible for the death of those dear little baby elephants!"

"Oh yes, we've always known Betsy was a help to Pettison in more ways than one. We're not sure about Ted, but he must have known what was going on with the strange animals Betsy brought home on occasion."

"I remember you saying," Lois said slowly, "that you weren't taking Betsy in for questioning, because you wanted to get the head of the snake. What exactly did you mean?"

Cowgill sighed. "I did say that, I know. And I see now that I was wrong. My idea was that as long as Pettison didn't suspect we were on to him, very close on his tail, we stood a good chance of catching him in an illegal act. But if Betsy had twigged and been able to warn him, he was clever enough to destroy all his records and do enough to make it very difficult for us to make a good case against him. It never occurred to me that he would be killed first."

"And now, could it have been an accident? Who was that care attendant who drove him to Farnden and then took him behind the shop to look at a hive full of killer bees? No official volunteer drivers would have done that."

"Right as ever, my dear Lois. We are well on the way to discovering who he was. I won't keep you much longer, my dear. You are looking exhausted, and should go home to have a good rest. I wouldn't have asked you to come in if I'd known."

"So what else, Cowgill? I'm still wide awake."

"Justin and Betsy? I understand there's something between them, running the zoo while Pettison was out of action?"

Lois nodded. "Mm, but nothing more than that, I think. I actually think he fancies my daughter. I'm good at seeing the signs of a predatory male."

Cowgill smiled at her. "Oh dear," he said. "Does it show?"

"Back to business," said Lois sternly. "There is one more thing Justin said. The lower half door to the pigsty was locked, and he opened it reluctantly, leaving the key in the padlock. The mystery attendant pushed Pettison in, then almost immediately ran out, shut the door and locked him in, and, as Justin discovered, took the key with him. That's why he couldn't get Pettison out quickly enough. Justin hasn't forgiven himself for that."

"So we're looking for a heavily wrapped-up driver with an adapted vehicle, and a padlock key in his pocket? Shouldn't be too difficult to trace."

"And, surely, one who had evil intentions towards Pettison.

And who knew the bees were killers. That narrows it down," said Lois. "I must go now. Gran is still cross with me, and if I'm late for tea she'll kill me. Oh God," she said, putting her hand to her mouth. "I shouldn't have said that. Sorry. I'm off. Bye."

IT SHOULD HAVE BEEN EASY TO TRACE A SPECIALLY ADAPTED TAXI and its driver, but when Cowgill instigated the search, it proved more difficult. There was only one hire company in Tresham owning a specially adapted vehicle, and that was in a repair shop, being overhauled to have new harnesses fitted. He directed a search further afield, and then packed up and went home.

THE MEADE FAMILY WERE SEATED ROUND THE SUPPER TABLE when a knock at the door brought Mrs Tollervey-Jones into the kitchen. Gran looked cross at the interruption, but Derek pulled up a chair and invited her to sit down.

"I just couldn't settle, my dear, worrying about you," she said to Lois. "Are you sure you are all right? There is such a thing as delayed shock, you know. But I see that you are being well looked after, and I apologise for bursting in. Stupid of me, but it was such an awful thing. Anyway, I'll be going now."

Derek, recognising that the old lady had had something of a shock herself, standing by the ambulance as the wheelchair with its tragic occupant was loaded in, said she must stay and have a snack with them. "I don't suppose you've eaten this evening?" he said.

The conversation inevitably centred on the accident, and after ten minutes or so, Lois suddenly banged the table with her hand. "It was *not* an accident!" she said. "Robert Pettison was *murdered* by that attendant, who locked him in and took away the key. He's got to be found, and although Cowgill's lot are all looking, I think we should think about it seriously, too."

"Did Justin say he saw the vehicle? It was quite dark by that time." Mrs T-J looked around the table. "I know he was a sort of protégé of his uncle, and is very cut up about it all, but perhaps there is something . . . ?"

"You mean he could have organised it?" Lois frowned. This had not occurred to her, and seeing Justin in a state of collapse after it had happened, she could not imagine that he had had anything to do with it.

"It is possible, Lois," said Derek. "He might not have realised just how appalling the whole thing would turn out. Perhaps he thought it would frighten his uncle into agreeing to take some different course of action with the zoo."

Lois could see that this conclusion would probably have been arrived at by the police, and decided to ring Cowgill tomorrow to see if this was so. Now she changed the subject to the small-animals racket that had been carried on by Pettison. "Thank heavens there won't be any more of that," she said.

"Not from the zoo, I hope," said Mrs T-J. "Unfortunately, it goes on in many places, here and abroad. There's big money in it, and once a network is set up, with the right connections and runners, the illegal nature of it is hard to prove. Pettison's contacts will regroup and carry on, I expect. They are well organised, particularly with the small creatures, which are easy to hide."

"Mm, and not all of them are cuddly little treasures," said Lois feelingly. "That snake, for instance. And the toad and the frog. And that amazing spider with her babies. That one was quite sweet, so long as you forgot it was a spider!"

"Why was the flat targeted, do you think?" Derek said.

"Because Pettison really wanted Justin to live there, to keep his ear to the ground, especially when I was around, I suppose," said Lois. "And the reptiles were to put off other prospective tenants."

"And the other stories of reptiles poisoning dogs and people?"

"Nothing to do with Pettison, so Justin said. Just coincidence. There are plenty of other sources of supply. You can see them on the internet."

Mrs T-J spoke into a moment's silence. "Speaking of rare animals," she said, "did any of you ever see Pettison's private mausoleum? It is grisly, but quite remarkable."

Lois thought that the less said about that the better, and turned the conversation back to the zoo. They speculated about what would happen to it, and Derek said he thought it would probably be closed. "After all," he said, "Pettison's dead, and the Brierleys and Brookeses could well have a spell cooped up in jail. Unless, of course, they get heavily fined. Even then, they'll have no money to run it."

"Well," said Mrs T-J, rising to her feet, "I suppose that's the end of it now. For us anyway, Lois dear. The villain Pettison has got his just deserts, and when the mysterious attendant is found, and I'm sure the police will soon do that, life can return to normal."

"And so say all of us," said Derek, seeing her to the door. "Lois is exhausted, and I hope New Brooms will be her priority from now on."

A forlorn hope, thought Mrs Tollervey-Jones, and smiled her farewell.

Fifty-Four

A week later, Dot Nimmo sat at her window, looking over the road to the Brierleys' house. All the curtains were drawn across, and Dot had seen few comings or goings since the terrible news about the zoo owner. She supposed Betsy had imposed total mourning on the house. Only once had the front door opened, and that was to permit Ted, resplendent in his undertakers' black, to march off briskly.

Pettison was to be buried in a leafy glade behind Cameroon Hall, where a handful of people would attend a brief ceremony of committal to the grave. Justin, and his mother, Pettison's sister on a flying visit, stood amongst the leafless trees. He bowed his head and tried to think of good things his uncle had done. He had had his moments of kindness and affection, but these had been sadly outweighed by his unashamed cruelty in handling little animals which were almost certain to die in captivity, away from their natural homes. Now the unfortunate man was decently buried and covered by loamy earth. Dust to dust, thought Justin.

AFTER THE FUNERAL SERVICE, WHICH LOIS ATTENDED AGAINST Derek's wishes, and, as she said, representing New Brooms, a few people gathered in the zoo café to drink a warming glass of punch.

Lois found herself sitting by Betsy Brierley, who was being obviously shunned by a few stalwarts of Tresham's blameless citizens who attended more out of curiosity than respect.

"It must have been a shock, Mrs Brierley," she said. "He was a good friend, I believe?"

"You believe right," said Betsy, with a sulky look. "And you needn't bother to pussyfoot around it. I was his mistress, and we had good times together."

"Of course," said Lois blandly. "And isn't that your husband with the undertaker's men? They do a really good job, don't they? Dignified, an' that. I reckon it's nice to give a good send-off."

"You're not saying his death was a good send-off, are you?" said Betsy in a loud voice. Everyone turned to look at her. "The poor old bugger died a horrible death, and the sooner the police find that sod who pushed him into a bees' nest, the sooner I can sleep at nights." She stood up, adjusted her tight skirt, and strutted away.

"Straight in it," Lois muttered to Justin, who came to sit by her and introduce his mother.

"Don't worry, Mrs Meade," he said. "She had to explode sooner or later. I've been in touch with her, as there's going to be a court hearing soon, and she and I will be in starring roles. I don't think she and Ted talked much, so it's probably done her a bit of good. Don't take it personally!"

As Lois walked away from the zoo and up to the house to collect her car, she was passed by the hearse returning to base. She remembered reading about black horses with plumes of feathers on their heads, pulling a special carriage for the coffin. And in those days, you could hire mourners! Maybe Pettison would have liked that. Or perhaps he would have preferred to be drawn by a harnessed gorilla, pounding its way round the streets of Tresham.

Driving home, she thought again of Betsy's outburst. She had probably loved Pettison, in her way. She might decide to give up selling herself, and concentrate on working with Justin in the zoo instead. If they got off with only a fine, of course.

As she walked into her kitchen, Gran stood by the cooker, stirring vigorously. "I expect you've had something to eat?" she said crossly.

Lois shook her head. "No, nothing to eat. I'm ravenous!" she added.

"Well you'd better get your coat off and go and ring Inspector Cowgill. He's been on the phone. I told him where you'd gone, and he said to ring him back as soon as you got in."

"And *I* say," Derek added, "you will have your lunch properly, and after that you can ring him. Agreed?"

"Agreed," said Gran.

"Mm, thanks, Mum," said Lois.

"AND NOW CAN WE GET ON WITH OUR LIVES?" TED BRIERLEY stood with his back to the fire, glaring at his Betsy. Her face was ravaged by constant crying, and he was thoroughly fed up. Okay, so it was natural for her to be sorry, but not this great rush of mourning! She had embarrassed him at the funeral, sniffing and snorting! Half the time at home now, she was looking through albums of photos she had filched from the hall, weeping over photographs of Pettison, from golden-haired youth to cheerful-looking zoo owner, carrying a grinning chimpanzee on his arm.

And the other half of the time, she sat in an armchair, refusing to eat, and rejecting any attempts at conversation or comfort.

"I've had quite enough of this," he continued. "You gave him a service, and he paid for it. I fixed it up, kept him happy and benefited financially. That's all there was to it, as far as I'm concerned. A business arrangement. But no, you had to fall for him, and I suppose he fell for you, and I was forced to get rid of all your other clients. He wanted sole possession, and I had to agree. You made that quite clear. Now both our jobs are gone, and we can't live on my undertaking money."

"We could be out of a job anyway," muttered Betsy. "There'll be a case against us for trading in them animals. Aiding and abetting, I suppose."

"Why don't we cross that when we come to it? We're well rid of him, and we've still got a future together. He wasn't the only one who grew fond of you, silly girl! So can we start again? You can give up hiring yourself out, if you want, and I'll ferret about for work where I can. We can be a proper couple. If you and young Brookes want to work together at the zoo, fine. I can help out there as well. As long as we are paid a reasonable sum. There should be money in the bank there, when Pettison's financial affairs are sorted out. What do you say, Betsy?"

Betsy shook her head, sniffed and said nothing.

Lois duly rang Cowgill after she had had her lunch, and he had been brisk.

"Sorry to disturb you," he said. "Something has come up, and I do need to talk to you. Say tomorrow, at about three? I have to come over to Fletching, so I'll call on you, if that's convenient?"

"Derek is going out, but I shall be here. Him and Gran are conducting a campaign to keep me away from anything to do with ferretin', so don't be put off if she's grumpy when she opens the door. I'll be in my office, so if I see you coming, I'll make a dash to let you in!"

Cowgill put down the phone with a smile. He was glad and relieved to hear Lois sounding back to her old self. Seeing her so exhausted and shocked, he had worried. He could not bear to lose contact with her, however seldom they should meet. Now that they were almost related, with Josie's husband being his nephew, he hoped that this alone would mean seeing her occasionally. He did not think of Derek as an obstacle in any way, he realised as he went off to find Matthew. He was content to be on the periphery of Lois's life.

WONDERING WHAT HE WANTED TO TALK ABOUT, LOIS STAYED IN her office, sorting through New Brooms schedules for the coming week. She was finding it hard to concentrate, and decided to walk down to the shop with Jeems, call in to see Josie and then continue with a dog walk round the playing field.

"Don't be too long," said Gran, as she returned to the kitchen. "It gets dark really early, and very cold with it."

"I'll be fine," Lois replied. "And I'm not a kid anymore. I appreciate your concern, but I am a grandmother myself."

"And so you are!" said Gran. "You'd do better to concentrate on being a good grandmother instead of mixing yourself up with nasty animals and that inspector."

"Bye, Mum," said Lois cheerfully, and unhooking Jeems's lead, she set out for the shop.

"Hi, Mother!" said Josie. "You're looking very healthy with your warm scarf and rabbit-fur gloves. Are they rabbit, or one of Justin's foreign things?"

"Enough, Josie! I'm up to here with wisecracks from Derek and Gran."

"Sorry! What can I get you?"

"Nothing. I just called in to see you. I'll go the minute a customer arrives."

"Don't be daft. I'm very glad to see you. How's everything?"

"All right. I went to Pettison's funeral. It was quite dignified, actually. Poor old Betsy Brierley was very upset."

"Naturally," said Josie. "She was his longtime fancy woman, wasn't she? It must have been a great shock to her when she heard about it."

"Yep, I'm sure. Josie . . ."

"Yes, what?"

"Have you talked to anyone in the shop who actually saw that taxi they said brought Pettison here that night? There were quite a lot of people gathered around to see what was going on."

"Not really. The neighbours came running out when they heard the shouting, and people who were really close could hear the bees as well. But I reckon the taxi had driven off by then."

"Mm, well, I just wondered."

"Why don't you ask Joan, Gran's friend? She must have been one of the first to come running round. Her garden backs onto the shop's patch. She could have seen or heard something."

"Good idea. Thanks, love. Here comes the vicar, so I'll be on my way. Take care of yourself, and don't allow any buzzing insects into the shop."

She walked around into Blackberry Gardens, and knocked at Joan's door. It was answered immediately, with a warm invitation to go in and have a cup of tea.

"Jeems will be fine. I keep a few dog biscuits for visiting pooches," she said. "How's your mother?"

"On top form, thanks," Lois said. "I was hoping I could ask you one or two questions about that terrible night. You must have seen quite a lot of the goings-on?"

"Yes, I did. I saw some of it from the bottom of the garden, but I did run round quickly to see if I could help."

"Did you by any chance see a taxi leaving the scene?"

"No, no taxi. There was only one vehicle going by at twice its usual speed!"

"What d'you mean, Joan?" Lois said urgently.

"Well, believe it or not, I saw the tail end of a hearse! A great long black thing, and it shot off in the Tresham direction. Funny, that."

Fifty-Five

Inspector Cowgill arrived on time next day, and Lois saw his car drawing up. She rushed to the door, but collided with Gran coming at speed from the kitchen.

"You win," said Lois, and retired to her office.

Gran straightened herself up, and then opened the door. "Good afternoon, Inspector, can I help you? My daughter's rather busy at the moment."

"She's expecting me, Mrs Weedon," said Cowgill, with his most charming smile. "I am sure she will spare me a few minutes."

"Oh, very well. You'd better come in."

At this point, Lois came out and said that Inspector Cowgill had made an appointment with her, and they were not to be disturbed. Gran sniffed, and said in that case, they would probably want cups of tea, unless Lois called that an interruption. Lois resisted a temptation to give her mother a sharp response, and eventually she and Cowgill were left alone.

"So how are you feeling today?" he asked, though he could see from her smile that she was her old self.

"Fine, and you?"

"Haven't had time to ask myself!" he said. "We've had a lot of thinking and discussion. Going back to Pettison's funeral, what did you think of it? Not bad, I thought, under the circumstances."

"Yep. I thought Betsy Brierley was very dignified, until she snapped in the café."

"Snapped? I saw her stalking off."

"Yeah, it was something I said, about giving him a good send-off. She must have loved him, I reckon, Hunter. Very sad, really."

"Mm, well, not many would agree with you. Betsy is considered to be hard as nails. Still, no reason why she should not mourn him. She'll get over it, one way or another. Now," he continued, "we've trawled all round the county, but found first of all that there are very few adapted taxis, and second, they were all either being repaired, or in use by reputable folk unconnected with our enquiry. In other words, we've drawn a blank, so far."

"Oh dear. Well, this may mean nothing, but I went round to Gran's friend Joan, who lives in Blackberry Gardens, and asked her if she had spotted a taxi leaving that night. She said no, and then she laughed and said that on her way round to see if she could help at the shop, she saw a hearse—yes, a hearse!—vanishing at speed. It wasn't until now, before you came, that it dawned on me that it could have had something to do with Pettison."

Cowgill said nothing for a few minutes. Then he opened his briefcase and withdrew a small plastic bag, securely sealed, and put it down in front of her.

"Ever seen this before?" he said.

"It's a padlock," said Lois flatly. "And there's a small key in the keyhole."

"Correct," said Cowgill. "The padlock has been taken from the pigsty at the back of Josie's shop."

"And the key?"

"Brought in by Betsy Brierley. She found it in the pocket of Ted's black undertaker's coat. It has been checked over thoroughly, and it is definitely the one."

"Oh my God! What did she say when she brought it in?"

"Not very much. She was very upset, but tried to explain that she had to decide between loyalty to Pettison or to Ted."

"And Pettison won?"

Cowgill nodded.

"But why would Ted have wanted to do such a terrible thing? He'd lived alongside Pettison for long enough. They must have had a sort of tolerance of each other?"

"Not necessarily. Ted could have been like a simmering kettle all these years, and suddenly boiled over."

"Boiled dry, more like," said Lois, unimpressed. "But kettle or no kettle, he had put up with a lot, including being mocked by Pettison. Poor sod, he must have suffered. I suppose he could have walked out on Betsy, but maybe he loved her. Loves her, I should say. He started as her pimp, so I'm told, but they've lived together for years, and she's not unattractive. So does he think he's got away with it? What are you going to do?"

"Pull him in for interview, of course. But first, I hear Mrs Weedon approaching with a tea tray, so you and I can exchange sweet nothings for a short while longer."

Lois sighed. "You really are an old softie," she said. "But there is something tragic and romantic about all this, isn't there? Too much misplaced love. I must say, and please don't use this in evidence against me, that Pettison was an evil old devil."

"Maybe, but there could have been other ways of putting him out of action, such as a long stretch in prison for breaking the law relating to trafficking in rare species. But now he is dead, and we don't have to think about that. We have to take care that Betsy Brierley doesn't do anything stupid."

LATER THAT DAY, COWGILL SAT IN HIS OFFICE, FACING A RESENTFUL Ted Brierley.

"What do you mean, was I out that night driving a hearse? Of course I bloody wasn't! There's no call for a hearse at that time of day. Unless it's for the Hell Fire Club. They have nasty rituals, but our lot won't have nothing to do with that!"

"Do you have someone to vouch for you being at home all evening, as you say?"

Ted thought quickly. He would have to risk this, and tell Betsy as soon as he got home. "Betsy, of course. She'll know I was at home with her. I can even tell you what we had for supper."

"Very well, tell me." Inspector Cowgill sat back in his chair, and looked interested.

"Steak and kidney pie," Ted said. "With chips and peas, and ice-cream with fruit cocktail for pudding. Most of it came from the supermarket, but we're both busy people. Sir."

"Excellent recall!" Cowgill said. "Do you pride yourself on your good memory?"

Ted visibly relaxed. "Oh yeah, me and Betsy do the crossword every day to keep our brains sharp."

"So were you able to find some time to help out at the zoo, when Pettison went into hospital?"

"No, they didn't need me. And, I don't mind telling you, I am not that keen on zoo animals. There's always that smell of doings and disinfectant mixed. So no, I kept out of the way and left it to Betsy. She and that Justin Brookes seemed to be coping all right. Is it something to do with the zoo that you got me in here for?"

"Possibly. Or it might be a charge of driving a hearse without due care and attention, and exceeding the speed limit in a built-up area."

Ted laughed at what he thought was a joke. "I'd not call Long Farnden a very built-up area!" he said.

"I see," said Cowgill, and made a note. "I suppose you must have attended several funerals there, over the years?"

"Oh yeah. I know the area well. Those little lanes an' village greens, an' that. Sometimes difficult to manoeuvre round. You get used to it, though."

"So I expect you'd be good at driving in the dark around there?"

"Oh yeah," Ted said proudly. "They always ask me to drive, if there's tricky jobs to be done."

Silence. Cowgill said nothing, and the atmosphere was heavy with tension.

"Can I go now, inspector?" Ted said.

"No, not yet, Mr Brierley. Not yet," he repeated, opening his desk drawer. He carefully placed the small plastic bag on the desk in front of him and slid it towards Ted.

"They've kept him in, Justin, and it's all my fault! What am I going to do?" Betsy was gripping her telephone, trying to speak calmly, but failing miserably.

Her voice was hoarse, and Justin did his best to make sense of what she was saying.

"You mean the police have taken Ted in for questioning, and have not released him yet? Do you know what they are asking him?"

There was the sound of sobbing, and Justin was puzzled. "What's been going on, Betsy?" he said.

There was no reply, and he realised Betsy had cut off the call. He frowned. This was not like her. Perhaps he should drive over and make sure she was okay. If they had taken Ted into the police station, something new must have come up.

BETSY SAT WITH THE PHONE IN HER HAND, STARING INTO SPACE. She had done it. She had agonised over what she should do since she had brushed Ted's overcoat, ready to put it back in the wardrobe, and felt the key in the pocket.

Not that she hadn't already suspected him of being involved in something fishy. Twice lately, Ted had gone out unexpectedly in the evening, dressed in his black undertaking clothes, and had returned later than usual.

The first time, it was the night before she discovered Pettison had been humiliated in the hospital. A man in black had been spotted running away, the receptionist had said. And the second time was the night of the killer bees.

Again, he had been wearing his black suit and overcoat, and she had noticed him taking the emergency hearse key from its hook in the kitchen. He had said next day he'd been meeting some of the lads for a special get-together in the Royal Oak pub in town. They'd agreed to wear their funeral gear to play a trick on the publican, he'd said. But she had met the wife of one of his undertaker mates in the supermarket next morning, and she had said her man had stayed at home all evening.

Betsy had tried to put all this from her mind, but now Ted was in custody, and it was her fault. She had tried to deliver the padlock key to the police station anonymously, but they had insisted on taking her name and contact details. So now he would know she had shopped him.

She drifted upstairs and found herself staring again at the black overcoat. He had been so proud of it, but in the end he had used it as a disguise for a horrible crime. She had always said he looked his responsible best when fully kitted out. She put her face to the warmth of the coat and noticed a stain on the cuff of one sleeve. She wished she was dead.

Ted Brierley. She sat down on the bed, and let her thoughts carry on remorselessly. They had never married, although after a while she took his name. He had managed her life, along with several other girls, and he was a careful and considerate protector. Provided the girls made no trouble. For her it was easy. Being on the game ran in her family, and she'd drifted into it without thinking too much about it. Then when Ted took her on, it had been convenient for both to live together, especially when Pettison had said he wanted to be her only lover.

Like an old married couple, Ted and she had got used to one another, and he was still protective towards her. What a mess! She caught sight of herself in the mirror on the wardrobe door. What a ravaged, awful face! Prostitution showed in the end, didn't it? It might have started as a game, but ended in disaster. Best to end it. End it for good.

"It's all my fault, and there's only one thing I can do about it," she shouted to the image in the looking glass.

Then the doorbell rang, and she went to open it. It was Dot Nimmo and Justin Brookes.

"Can we come in?" Dot said. "We've brought a bottle."

Fifty-Six

THEY SAT IN THE SMALL BACK ROOM, GLASSES OF WHISKEY IN front of them, and Betsy did most of the talking, spilling out the whole story, with Dot and Justin asking questions now and then.

"Why did he do it, Betsy? I thought you and him rubbed along together quite happily. After all, you were only one of his girls," said Dot. She was trying to be tactful, but it was not in her nature.

"So we did, Dottie. He had to get rid of the other girls, and look after only me. Pettison organised all that. O'course, I knew he didn't like Pettison. Not many people did! But Pettison was money, and we needed it."

"If you don't mind my asking, Mrs Brierley, do you think Ted was jealous of you and Uncle Robert being together so much in that way? Do you know what I mean?"

"No need to be polite, Justin. I made an early start. Mum hired us girls out. Wouldn't be allowed now, would it? I was always the prettiest one, and did well. Then Ted came along and wanted me to join his group of girls. A pimp, he was, but known for being fair and professional. Pro can mean professional as well as prostitute, you know, Dottie Nimmo! We were professionals at what we did, and saved many a failing marriage, I reckon. An' if you're asking if Ted loves me, I expect he does, in his way. But jealous? I dunno. Maybe."

"So when Uncle Robert first appeared, was he a regular client? I think our family had more or less decided he was gay."

Betsy laughed. "Don't you believe it!" she said. "I taught him a trick or two, but he knew most of them, and they had to do with girls like me. I was very pretty, you know, and he fell in love with me. He admitted it, and after a while he asked Ted if he could pay to have me all to himself. And Ted had to get rid of the other girls, so it was all confidential, an' that. That was quite a long while ago, and we've carried on like that ever since."

"And what about Ted?" asked Dot. "I expect he thought it was a good deal? One regular client, no trouble, payed up regular. It meant he could get himself a job on the side. What went wrong, Betsy?"

"Well, o'course I knew Ted was fond of me, like I said, but it was more like a father. Him and me never had no close relations, as you might say. Except for the last year or two, when he needed a cuddle in the middle of the night. And to tell the truth, Pettison was getting a bit past it. So there we were, a right triangle, and I think Ted had had enough of being beholden to Petti."

"What did he think of the animal trade?" Justin was amused at Betsy's account of what could hardly be called a romance, and had a sneaking admiration for her practical, straightforward way of looking at it. He had never met anybody quite like her.

"Oh, Ted disapproved of that. Reckoned it was too risky, an' he'll probably be proved right. Not that he had much to do with it, but he knew I helped out quite a bit. So I suppose he decided to put a stop to it. I reckon he wasn't thinking quite straight. When Pettison asked Ted to take him to Farnden to see the bees, I reckon he saw a golden opportunity and didn't see straight until he'd done the deed."

Her face crumpled, and she began to cry silently. Justin reached out and took her hand. "Don't worry, Betsy," he said. "We'll take care of you."

Dot looked at him in surprise. As far as she could tell, Betsy Brierley was quite capable of taking care of herself.

"But how did he get hold of the hearse?" continued Justin. "I know he was a part-time undertaker, but this was in the evening. Not many funerals at that time."

"Not sure," said Betsy, "but it must have been the hearse he's been working on. Refitting it inside, they are. Poshing it up with red velvet and brass handles an' that. He could easily have got a wheelchair into that one."

"Wouldn't it all have been locked up, standing there in the workshop?"

"Oh, no problem. He had access to all the keys. They trusted him, poor saps," she said.

Fifty-Seven

Winter had finally ended, and there were signs of spring everywhere in Long Farnden. Lois's garden was full of snowdrops, and the children in the village school were leaping about like young lambs, reviving old playground rituals with skipping ropes and coloured balls. Gran spent minutes at a time outside the school gates, listening to chants of "Nebuchadnezzar, the king of the Jews, bought his wife a new pair of shoes."

"When the shoes began to wear, Nebuchadnezzar began to swear," she sang now to her friend Joan in her neighbour's kitchen.

"When the swear began to stop," chanted Joan back to her, "Nebuchadnezzar bought a shop."

"When the shop began to sell, Nebuchadnezzar bought a bell," tootled Gran, in a high soprano.

"When the bell began to ring," they ended in unison, "Nebuchadnezzar began to sing, GOD SAVE THE KING!"

"We shouldn't be singing today, I suppose," said Gran, when they'd stopped laughing. "It's the anniversary of that horrible killer-bees incident. Six months to the day. Or night."

"Yep. Well, that Ted Brierley's safely put away, and Betsy and Justin Brookes paid enormous fines. Just as well young Justin's got all that money! I reckon they got away with a lot, them two. And that Betsy, who's no better than she should be, shacking up with young Brookes! She's old enough to be his mother! It's a funny old world. There's the grand opening of the refurbished zoo this afternoon. Shall we go? I can drive us."

THE SUN SHONE ON THE NEWLY PAINTED ENTRY BOX, WHERE Margie Turner, in a new frilly dress for the occasion, welcomed visitors in. "Free entry today, dears," she said, as family after family passed through. The town band was playing a selection from *The Sound of Music*, and refreshment stalls had been set out on the lawns behind the zoo.

Cameroon Hall was still empty, and it had a sad, neglected look, with the blinds pulled down over the big windows. But rumour had it that Justin Brookes, who had been given by his mother a goodly sum from the sale of his family farm, as well as inheriting Pettison's entire estate, would be moving in shortly.

"He's still in our flat at the moment," said Gran tartly, as she and Joan walked into the zoo. "Betsy Brierley has moved in with him. I told Lois she ought to forbid it."

"I expect they'll marry and have a family in due course," Joan said kindly.

"I hope she'll give up the game, then! Mind you, she and that Ted were never married, you know, so there'll be no problem there. Justin Brookes is welcome to her," Gran added. "The sooner they're out of the flat and we can get a nice middle-aged couple in there, the better I shall like it."

"Oh look," said Joan, trying to change the subject. "There's the maypole set up, ready for the schoolchildren. Shall we sit over there and get a good view when they start dancing?"

Inside the zoo and officiating beside the animal enclosures, Justin and Betsy were talking pleasantly to visitors about the habits of chimpanzees. "You have to be careful with them," he said. "They are easily offended, and then you have to run!"

"That applies to several people I know," muttered Betsy in his ear.

"And now, let's go and see the snakes," said Justin to the small group of onlookers. Shrieks from the children greeted this, and his eye was caught by a familiar figure "Hi, Josie!" he called. "We're just off to see some lovely snakes. Will you join us?"

"You know what you can do with your snakes!" she yelled back, and she and Matthew walked off towards the new penguin pool.

"Mrs Meade!" shouted Betsy, spotting Lois and Derek approaching. "Come and say hello to someone you know."

"Pretend you haven't heard her," whispered Lois. "I know what she's up to. That snake that we found in Josie's stockroom."

But Betsy had walked towards them, and they couldn't avoid her. "Nice of you both to come along," she said, taking Derek's arm, and moving them towards the snake house.

Lois detached herself, and veered off to the small-animals section. "See you later," she called back. "Say hello to Flatface for me, Derek. And I don't mean the one hanging on your arm. Ah," she continued, seeing her mother and Joan watching the dancing. "There's Gran."

"Lois! Come over here! Now then, gel, sit between me and Joan and enjoy the maypole children. I was just telling her you've given up ferretin' for good."

"Whatever that was!" said Joan, laughing.

"What indeed," answered Lois. "Oh, there's someone over there I must have a word with. See you in a minute." She stood up and, turning round, waved to a solitary figure standing by the entrance kiosk.

"AFTERNOON, COWGILL," SHE SAID. "YOU'RE NOT ON DUTY, surely?"

"No, just hanging around hoping to catch a glimpse of my favourite new broom."

"Not so new now," Lois said. "Anyway, come on in and sit with me and Gran. Derek's been kidnapped by Betsy Brierley, and the maypole dancing is about to begin. Josie and Matthew are somewhere, keeping well away from the reptiles. Come and join us, why don't you?"

"Well, actually, my dear Lois, as far as I can see, you're not coming apart."

"Cowgill! You made a joke! First time ever. Must be a good omen. Now come along with me."

She took his hand and he squeezed it. "We are almost related," she added, and they walked away together. Not quite into the sunset, but to join Gran and Joan, which was almost as good.